Knock on Wood

Also by Claire Dean

Girlwood
Spirit Caller
Good Boy

Writing as Christy Yorke

Magic Spells
The Wishing Garden
Song of the Seals
The Secret Lives of the Sushi Club
Summer of Glorious Madness

Knock on Wood

Claire Dean

Long Creek Books edition 2026

ISBN 978-0-9986025-5-4

1. Fiction Fantasy General 2. Nature

Printed in the United States of America

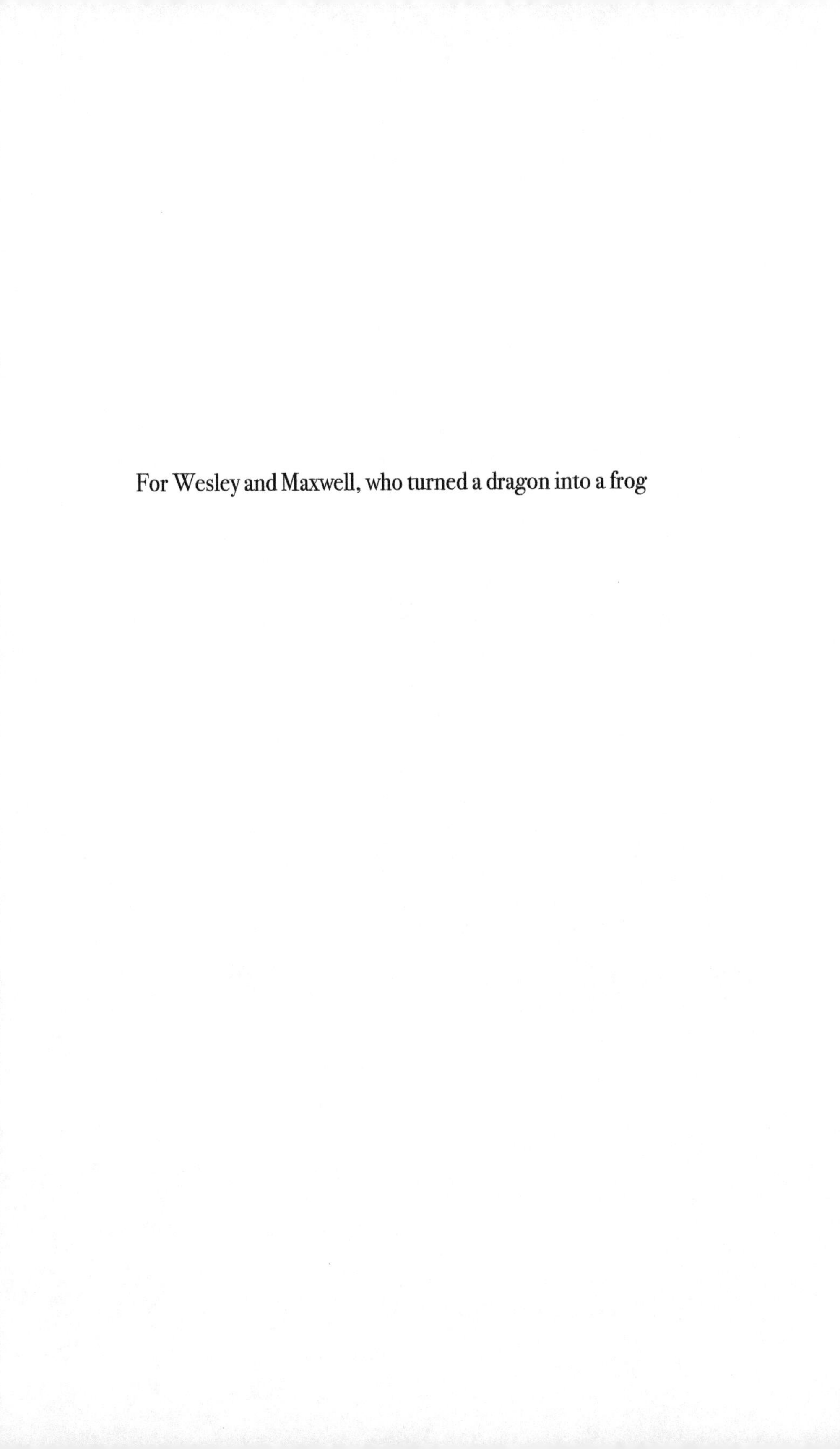

For Wesley and Maxwell, who turned a dragon into a frog

ONE

Western Larch
(Larix occidentalis)

People need to get their facts straight: Black walnut bark isn't black, olivewood and ebony make harder wood floors than the oak everyone raves about, and not all conifers are evergreen. The ten species of larch, including the largest, most spectacular variety known as Western Larch, sport bright, almost iridescent green needles in spring and summer that change to a brilliant yellow-gold before they drop in the fall. All winter, surrounded by chunky, gray green pines and firs, the larch bares her model-thin trunk and naked limbs like the diva she is. From a distance, her branches look feathery, as if she could lift herself off the ground and fly away at any moment. But, of course, that's just wishful thinking—the stuff of a good, long fairy tale.

✦

EIGHTY YEARS AGO . . .

The day she first feels pain begins like every other. The scramble of a chipmunk up her limbs, the taunting screech of a magpie, the sun rising a minute later than the day before. Autumn has already spun her needles into gold, a dazzling display in an otherwise dusty green forest. Crisp, pine-scented wind blows up the canyon; a rainstorm pelts the earth and scours the sky into a brilliant, robin's egg blue. After the hot, drowsy days of summer, fall brings the one-eared bear back to her trunk to feast on her sapwood while her sisters doze. They sleep through the blasts of gunshots across the valley and the bear loping away for cover, even the crunching of small, human footsteps as someone tramples, for the very first time, through their grove.

It is a boy. She has no idea how old he is; she's never seen anyone before. Some of her sisters are larger, but she is closing in on two centuries, her gnarled bark impervious to all but bear claws and red hot flames, while the boy is young enough to cry at the tiniest scrape of thistle across his knee, swiping his tears with his dirty sleeve. Burrs dot his short brown hair. He's covered in greens and grays, as if he's trying to blend into the forest without realizing how colorful the natural world really is. His black lace-up boots are too big for him and cause him to stumble. When a man calls out from somewhere down the mountain, the boy wails in fear and lands in a heap in her lap.

The weight of him is nothing. More than a field mouse but far less than the bear who has already clawed out a cozy den in her flank. When the man in the distance shouts again, ugly staccato sounds—"Boy . . . Coward . . . Hell to pay . . ."—the boy pulls his knees to his chest. No thistles poke him here, but he whimpers just the same, burying his head between his knees. He shakes so hard, her lowest branches tremble.

In the distance, a gunshot hits its mark. There is a quick, tortured animal cry, then nothing, not even birds. She is no stranger to destruction. She's suffered cracked limbs and woodpecker holes, bark and roots eaten away by starving wolverines, but the boy appears to be suffering from damage she cannot see. He cries himself to sleep, the warmth of his little body scorching her like a grass fire—not lethal by any means, but singeing off her toughest bark.

The pain she has never felt before is sudden and strange—an ache for something she can't define, a longing from somewhere down deep. She is glad her sisters sleep. They never question whether it's the wind that makes one of her limbs move closer to him. They can't tell the difference between a breeze and a sigh.

Two

Black Walnut
(Juglans Nigra)

Don't be fooled by the beauty of trees—some of them are out to get you. The honey locust, for one, with its 8-inch long thorns, and the toxic Manchineel tree, also known as "little apple of death." Just standing beneath this tree during a rainstorm will cause your skin to blister. One bite of the apple-like fruit will taste sweet, then gradually progress to a burning, tearing of the throat and the inability to swallow. The worst tree of all, though, is the insidious black walnut. Reaching a hundred feet tall with a beautiful oval crown and diamond-shaped bark, it's the black widow of trees. Humans may prize the tree for its fruit and dark, straight grained heartwood, but they wonder why everything they plant around it dies. Someone ought to warn them that the black walnut excretes a chemical meant to obliterate the competition, basically suffocating every other green thing until it dies. Even after the walnut is gone, the soil remains a death zone for years; throw walnut husks into a pond and you'll poison the fish.

✦

The next time the boy comes, he is covered in blood.

It is another autumn, when the woods are at their most beautiful—and lethal. A haven for the one-eared bear who bulks up on salmon and serviceberries, then digs a winter den under her roots, and a slaughterhouse for elk. Her sisters try to doze, but even the oldest and hardest of them quickens with the seemingly endless barrage of gunfire and the thuds of bucks falling onto the frosted earth.

He carries a shotgun and is bigger than he was, not yet a young man but not a boy either. His brown hair has grown long and wavy; his eyes are swollen and red, but he no longer cries when he yanks away a thistle leaf embedded in his ankle. He tosses the gun on the ground and doesn't fall into the lap of her roots so much as throw himself against her, looking at the hole in her trunk where the one-eared bear has feasted on her, at her long limbs and golden needles—everywhere except at his own bloody palms. Tears may not fall, but he grimaces as if something pains him. Then he scoops up handfuls of black soil and scours his hands clean.

The forest, like anything else that's alive, can't exist without dead things. Essential microbes dine on decaying leaves and fruit; rotting wood, ash and bone create rich, black humus; flesh and blood add a flush of nutrients to the soil, which eventually make their way down to her own lateral roots. She sprouted from the light, long-winged seeds of her long-dead sisters. Everything and everyone, no matter how small, mean or inconsequential, eventually becomes a blessing to those who come after.

But perhaps the boy-man doesn't know this. The blood he can't scrub from beneath his fingernails seems to make him unsteady. He sways for a moment and, when he finally rests his head against her trunk, trembles. It's the lightest touch—less than a chipmunk skittering across her boughs—

but the feel of him makes her quake from her roots to the tips of her golden needles. He is the rarest thing, a winter thunderstorm or a warm wind from the north. If she were human, she might whisper a word: *Mine*.

The moment the thought comes, her sisters release a rush of pheromones to warn her and the rest of the forest of danger. Some trees emit ethylene gas when their leaves are chewed, causing their neighbors to pump so much tannin into their own leaves, they can kill the next herbivore who tries to graze. When under attack from leaf-eating caterpillars, certain trees can release a hormone that attracts parasitic wasps—the kind that lay their eggs inside the caterpillars themselves, so they will be eaten from the inside out. Some of the deadliest creatures on the planet are stone silent.

But today, she isn't listening to the distress signals from her sisters. For the first time in her long life, she stands alone.

The boy-man looks up. His eyes are as brown as heartwood. He has a spattering of freckles across his nose and cheeks.

"I'm so sorry," he says, and though the words mean nothing to her, she understands that he doesn't lie. He isn't like the bobcat who feigns sleep, then pounces on an unsuspecting doe. He is just as much a predator, but he doesn't want to be.

He stares at her sisters, perhaps sensing their hostility, the dropping of their golden needles despite a lack of wind. Somewhere in the distance a buck bleeds out; she hears the distant echo of men's harsh laughter. The boy-man grimaces as if the sounds pain him and all he wants in this world is to never go back.

Her sisters spray the air with pheromones, but the only thing she's afraid of is him leaving. The boy-man will return to his world, and when autumn comes next year, he'll hold the shotgun steady. He will toughen up and stop crying when things die. She might live another 100 years exactly like this—rooted, nearly unbreakable, part of something bigger than herself. He'll be lonely and she'll never be alone.

People, like trees, often fall right where they're planted. It's as hard to change their nature as it is to wrench a massive root from the ground. She stiffens against the crisp, unyielding air, draws the heat of him through her bark and cambium, to the heartwood at her core. She feels the weight of herself as she never has before: Eight thousand pounds of inflexibility, her oldest branches hardened almost to stone, roots so immobile they could have been set in concrete. The only give in her is the fragile new bark that keeps trying to grow over her bear wound, and which now, suddenly, burns. The pain is worse than the wildfire that once scorched her trunk; it sends shockwaves through bark and sapwood to her innermost pith. Yet it is that pain that reaches her roots and propels the smallest tendril up through a thin patch of soil.

It is hardly a change at all—just a tiny root where there was nothing before—but the boy-man jumps to his feet.

"Jesus," he says.

All her life, she has breathed out what other creatures need to breathe in to live; she's given far more than she's taken. Now the soil in the grove, the moist, steady diet of nitrogen and microbes, no longer seems enough for her to survive. The air is still rich with carbon dioxide, but she shudders as if she's suffocating. The tips of her needles curl. She feels starved, airless, empty. She wants him to speak again, to see her.

Instead, he runs his hand through his long hair and laughs shakily. He picks up the shotgun and, with a nervous glance at her sisters, walks out of the grove.

She feels his footsteps through the earth, hears the men in the distance cheer when he returns before popping the tabs off beer cans, handing one to him in triumph. The men stay in camp for a week, staining the silence with their saws and gunshots. They shoot deer, moose, bear, and, when there's nothing more to kill, the targets they tape to trees. When they finally leave, her sisters do not sleep. Trees are slow to grow and even slower to forgive. They are watching her.

✦

He doesn't come for the next few seasons, but the path he blazed brings others.

Men with compasses and surveying chains mark a line through her sisters with orange paint, black dogs bound into the brush and giddily return to their bearded companions with thrashing, bloody turkeys in their mouths. Once, an out of breath family of three—red-faced parents and a teary teenage girl—search the needle-covered ground as if expecting to find an arrow pointing the way home. With a worried glance at the man, the woman gives the last drops of water in her canteen to the girl, who guzzles it down. The man's face is grave as he studies a topographical map, while the woman gathers moist branches and tries without success to start a fire. Even an hour's smoke will reduce photosynthesis in trees by half and lessen that season's growth, but perhaps the family doesn't know this.

"Where *are* we?" the teenager wails, her gaze flitting from tree to tree as if she can't tell the difference between old growth and sapling. She hunches her shoulders and curls in on herself, her cries much louder than the boy's, as if she wants to make sure the whole forest can hear her. Tears and sweat coat her skin; she is all slickness and smooth angles, without a blemish or bear wound in sight.

The one-eared bear has not come for three autumns and the wound he left behind has scabbed over with pale callus—something far softer and more skin-like than her trunk has ever produced before. With all these people entering the forest, her sisters send out distress signals daily —not only to announce intruders, but also to proclaim that the air reeks of oil and gasoline. Below their grove, two hundred year old pines have given way to a winding dirt road. On a nearby ridge, an entire forest of firs fell to bulldozers, the earth shaking for miles when the titans fell. The birds are eerily quiet. All the ground squirrels have gone, scrambling for underground burrows somewhere safer, farther away. Trees can't scatter, but they feel fear in the same way the older man with the map must; in their deepest, darkest recesses, down where no one can see it.

Yet for some reason she is no longer afraid. For trees or people, the choice is the same: Embrace change or deny it. Adapt or die. She studies the girl, memorizing her smooth lines, the curve of her quivering jaw, the shadowy gaps between arms and torso. She watches the girl raise a hand to her mouth, pace on long, shapely legs, cry out in relief when the man finally says, "Oh my God, the path is right here. Just below us. Everything's going to be okay."

It's as the three of them rush out of the grove—even their weary legs marvels of strength and agility—that it happens. That newly formed callus, her wound wood, pools just enough to form a slight mound—right where a girl's hips would be. It's the smallest shift, a barely perceptible curve where there was none before, but it changes everything. Suddenly, she can no longer hear her sisters' alarms or feel the hum of water and nutrients moving through her xylem. The smallest shift, and she's on the outside looking in.

Her sisters don't—won't—move an inch, yet it feels as if they are suddenly miles away.

✦

When the boy finally returns, he is a handsome teenager. And he isn't alone.

The girl he drapes his arm around has long brown hair that she swats constantly, to scatter the horseflies. Below a pair of frayed denim shorts, her dark legs are marred with cuts and bruises, her ankles a bloody dartboard studded with cheatgrass and thorns. He smiles, but she doesn't.

"Why did we have to walk so far?" she asks.

"It's only a quarter mile from the car."

"Yeah, uphill. And you know I h—" Her words end in a scream. A pair of bees are drinking the sweat on her neck and the girl runs in circles, shrieking. The young man turns aside to hide his laughter. He is taller than he was, more muscular, but with the same pine-brown hair and heartwood eyes. She misses his freckles, hidden now beneath sunburn and a very thin stubble of beard.

"It's okay," he says. "Calm down. They're just bees."

But the girl cries until he swats away the insects and loops his arms around her waist. Like the bees, he licks the moisture from her neck, but this time, instead of screaming, she closes her eyes. When she lifts her chin, he presses his lips to hers. His hands find the buttons on her shirt, turning the last of her cries to moans. The young man kisses each piece of skin he unveils. He lays his own shirt on the ground and her atop it, then speaks tenderly when she crosses her legs. Their conversation starts and stops like birdcalls—alarms, invitations, quick, throaty pleas. It may be a language she's not meant to know, but one word comes through.

"Edward," the girl says over and over. "Edward. Edward."

The grove is still and wary. A teenager is as much a predator to trees as a deer with a taste for tender branches, but it seems that the girl has claimed him and will take him away.

"Edward," the girl says again, this time with tears in her eyes, "I love you."

This particular trill rises at the end, more of a question than anything else. Most of the words they say seem to mean nothing at all, while a chosen few carry all the weight in the world. The girl stiffens, waiting, but it's obvious from the way the young man turns his back to her and gathers their clothes that he's not going to respond.

The silence in the grove has never felt lonely before. If her sisters are sending out phytohormones or ethylene gas, she doesn't feel it. She stands where she always has but somehow apart, listening to things she's never heard before —the girl swallowing nervously, the jingle of keys in the young man's pocket as he stands and casually tosses the girl her blouse. Even the quietest human things drown out the communal breathing of trees.

"Edward?" the girl says.

The smile he carried into the grove has been replaced by a set jaw, impatience. His gaze travels past the girl to the bear wound, perhaps to the callus curves that weren't there before. She is an ancient larch tree, rising over one hundred and fifty feet into the sky, but suddenly she can't sense anything above the level of his eyes. When he rakes his gaze across her, his stare feels like the heat of the sun.

Whatever her sisters feel is immaterial. In the dark hollow of that bear wound, she breathes.

Three

Weeping Willow
(Salix babylonica)

The name Weeping Willow is a misnomer. Certainly, their long branches and delicate silver-tinged leaves weep into graceful arches, but unlike the sap-filled maple, they never cry. Willows grow fast, tolerate most kinds of soil, and spread their roots to three times the height of the tree itself, allowing them to crack pavement, damage foundations, and infiltrate pipes and water lines. Stunning trees, really, but brats. Targets for gypsy moths, sawflies, beetles, aphids, willow scab, black canker, leaf spot, and crown gall, weeping willows expect to be tended to continually. But in return for the headaches they cause, they offer salicin, a natural form of aspirin.

✦

He never brings the girl again.

Instead he comes with a man who would look just like him, if decades of sun and wind hadn't tanned the man's skin into leather. Both dressed in dull green, the two men creep lightly across the forest floor, careful not to snap any twigs. They don't speak; when the older man decides to stop, he merely holds out his hand. Perhaps they don't realize that every animal in the vicinity has long since smelled them coming and taken off for places they'll never find.

The young man still looks like a sapling, barely leafed out and spindly, but his hands, as she predicted, no longer shake when he lifts a rifle. The two of them stand silently atop her roots for one hour, then two, their breathing eventually blending into the wind—which might explain why the young doe makes the mistake of returning to the grove. With one shot, the young man kills her. He doesn't cry at all.

The older man examines the carcass. "She's barely got any meat on her," he says. "Hardly worth the effort of hauling her back."

His voice is gruff, as if the air he breathes is full of sawdust. He kicks the doe's lifeless chest in disgust, then turns his gaze to her sisters, assessing them from root to crown. He raps on their trunks not to wake them, but to gauge their density. He is interested in board feet, not the secrets trees will share if you stay still long enough. How to bend but not break, for instance, and the importance of rest and a little sunshine. How much easier it is to survive when your roots are intertwined with others.

But the older man merely rips a sprig of golden needles off one of her sister's limbs and says, "Lumber futures are trading higher. Nine hundred dollars a thousand board feet for that hillside we logged in town."

The young man isn't listening. He refuses to look at the doe he shot and focuses instead on her bear wound, which doubled in size last fall, when the one-eared bear finally returned and feasted on her for weeks. Ever since, her callus tissue has kicked into overdrive in an attempt to heal her, creating smooth lines and curves where there'd been only brittle bark before. When the sun is low and shadows long, no other animals will come near her, mistaking the glowing wound wood for a pair of luminous eyes.

She's not sure what he sees, or believes, but the longer he watches her, the more her wound wood burns. She's been dropping green needles all summer and her bark has turned an ominous shade of rust. If trees could talk, her sisters would be screaming at her, but their constant distress signals are little more than background noise to her now.

Edward. She hears the name even when no one speaks it. Hears it in the wind through her needles, hears it when the crows cry. She's been dreaming of him, of where he goes when he's not with her. The first time she tried to imagine what lies beyond the grove her pith, the oldest wood at the center of her, cracked. Now there are gaps between her core and sapwood. She imagines the openings are like the spaces between a girl's slender fingers, just wide enough for sunlight to break through.

The older man sees none of this as he squints into the sun and calculates board feet. "We haven't got the capital to buy the land here outright, but I'll bet we could get logging rights," he says. "The owner just brought his sons into the business. That's why you're coming to the meeting I set up. Gotta show 'em we're family-run too."

Edward finally turns. "Are we?"

The older man pulls a cigarette from his shirt pocket and strikes a match. Years ago, flames scorched her trunk, but moved on quickly through the dry grass without reaching her canopy. She remembers the searing heat though. Parts of her are still covered in soot.

The older man squints through the smoke. "I'm paying you, aren't I? You're up on this mountain and not at that fancy college that you couldn't get into."

Edward jams his hands in his pockets. "The advisor said they might take me if I go to community college for a semester or two. I could still work for you part time."

"Degrees are worthless around here, boy." The older man's lip curls meanly around his cigarette. "Look around you. Men here cut trees and pack their freezers with elk meat. You need to stop thinking you're better than everyone else and learn how to kill a buck without fainting."

Edward stiffens. "I've never fainted."

"But you've run off on our hunting trips. Bawled your eyes out to the trees." The older man smirks. "You gotta toughen up, boy. Jesus, Edward, don't you know who you are?"

She hears Edward's name, but it doesn't sound the same. The girl had spoken it like a plea, while this is a condemnation. It's a wonder that anyone can tell truth from lies.

Edward juts out his chest. She's watched dozens of standoffs in her grove—bull elks fighting over territory, manic magpies pecking at intruders, moose versus wolf. The same one wins every time—the one who doesn't care about the outcome, who would rather die than lose.

Edward holds out for a few moments, then drops his shoulders.

"I'm the same as you," he says, and there is such sadness in his voice she feels a strange, new twitch at the core of her. A flicker of compassion, the first beat of a fierce young heart.

"That's right," the older man says, throwing his smoldering cigarette onto a pile of brown needles. "You're a *logger*. That means you work your ass off and cut whatever's in front you."

He narrows his eyes at Edward as the dry larch needles begin to smolder. A thin plume of smoke snakes up between them, but only Edward's gaze falls to the lick of flame by their feet. The old man smirks as Edward crushes the fire beneath his boot.

"Go back to the truck and get the saw," the old man says.

Edward's gaze flicks first toward her bear wound, then to the fallen deer. But when the older man lights a second cigarette, Edward nods and walks out of the grove.

She and her sisters absorb the gray cigarette smoke through their needles and bark. The man inhales deeply before removing the glowing cigarette from his lips and pressing it to her bark. She reacts to the burn the way all trees do, by sending out a distress signal to warn her sisters of danger and closing her stomata—basically holding her breath to avoid inhaling the smoke particles. She's been pummeled by ice and wind storms, mauled by the one-eared, yet this is the first time she's been harmed for sport. As the man brands her, she marks the moment in her xylem. She will not forget.

When Edward returns, he carries a chainsaw instead of his rifle. The older man finally removes the cigarette from her bark, leaving a smoldering, black wound behind. He pulls the starter and the stench of gasoline floods the air. Razor sharp teeth spin and she braces for the pain she knows is coming, then he turns and puts the blade to her oldest sister's trunk.

The saw wails like a dying animal; even the fearless magpies take flight. As the man carves a deep V into her sister, the ground shudders and sawdust settles into the creases of her bark. Her sister does all she can, dulling the chain with her hardwood, but still the gouge in her trunk grows bigger until her canopy sways precariously in the wind. But before she falls there is silence; the man sets down the saw.

Nothing else in the forest makes a sound. The older man turns to Edward and smiles.

"Finish it," he says.

Edward stares at her nearly eviscerated sister without moving, except for the hands he clenches into fists. "Dad," he says, "you know this is private property. You shouldn't have—"

"You think I built this company, this life, by asking for permission?" the older man asks. "If you don't take what you want, you're handing it to somebody else."

Edward says nothing, but a muscle tics in his jaw. The afternoon wind picks up, testing itself against her sister's spine, but otherwise everything in the forest is hushed, waiting. Edward looks around the grove as if he can't remember how he got here, or if there is even a way out. And for the first time in her life, she wishes for some of the words these humans are so fond of. Just a few will do: *Start walking and don't stop.*

But like her sisters, she's silent, even when Edward grabs the saw. Somehow the noise is more deafening when he's the one revving the engine. When he sets the blade to her sister's trunk, it's possible that she grows ears just to hear him.

It takes only seconds for the saw's teeth to sink deep enough to crack through her sister's core. Sinews snap, her sister teeters, Edward and his father step nimbly to the side. The men are woodsmen, after all, felling the 250 year old larch right where they want it, into the open space at her feet. The ground shakes for miles when her sister hits the earth.

✦

The last bit takes the longest. It's easy to decide to be something different. The hard part is letting go of whatever you were before.

She is a marker of time and seasons—every ring in her trunk a snapshot of another year's survival. She lives so that others may breathe, every part of her designed to maximize photosynthesis—xylem whisking water and nutrients to her needles, roots supplying carbohydrates to fungi, which return the favor by increasing hydration and mineral uptake to her feeder hairs, chloroplasts storing the energy of sunlight. Alone, she can provide enough oxygen for a family of four. But she will still be alone.

So she chooses. Capillaries instead of cambium. Blood and bone over heartwood and sap. Nature has always known the secret: The key to changing everything is changing slowly, one small step at a time. Female wasps attacked no one for centuries before developing stingers and becoming queens. A single poplar seed turns a meadow to woodland—over millennia. Nature favors the slow, and she is in no hurry.

Like always, her golden needles drop beneath the autumn gloom, then at the first blast of winter, the water in her cells turns to sap to keep from freezing. Even when the spring rains come, she looks the same—her limbs sprouting their usual pink, rose-like cones and lime green needles. But when the one-eared bear appears in the grove, he takes one whiff of her old wound and quickly lopes away. It's only then that she wonders at her smell. What was once the earthy scent of bark and wound wood has become the stink of sweat. She reeks of something that doesn't belong in the forest.

Throughout the spring, a layer of light, soft wood accumulates in her trunk, followed by a denser, darker ring of summer, but she hardly notices the added weight. Parts of her grow, die, and turn toward the sun, but it's all by rote. She no longer senses anything except what's happening inside the dark hollow of her bear wound. Strange things, things that make her sisters go eerily still. Wood grain that no longer aligns with her axis but settles instead into the shape of slender fingers. Callus tissue stretching and softening to something akin to freckled skin.

Whatever she is becoming aches. The following autumn, despite fallen needles protecting her roots from the first frosts and her branches using resin as their own form of antifreeze, her wound wood prickles for the very first time. She used to doze through winter, but now her outer bark sloughs away and the soft, tender layer beneath it shivers. Every day, there is a new, delicious sting—fingernails erupting from knots, xylem expanding painfully as something thicker than water flows through its cells, a deafening crack as a gnarled whorl splits lengthwise between two forming lips, allowing her to breathe in the very oxygen she was born to give away. She tries to master a clunky new tongue while an unfamiliar instinct makes her swallow. Saliva floods her mouth, saltier than rainwater, enough to swirl.

Her supple new skin crinkles upward. Inside her bear wound, she opens a pair of blue eyes.

The first time she wiggles her newly formed toes, the crows take flight and don't return. No deer have grazed in the grove since she opened her eyes. Her oldest sister's corpse still lies where it was felled, abandoned like worthless bone.

The human body is a marvel of engineering but she's not sure it knows what it's doing. Rootless and top-heavy, every time she tries to lift a brown foot from the ground she merely trembles. Arms bend one way but not the other, hands go numb for no reason, heels and lips crack open in the dry air and bleed. Her sisters sway with the wind while her newly formed bones struggle for balance. Even at rest, her body gurgles, itches, and throbs. Yet when a wolf slinks into the grove, enticed by the scent of her, she can't help but admire the pounding of her new heart. Each beat slams against her chest, warning her of danger but also marking every second she's alive. *Alive*, she thinks, and lets loose a rumble from the back of her throat. The wolf's ears prick up; his yellow eyes peer into the gloom of her bear wound, unable to tell if she's predator or prey. Her rumble becomes a ragged growl, a sound neither one of them have heard before. His ruff up, the wolf retreats, disappearing into the brush.

Edward returns in mid-spring, carrying the saw he used to fell her sister. He looks much the same, aside from a broader chest and more muscular physique. She's been testing her own muscles, flexing and stretching, leaning forward toward the light beyond the bear wound. Waiting for him.

Edward climbs atop her sister's carcass, snapping brittle branches with the heel of his boot. His jawline and heartwood eyes are exactly as she remembers them, yet something has changed. There's no more give to the corners of his mouth; when he breaks the last branch, he glares at the trees around him in search of something else to destroy. He sizes up her smallest sister, who would be the easiest to fell, but settles on the tallest in the center of the grove, the one who will take a dozen others down with her no matter which way she falls.

Edward clutches the saw so tightly his knuckles turn white, then lifts his face toward the sky. When his shoulders tremble, she can't help but lean toward him, and his head snaps in her direction. His eyes are as hard and dry as the branches he snapped. She remembers his tears and wonders where they've all gone now. He squints at her as if she's a little blurry around the edges, then shakes his head and starts the saw.

There is no one to goad him this time, no reason to set a blade to another sister when the first one he felled still lies unharvested on the ground. Approaching the tallest tree in the grove merely confirms that he's lost his way. If he were a larch, he might be able to transform himself into what he wants to be, but changing a broken man is harder.

He puts the blade to her sister at the same moment she slides out of the bear wound and into the sun. Her untested legs struggle to hold her, the needles she shed last fall stab the tender soles of her feet. Since the moment Edward first stumbled into the grove, she's wanted nothing more than to be with him. But now all she wants is to make him stop.

She tries to take a step and has to grab the trunk of her tree not to stumble, but it is enough. It's possible that he senses her, or has always known she was there. His shoulders stiffen as he pulls the blade away from her sister. A moment later, he turns.

Four

Ponderosa Pine
(Pinus ponderosa)

Loggers value the 150 feet tall Ponderosa for the window frames and cabinetry made from its knot-free lumber, but the tree is worth far more alive. The white-headed woodpecker and pygmy nuthatch depend on pine forests for food and shelter; the Pawnee montane skipper butterfly exists only where Ponderosas meet an understory of blue grama grass. It's a humble, friendly tree, giving way to Douglas fir in moist climates, welcoming a company of bitterbrush and snowberry on drier slopes. Even fire is treated like an old, dear friend—the Ponderosa carpets the forest floor with its dry, brittle needles, facilitating surface fires that never reach the tree's higher, healthy boughs.

✦

For almost two centuries, she's stood in the same place, everything she needed within reach. Sunshine, water, nutrients, soil, fungi. Nothing, it seems, can change until you need more.

As Edward's gaze meets hers the saw he wields sputters into silence. Trees are born with a purpose, but even in this new form she knows what she's meant to do. Whatever else happens, her sister will remain standing.

Edward stares at her, transfixed, and the first emotion she feels as a woman is pleasure. He is, and always has been, hers.

His gaze travels from her bare breasts to her dirt-stained feet and back up again, his face turning red. He drops the saw and quickly sheds his flannel jacket.

"Miss?" he says, holding out the coat. He takes a step toward her but turns his head sideways to look somewhere else. "Are you all right?" he asks the trees. "Are you hurt?"

She can't believe the scents! She'd had no idea that she and her sisters released such strong, resinous, almost citrusy aromas. Her newly formed nostrils flare at the vinegary stink of Edward's sweat, but then the canyon breeze replaces the odor with a heady swirl of mint, sage, syringa, and decomposing humus. She takes the deepest breath she can, flooding her magnificent new lungs with fragrance and larch-sent oxygen. Then she turns to the trees and bows her head. She left them, yet they still offer freely what she needs to survive.

Edward jiggles the coat, or his hand is shaking. She tests her lips and finds that she can smile.

"Put this on," he says. "Please."

Before, his voice was like every other sound outside of her—mostly indistinguishable buzzing funneled through bark and pith. Without a shell of hardwood around her, she hears the catch in his throat, the rise and fall of every syllable. His voice is deep and a little unsteady. He sidesteps closer to her, still looking away.

"Please," he repeats, and she finds she likes the sound of that word.

He glances at her briefly, then drapes the jacket between them like a shield. She's mesmerized by his movements—an elbow bent to hold the fabric, his back leg bending before swinging forward, muscles and kneecaps always in motion, heel hitting first before rolling up to his toe. She wonders if he knows how remarkable a creature he really is.

But then his fingers swipe her shoulder and she jumps.

"I'm sorry!" he cries. "I just . . . Here."

He presses the flannel to her skin. It's the softest thing she's ever encountered, and her astonishing layer of skin prickles—whether in pleasure or apprehension she can't tell.

He raises his hands. "I'm not going to hurt you," he says softly.

It's the first decision she will make: Move toward him or away. He stands still and quiet, watching her. His eyes are wide again, the color of pine. Suddenly something obstructs her view of him and remarkably she can lift her own hand and reach for what turns out to be an errant lock of her own hair. It is bark-brown and silky—another soft thing. Her legs, however unwieldy, are long and smooth, the light brown color of one of her winged seeds. *I'm young,* she thinks. *Like the girl he brought to the grove. I might even be beautiful.*

She looks around the grove, taking in each of her sisters, memorizing them from the outside in now, memorizing all of it. She can never go back.

She leans toward him.

When he touches her again, it's to slide a flannel sleeve over one shoulder, then the other. He gestures at the front of the jacket and, when she doesn't move, he fumbles with the buttons. As he fastens the ones near her chest, his hands begin to shake.

He steps back abruptly, as if she spooked him. She notices that needles, her needles, have fallen into his brown hair.

"Who are you?" he asks. "What are you doing here?"

She cocks her head. There's no warble to his voice, no hoot or trill to mark his territory or announce the sunrise. But the longer he looks at her, the more she wants to know the meaning behind his sounds—his particular lilt and intonation, every change in pitch and tone. He takes another step back, glancing at his saw, the way he came, one side of his mouth pinched in indecision. He has choices to make, too.

So she tests her toes, wriggling them into the dirt. She doesn't dare lift a foot completely from the ground, but she can slide forward—one foot scraping the earth, then the other. Newborn elk have more grace than she does, but she doubts any of them have been as delighted as she is to take their first steps. He watches her warily as she inches toward him, until her toe hits a rock and she stumbles. With one quick motion, he catches her by the elbow. Her lovely new skin warms beneath his touch.

"Can you speak?" he asks. "Did someone hurt you?"

He looks her over, his gaze lingering on her long legs until he notices her watching him. He looks away quickly.

"Where are your clothes?" he asks. "Should I call the police? What am I supposed to do here?"

Her lips curl upward whenever she looks at him. He still holds her elbow, and she hopes he never stops. How wonderful to have only a thin layer of skin between her and everything else—the gentle breeze on her neck, his red hot fingers, even the things that hurt, every needle and jagged rock.

"You've got to help me out here," he says.

His voice, she decides, sounds most like the mountain bluebird. A non-musical "tew tew tew" coupled with the occasional "tink" of alarm. With him holding her steady, it's the easiest thing in the world to lift her hand to his chest. Another tendril of wavy brown hair falls across her fingers. Her *hair*. She stares at it, delighted.

He opens his mouth as if he might speak, but he seems to have run out of words. She remembers that girl he once brought into the grove, the way her lips moved, the sounds she made. She taps her tongue against the roof of her mouth, focuses on the back of her throat until she finally produces a hum. She's been dreaming of his name for years now. When he squeezes her elbow tighter, the rest is easy.

"Ed-ward," she says.

Turns out that stopping Edward from harming her sister is the easy part. Once she speaks his name, he steps away from her and looks warily around the grove. He might leave at any moment and never come back. Or return in the night to do more damage. Trees stand guard, but she has no idea what people do.

"How do you know my name?" he asks.

When she only stares at him, he retreats another step, back toward wherever he came from. She has already made her decision—toward him instead of away. So she takes one last, long look at her sisters before attempting to follow him.

If her sisters are sending out a warning flash of hormones and chemical signals, she feels nothing but a slight unease. Her right leg buckles and she falls hard on one knee. When she cries out, Edward hesitates for a moment before turning back.

"This is crazy," he says, helping her to her feet.

She clings to his arm while studying how he lifts one foot then the other without falling. She concentrates so hard on mimicking his stride that she fails to notice the moment they leave the grove. By the time she finally masters two steps on her own without stumbling, her sisters are well behind her, hidden by a wall of pines. The only sound is the wind through the trees.

It takes them most of the morning to walk down the mountain. Not only are her muscles untested and weak, she keeps stopping to gawk at the landscape. Dark pine forests, sunny hillsides blanketed with lupine and yellow balsamroot, bright green marshland humming with insects, a boisterous river that drowns out everything else. With their sturdy legs, humans can always find a path to something beautiful. She wonders if they realize how lucky they are.

Edward barely glances around him as he leads her to a hard-packed dirt road. Parked there is a battered pick-up truck dripping oil onto the earth. Even with a thick coating of mud on the tires, the truck reeks of gasoline.

She releases Edward's arm and steps backwards. Edward opens the truck door, swiping crumpled wrappers onto the floor. When he notices she hasn't moved, he holds up a set of shiny keys.

"Are you getting in?"

She takes another step backwards, toward the forest, toward things that smell right, and he throws up his hands.

"I live eight miles from here," he says. "You're in no shape to walk."

She cocks her head, disliking the new, disagreeable tone of his voice. He taps his foot on the ground, then slams the truck door shut, the thud echoing up the mountain, where she's sure her sisters can hear it. This far from them, the only thing she senses from the grove is wariness, not only of Edward, but of her. She will always be their sister, but what she's become could also be a threat. They've gone still, waiting for the danger to pass.

As Edward paces around the truck, she remains by the trees, as still as her sisters, wondering if she's safer with him or left alone. He mumbles something she can't hear, then tosses the keys on the hood of the truck. He looks down the dirt road that's been carved straight through a stand of willows, for no reason that she can see, and takes a deep breath. He glances at her nervously and shoves his hands into his pants pockets, so much like the timid boy she remembers that her lips curl upward.

"What do you expect me to do?" he asks. "I can't just leave you here."

This tone is better—softer, almost pleading. She likes how slowly he approaches her, as if he worries that she might flee at any moment, and how, when she looks up into his eyes, she also gets to see the sky above him, every passing cloud. She reaches up to touch the whiskers on his cheek, remembering the freckles he had before. He hardly breathes as she runs a thumb across the bristles. He knows almost nothing about her, while he is the only thing in this new world that she really knows.

So she lets him lead her to the truck. He helps her into the cab, pulling a band across her stomach and belting her in. It smells horrible—vinegary, stale, like something beneath the seat is rotting. Bird splatter and dried mud mars the windshield. The seat fabric is ripped and scratches at her bare legs.

When Edward turns the key, the engine rumbles like the earthquakes that occasionally thunder through the mountains. She cries out, but they're already moving. She chews on the cuffs of the flannel coat.

At first, she thinks it might be all right. The dirt road is an obstacle course of rocks and washboards, so they move cautiously. She can look out her window and still make out every willow tree and birch.

It's only when Edward turns onto pavement and enters the highway that she covers her face with her hands. There is no point trying to identify the trees they pass because everything flies by in a blur. Edward says something to try to soothe her, but she can't hear him over the roar of the engine. When he swerves to avoid a pothole, the first tears she's ever shed slide down her cheeks.

She closes her eyes and remembers a world of stillness. Heartwood clogged with so much resin, sound waves can't penetrate it. Roots strong enough to anchor an 8,000 pound tamarack to the ground. There's a palm tree in the South American rainforest that walks from shade to sunlight by growing roots in the direction it wants to travel, then allowing the old roots to lift into the air and die. But no other tree will grow near it. Aside from a few rebels, most trees don't want to flourish somewhere better. They die where they were planted, so that everything that comes after them there can thrive.

She hasn't forgotten where she came from, 200 years of going nowhere at all. She keeps her eyes tightly closed and imagines roots growing from the soles of her new feet toward the truck floor, then wriggling through the tiniest metal seams. When Edward slows for a turn, a thick taproot latches onto a pothole in the gray pavement and tunnels quickly downward into cool, nourishing dirt. She likes this new, human imagination. It works so well that the truck's wheels begin to slow. Edward makes a gentle turn, then another, then the deafening engine suddenly going quiet.

She opens her eyes. They've parked in front of a small white house with peeling paint and a porch that is sinking on one side. Edward releases her seat belt and leans across her to open the truck door.

She launches herself from the cab, falling to the ground then stumbling toward the only thing she trusts—the elm tree in the middle of the yard. She wraps her arms around the trunk, presses her cheek to the rough bark, and the elm's rippled leaves cluck their sympathy. Here, she sniffs for the familiar—grass, sagebrush, damp, fallen leaves. Way off in the distance, above the roofline of the dilapidated house, she spies a sliver of dark woods.

Edward approaches her hesitantly, as if she might bolt. But she has nowhere to go now except to him. She takes a deep, steadying breath and turns from the tree. When he doesn't come close enough, she holds out her hand until, with a quick look around to see who's watching, he takes it.

✦

Inside.

It is unpleasant.

Dark even though it's light outside, unnaturally warm despite spring frost on the window panes. Nothing moves. A pair of curtains hang limply, the head of a bull elk stares lifelessly from the wall. She doubts that a window has ever been opened; the very walls reek of charred meats, cigarette smoke, dry rot. Even the dust in the air is listless, floating aimlessly in the single beam of sunlight that makes it inside.

Despite a mountain view through the window, caricatures of forests adorn the walls. The floor is the color of dirt but too soft, with wooly fuzz that tickles the soles of her feet. The glossy brown planks on the walls are painted to look like wood—if trees grew straight and flat, with identical knots every few inches. Her own grain twisted and shifted with every change in temperature and nutrients, so she has no idea what the walls are actually made of. She does, however, make sure that she doesn't touch them as she takes a hesitant step into the room.

There are too many things. Cushy things, hard things, things that tick and glow and hiss. If she moves another inch, she will brush into something else, so she stops. The only familiar thing is also the worst one: a pile of still smoldering wood ash in the fireplace.

Edward closes the door behind her and she wills herself not to jump. In this closed space, everything he does is deafening, from the racket of the keys in his hand to his boots thumping across the brown, fuzzy floor. He gestures toward a chair covered in scratchy-looking blue fabric, and she thinks of the soft seat where her trunk met the earth. Another chair has real wooden feet and cushions of red and gold, like the amur maples that used to live in the grove, before the creek that once ran there dried up.

"You look . . . Are you from here?" he asks. "Where's your family?" He points at her and slows his speech. "Do . . . you . . . speak . . . English?"

She turns toward the window. A sliver of sunlight breaks through the gap between the listless curtains. There, through the dirty glass, is the distant view of forests.

She has no choice but to inhale the stale, lifeless air. The biggest metamorphosis isn't the creation of her hands and legs, or even the heart that beats inside her. It's turning from the window, trying to find something beautiful inside.

She looks at Edward.

He walks toward her, gently touches her upper arm. "Come sit," he says, patting the back of the scratchy blue chair and sending up another plume of dust.

When she only stares at him, he sighs and walks to the chair. He turns his back to it, then lowers himself slowly onto the cushions. "Like this," he says.

She smiles at him, trying not to wish for birdsong or the distant crack of thunder. With the walls and thick panes of glass, it could storm outside, the elm could fall, and nobody in the house would know it.

Edward returns to her side. This time, he takes her by the elbow to guide her to the chair. He positions her with her back to the seat, then pretends there is a chair behind him and mimes folding himself into it. She tries to reach out and touch his whiskers again, but he shakes his head and mimes sitting again. So, to make him happy, she folds her new body until her rump touches the chair. Though the fabric scratches the back of her bare legs, the cushion is surprisingly plump and comfortable. She smiles up at him in delight.

"Jesus," he says, crossing the room to sit in the maple chair opposite her.

She assumes this is his home, but there is no scent of him in the beer cans on the table or the ash tray piled high with crushed cigarette butts. She believes that the boy who stumbled into her grove would never hang an elk's head on the wall or choose the spindly tree in the corner—the one with plastic leaves and no odor at all.

She doesn't like it here, but sitting in the chair allows her to bend her legs farther than she realized they could go. She lifts her feet off the floor, marveling at the flexibility of her kneecaps. Not to mention the things her hands can do! She can reach, bend, flex, pull, even push the ash tray away from her, so she doesn't have to suffer its stench.

She looks up to find him watching her, his face so concerned and serious she decides the first words she'll learn will be the ones that make him smile.

"Edward," he says, tapping his chest. Then he leans forward and gently taps the hollow of her throat.

She understands what he's after. He believes that to know her, he has to give her a name. In his mind, 200 years of growth, stress, disease and survival can be summed up in one simple word. Yet she saw him, knew him, long before she learned his name. Trees use a network of soil fungi to find each other; wolves call their pack with distinctive howling; black bears identify a man by his particular odor the moment he enters the forest. She is what she is, though when he looks at her this way she wants to please him.

"Okay," he says. "Okay. So you don't understand."

He leaves his chair to crouch beside hers, and taps his chest again. "Edward," he says. He takes her hand and places it on his chest. "You know my name," he continues. "Edward."

She feels the flutter of his heart and smiles. "Ed-ward," she says.

When he smiles back at her, her heart races. She wonders how fast he can make it go. It's a marvel, all these things inside her—tears, heartbeats, sudden, aching desire.

He takes her hand from his chest and presses it to her collarbone. "May?" he says, tapping her gently. "Since I found you in May. May?"

She likes the sound of Edward better, but she tests the new word just the same.

"M-may," she says, and he releases her to clap his hands.

"May," he says, smiling at her.

He is smiling. She is May.

Five

Purple Ash
(Fraxinus americana)

The Purple Ash grows rapidly to 40 feet, with a dense canopy and stunning mahogany leaves in fall, but it doesn't care about that. The Ash is the guru of trees, a symbol of connections and creativity, and a passageway between worlds. Women who give birth at its base will have children who are protected forever, or so the tree would have you believe. It's a little full of itself, the ash—how could you not be when you began all things as Yggdrasil, the World Tree, with a trunk that stretched to the heavens, boughs that spread across the Earth, and roots penetrating the Underworld. The gods themselves held their councils under the ash's branches, and the tree has been going on and on about it ever since.

✦

The first word Edward teaches May is "Stay." As if she has anywhere else to go.

He walks to the door and turns the lock. "Stay," he says.

When she glances toward the window, he closes the curtains.

"Stay," he says again.

In her grove, the ceiling is made of traveling stars. Once impassable cliffs gradually crumble into talus pathways; rivers rise and fall and go dry. Nothing stays. But May doesn't tell him this. She likes the way he looks at her when she eyes the door.

He brings her a pair of large, fleece-lined pants. She runs a finger across the decadent fabric, remembering the year the poplars in the stream below the grove shed so much cotton, she and her sisters were coated in soft, white fluff until July. She laughs when he shows her how to put in one leg, then the other. Wherever the plush fabric brushes her skin, the hairs on her legs stand deliciously on end.

He guides her to the kitchen, where he fills the room with steam and an aroma that makes her stomach rumble. She puts a hand on her belly and marvels at the spasms and growls it makes. In the corner stands a circular wooden table—this one made of real oak—and two chairs. Edward pulls out one of the chairs for her and she remembers how to fold herself onto it. A few minutes later, he places a bowl of something slimy and red in front of her.

May pokes the steaming mound with her finger, but yelps and retracts it quickly when her skin burns.

"It's hot!" he says. "Haven't you ever heard of a fork?" He picks up a three-pronged dagger and stabs it into the bowl. He comes away with what looks like a sap-covered worm and pops it into his mouth.

"Mmmm," he says. "Yum."

Her finger still burning, she watches him chew. She likes the noises he makes—the clicking, slurps and sighs—and the way his Adam's apple bulges with every swallow. So much has changed since he first stumbled into her grove—his height, his strength, the timbre of his voice, not to mention every last bit of her. Yet her favorite transformation just might be being able to choose whether she leads or follows him. She'll never be somewhere she doesn't want to be again.

When Edward holds out the dagger, she flinches and leans away. With another sigh, he drops the dagger and dabs his finger into the steaming bowl. It must not burn him because he smiles as he comes away with a smear of red sauce.

"It's food, okay? F-o-o-d. I just want you to taste it."

She watches his finger as he moves it slowly toward her lips.

"Taste it," he says, opening his mouth and touching his tongue to his upper lip. "Like this."

She's not sure why, but her stomach tightens. When he dabs his finger into the bowl again and lifts it to her lips, she mimics him, opening her mouth and darting out her tongue. Her eyes widen in delight at the burst of flavor—sweetness and acidity all at once.

"Right?" he says. "Spaghetti sauce from a jar. One of my specialties."

He picks up the dagger again, but this time takes her hand.

"You hold it like this," he says, bending her fingers around the dull end, positioning her thumb on top. His skin is almost as hot as the worms. She likes the look of their hands together, beige and brown, like aspen bark.

"It's called a fork."

He keeps his hand over hers, guiding her toward the bowl until they stab another worm. When she only smiles at him, he turns the pointy end toward her mouth.

"Eat," he says.

May parts her lips eagerly this time, using her teeth to slide the worm off the dagger. Edward taps his teeth together and she mimics him again, chewing the worm and swallowing. It's so deliciously satisfying, she snatches the fork from his hand. Edward chuckles and shows her how to hold the utensil between her thumb and forefinger. After a few awkward attempts, she manages to stab a worm entirely on her own.

When the bowl is empty, she looks at him hopefully. Edward smiles as he takes the bowl to the stove.

"Food," he says, dishing out more worms and sauce.

Her mouth waters as he returns, but he holds the bowl just out of her reach.

"Food," he says again. "This is food."

Food, not worms. "Foo-duh," she says.

He shakes his head. "Food."

"Food," May replies, and he grins.

She learns half a dozen words that first night—*Stay, Food, Light, Blanket, Sleep, Water*. He shows her all the rooms she can't imagine he needs—three alone just for "sleep," one for food, two with knobs and pipes and floors that look like stone but aren't. He demonstrates how to turn nighttime into day with the flip of a switch, the magic box where food appears, faucets that channel cold and warm water from some distant river straight into the house.

"Toilet," he says, pressing a lever on the glistening white sculpture that whooshes foul smelling water away. She stares at him blankly, and he nervously runs his fingers through his hair. "You have to know about that."

He lifts the lid and flicks the roll of toilet paper until the needle-thin paper unwinds to the floor. May reaches around him to press the toilet lever again, laughing at the mini whirlpool in the bowl.

"Shit," he says, his cheeks turning pink.

He mumbles something she doesn't understand, then mimics pulling down his pants. He perches himself above the toilet, his face now a deep shade of red.

"Toilet," he says. "For when . . . you know."

She thinks she knows what he wants from her. The men who came to her grove urinated against her trunk; the girl whose family couldn't find their way dug a hole in the ground and squatted. She pulls down the pants he gave her, but Edward only shrieks and yanks them back up. She curls in on herself at the horrified look on his face. She's liked every emotion until now.

"Don't be crazy! Not . . . with me here."

He steps into the hallway and turns his back to her.

"Okay, now," he says, his voice unsteady. "Toilet."

She stares at the shiny "toilet," then at the brown curls that fall to the nape of Edward's neck. With everything he shows her, he hides something else. What he does in this room, for one thing, or the one down the hall with the lock on the door. Why he stopped crying and started acting exactly like the man he hates. Why he cuts down the things that give him solace.

She tugs down her pants and sits on the toilet. When the urine comes, his shoulders tense, as if the tinkle into the bowl is disgraceful. He waits for silence, then gestures toward the toilet paper without turning around. She doesn't need him to show her what to do. The moment he and the older man cut down her sister, she knew they believed that nature is something that needs to be tamed or wiped away. Edward may have brought her home with him, but she's not sure he's willing to keep her. Not unless she learns to hide things, too.

So she finishes quietly and doesn't pull the toilet lever, although Edward doesn't approve of that either. He shakes his head and flushes her urine away, then leads her into the backyard. It's an odd-shaped landscape, with identical, square bushes all lined up in rows.

"Outside," he says.

For some reason, the plants in the yard have no fragrance. Beyond the fence, though, a tangle of wild mint and bindweed perfumes the hillside, and she smiles as she aims for that. Before she can reach it, however, Edward grabs her by the elbow.

"Stay," he says. When she gazes toward the lone pine on the top of the hill, he adds, "Please."

May lets him lead her back inside, where he gestures toward the long brown lump he calls a "couch." He positions her on one end of the lump while he perches on the other.

She smiles whenever a tree branch scrapes against the house. Edward says nothing, but he's still noisy—fidgeting, swallowing, stifling a sneeze. She looks around the room, trying to figure out the reason for things. Half a dozen empty glass bottles emit a sour stench. A diamond-shaped saucer works as a catchall for dirty brown stubs and ash. She can't imagine why the bulky cabinet with its knobs and screen holds center stage in the room, but the contraption on the table is obviously some kind of alarm. She jumps to her feet when it suddenly starts squawking.

"Relax," Edward says. "It's just the phone."

He lifts the top half to his ear and the squawking stops. "See?" he says. "Phone."

He puts the "phone" to his ear and a disembodied voice floats into the room. It sounds like the girl he brought to the grove, except that the person in this phone is hysterical.

"Where have you been all day? You were supposed to pick me up. I've been calling and calling!"

May is reminded of the magpies that often roosted in her branches and cackled madly—wock, wock wock-a-wock. For hours on end.

"Calm down," Edward says. "I'm sorry I forgot to pick you up, but I was in the woods and this . . . person showed up. I had to bring her home."

The magpie girl goes silent for a moment, then erupts in another round of harsh alarms.

"What do you mean you brought someone home? Who is she? What was she doing in the woods? Is she there with you now?"

"It's not like that, Becca," Edward says. "I couldn't just leave her. Something happened to her. She seems . . . lost. She doesn't even know how to talk. Maybe it's amnesia. I don't know."

"Amnesia? Is that even a real thing? How old is she? Where's her family? What's your dad going to say?"

"I don't know!" he snaps, then runs his fingers through his hair. "I'm just . . . I'm trying to do the right thing here."

"The right thing is to call the police. Or take her to the hospital!"

Edward sags against the couch and closes his eyes. So far the things May loves best about his world are flannel pants, food from the magic box, and how there is nothing stopping her from scooting next to him and laying her palm against his cheek. When his eyes snap open, she smiles. The magpie girl is still chirping, but Edward lowers the noisy contraption from his ear. It seems the perfect time to lean in and press her lips to his, the way the girl in the grove once did.

It's strange at first, and a little wet. She's not sure what it's supposed to accomplish. Then he lets out a small moan and if there is anything left of her old life, it vanishes when he slips a hand behind her neck. His lips part slightly as he tilts her head backward. The girl is still trilling: "Edward? Edward, are you there?"

He pulls away, but not too far. She can still feel his warm breath on her cheek. His eyes search hers.

"Who are you?" he whispers.

"Edward!" the girl warbles. "Talk to me! Are you okay? What's she doing? Edward!'

He shakes his head as if coming out of a trance and brings the magpie girl back to his ear. "I gotta go," he says.

"But what are you going to do? Take her to the police, Edward! Let someone else figure it out!"

"Yeah," he says. "Maybe I'll do that. See you later, Becca."

He returns the phone to its cradle and rests his hands on his knees. His breathing comes quick and unevenly, as if he's exerting himself in some way she can't see. There are a million things she'll have to learn, but thankfully a few are instinctual. In times of uncertainty, it's best to stay still. Trees are slow to change, but humans might be even slower. Better to let them work things out themselves. She doesn't want to spook him.

So they sit. Edward stretches his neck left, then right. He taps his fingers against his knees. She matches her breathing to his, turns her head slightly away from him to hide her desires. When he finally gets to his feet, she does the same. Her heart races as he looks toward the door, then slows in relief as he turns the other way. Toward the hallway and the sleep rooms. Where there are no exits.

He's going to keep her.

In one of the sleep rooms, Edward pulls back the covers on the bed.

"My dad's out of town so you can sleep in here," he says.

May cocks her head quizzically, and he sighs.

"Bed? Sleep? You know, what you do at night? Wherever you're from, you have to close your eyes once in a while."

He gestures toward the bed and she mimics him, waving her hand toward the things he calls blankets and pillows, all of which are patterned with a species of black duck she's never seen in the wild.

"No, that's not—" He throws up his hands in frustration before lowering himself on the bed.

"Like this," he says, lying on his side and closing his eyes. "Sleep."

She remembers how he and the girl had sunk smoothly to the forest floor, their bodies intertwined. *Edward*, the girl kept saying. As if she didn't know any other word.

May doesn't have the girl's grace, but she manages to hoist herself onto the mattress, which is springy and decadently soft. She laughs as she rolls toward him, the warm, muscular side of him the perfect place to come to rest.

The moment she touches him, though, he flinches and scoots away.

"Whoa!" he says, leaping off the bed. "May, stop!"

The way he recoils from her, she knows she's supposed to feel shame again, but she doesn't. In fact, the only thing she does feel is that there are too many rules for what should and shouldn't be.

Edward's cheeks are red again. "You stay," he says, holding up his hands. He points down the hall. "I will be down there. In my room."

He backs up slowly, making sure she stays put. She watches him until he's out of her line of sight, then listens to his footsteps, a door opening and closing, then finally what passes for silence in his world. Things ticking and humming, people arguing in the house next door, the rumbling of trucks on a distant highway. And darkness isn't darkness at all, but merely a dimmer kind of daylight. A street lamp still shines through the window; the bathroom sports a cold blue light shaped like a shell.

May lies in the same spot he did, atop sheets still carrying a bit of his scent. It's almost too much pleasure to take in—the give of the downy mattress beneath her weary legs, billowy pillows to cradle her neck, layers of sweet-smelling sheets and blankets. She rolls around the bed, twisting the sheets into knots and testing the way her new body works. Trees stand or die, but now she can flip over onto her stomach or curl up into a ball. She can bend and straighten, flex or arch her back. With everything their bodies are capable of, it's a wonder that human beings ever stay still at all.

Eventually she hears Edward snoring—deep, grunting sounds like the feral boar that once migrated through her woods. That single male devoured the entire understory of grasses and shrubs in a day, then wallowed without food or water in the grove for six more as if he couldn't believe the damage he'd done.

She rises from the bed and walks down the hall. Edward's snorting has settled into rhythmic puffs as she opens his door. The street lamp guides her to his side, where she slips into bed beside him, sighing in pleasure when the pillow cradles her neck. He's turned away from her and doesn't stir when she presses herself against his back. He's so warm, she kicks away the blanket. As long as he's near her, she may never be cold again.

She is May now, but she's not so different from what she used to be. Trees relax their limbs at night, dropping their crowns and branches a few inches before raising them again at first light. Yet even while resting, they remain aware of their environment, just as she does now. She falls asleep for the very first time, but only for a few minutes. All night long, she frantically climbs out of slumber to assure herself that Edward is still there. Once, she opens her eyes to find that Edward has rolled over toward her. She smiles as she nestles into the curl of his arm. When she wakes next, he's holding her. She no longer hears the traffic roaring in the distance. There is only Edward's heartbeat, coming quicker now.

His arms are around her, but his body is tense.

He is trying not to breathe, as futile a task as a larch seed sprouting in pure shade. She opens her eyes to find her hand clasping his narrow waist, one leg thrown over his. His skin doesn't give as much as hers; he's all muscle and bones and nervous tension. She imagines that if he was a tree, he'd be something that grows fast and skinny—a cypress or skyrocket juniper.

She slides a finger over his hip bone and he gasps, but doesn't speak. She knows six words but will have to learn all the other ones quickly, because it's obvious she'll be the one who talks. She will learn the words that soothe him, the ones that make him smile. She will say them again and again and again.

She rises up on her elbow so she can see his face. He averts his gaze, as skittish as a wood mouse, but she puts a palm to his cheek and turns him toward her. His eyes are the color of heartwood, of home.

"Stay," she says.

He releases his breath in one long, slow exhalation. Now that he sees her, he never moves his gaze from her face.

"This is crazy."

She watches his lips closely, then tries to repeat the movements and sound. "This . . . cra-zee."

His mouth twitches. "You could be some lunatic murderer."

That one is harder. "Loon-tic mur-der."

He laughs out loud, the first real laugh, and her heart skips a beat. What else will keep him laughing? She'll learn every word.

But before she can, they hear a thud from outside the front door.

"Shit," Edward says, jumping out of bed and holding up his hands. "Stay. Shit. Shit. Shit."

He races out of the room, and May follows more slowly. She likes making him happy, but she likes doing what she wants to do more. She hears another man's gravelly voice and knows who it is before she steps into the room. He carries the stench of smoke and gasoline with him. Edward blocks the older man in the entry.

" . . . thought you were going to be out of town until Tuesday," Edward says.

The older man carries a bag on one shoulder and narrows his eyes. "And I thought I told you to get ready for our trip to California."

"I am ready. I headed up to the site yesterday."

"That so?" the older man asks. "And you didn't, by chance, take a chainsaw with you? Maybe to stick it to your old man and slice up his best lumber?"

"It's not our lumber yet. And I didn't cut anything."

"Yeah, I know. You lost your nerve. Jerrod Dempsey saw you. Said you went up with a chainsaw and came back with some girl."

Edward balls his hands into fists. May gives up trying to memorize the older's man's gritty words and steps forward. The man spots her instantly and lets out a harsh laugh.

"Oh-ho!" he says. "And here she is!"

"Dad, I can explain—"

"No need for that," the older man says. "You got yourself a little hot tamale. Nothin' wrong with that."

The older man looks her up and down, and though she knows instantly that this is someone to avoid, she also appreciates what he teaches her. Which words are cruel, for instance, and the only two choices offered when danger enters the room: Challenge or cower. Edward seems to have chosen submission, but the thing about being brand new is that nothing much has frightened her yet.

She crosses the room to stand between the man and Edward. The older man laughs, showing his teeth.

"Got some spice, huh?" he says. "Looks like you found yourself a pit bull, boy."

"Don't call her that," Edward replies. "She was in the woods, Dad. I couldn't just leave her. She's confused and can't really speak. We've got to help her."

The older man stares at her chest and May clutches instinctively at the clothes Edward gave her.

"Oh, believe me," he says, "I know exactly what kind of help she needs."

Rutting elks will trample each other for cows and dominance; foxes can be surplus killers, annihilating a whole den of rabbits to eat just one. Even the dainty hummingbird will kill any interloper who invades her patch of fireweed. The wild is full of bullies far more dangerous than one foul-smelling man.

When May steps forward, Edward puts a restraining hand on her shoulder. She smiles at him, but slips nimbly out of his grip. A tree must accept whatever happens to it, while a woman gets to wake up every morning and decide how hard she's going to fight.

She points a finger at the older man's throat.

"Not stay," she says.

His mean smile never falters. He stares at her finger, then disdainfully slaps it aside.

He turns to Edward. "We're going to California on Wednesday. I don't care what you do with your pit bull until then, as long as you help me get that deal signed and sealed."

Then, before May can brace herself, he pokes his own finger, hard, into her throat. She chokes on the pressure, and Edward lunges forward to knock the older man's hand away. She raises a hand to her throat while the older man drops his bag to the floor.

"Oh, I'm staying, sweetheart," he says. "This is my house."

Six

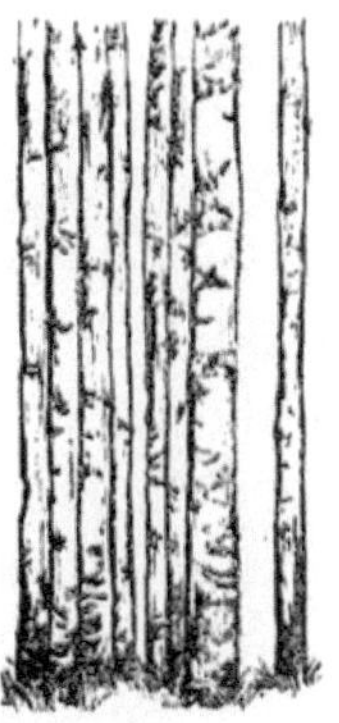

Quaking Aspen
(Populus tremuloides)

A stand of a hundred aspen trees is considered a single organism, and every tree in that stand a genetic clone of the rest. With their luminous white bark and chatty, round leaves that turn to gold in autumn, aspens are the beauties of the forest. They are also nearly impossible to kill. Years before a single aspen trunk grows, the root system lies dormant, waiting. This species of poplar feasts and grows constantly, even in winter, and is the only tree in the forest to not fear the axe. Chop them down and they'll merely spring up behind you.

✦

For three days, the older man stalks them. Not like a wolf or a cougar with a belly full of hunger, but as the man he is, the only species who hunts for sport. Edward and May play a constant game of keep away, hiding in the hallway when the man enters the living room, skirting from front yard to back when he steps out the door. But the old man is cunning, sometimes sitting in the dark of the kitchen so that they stumble upon him when they enter for a glass of water. He speaks only to Edward, but leers at May the whole time.

Edward teaches her the word "lock" and how to use one. May locks her bedroom door every night.

The older man yells often, but is scarier, somehow, when he's silent—sitting in his easy chair, watching her every move. May wonders if he knows what she is, or was, because he stares at her the same way he did when she stood tall in her grove—as if he's calculating how much usage he can get out of her. He drinks more than he eats—glass after glass of amber colored liquid—and one night as she walks past him in the living room he grabs her by the wrist. He smells bad and she pities him, all the time he spends lurking in the shadows, indoors. And maybe he knows this because he shoves her away and finishes the remainder of his drink in one angry gulp.

"Sweet dreams, pit bull," he says as he pours himself more.

The next day, Edward sports a bloody lip and a bruise on his cheek. He teaches her the word "father" and she points to the door.

"Not stay."

Edward shakes his head and the light in his eyes goes dim. Nature has a litany of defensive moves, everything from the Kallima butterfly tricking predators into thinking it's a dead leaf to acacia trees increasing the tannic acid in their leaves to ward off hungry herbivores. Humans can actually run to safety, yet something in Edward's nature makes him stay.

When May followed Edward out of the grove, she never expected him to lead her somewhere he didn't want to be. She didn't change everything to cower behind a locked door. And she hopes that, at some point, Edward will choose not to cower either.

So she waits until Edward goes to bed and the older man slumbers in his chair, glass in hand, then she slides open her bedroom window and climbs out. She's far from her forest, but with her first breath of fresh air she knows she's far safer outside than in.

She smiles at the stately elm towering over the house, then steps barefoot onto the grass. The blades are unnaturally even, a condition Edward calls a "lawn."

"Lawn," she says, before making her way around the yard, skimming her fingers across the feathery bottlebrush and practicing the words Edward has taught her.

"Porch. Drivey." She shakes her head. "Driveway. Truck. Street."

The street is an ugly swath of asphalt that hurts the soles of her feet, so she heads to the backyard. Two beheaded tree stumps stand sentry at each corner, while a line of stunted hedges Edward calls "boxwoods" serve as a pitiful fence between them. It appears that nothing in the yard, or the house for that matter, is allowed to grow to its full potential.

Things beyond the fence are far different. A tangle of grasses and vines growing boisterously up the hillside, a lone ponderosa pine on the ridge, glowing beneath the three quarter moon.

She pauses, wondering if Edward might sense her leaving and come after her. But the house remains dark and silent, curtains closed to block the brightness of the moon. May stares at the pine, growing far from her sisters. Things are different here. Full of life, but lonely.

Not stay. Instead, she will walk. Anywhere and everywhere she wants to go.

May steps over the stunted boxwood and onto a prickly carpet of burweed that stabs her tender feet. There are deer prints in the soil but no worn path; she doubts anyone on two legs has ever climbed the hill behind the house before. She heads up the slope, trying to keep to the soft patches of clover, then the carpet of fallen needles beneath the pine. Atop the ridge, a slope descends to a narrow ravine, then rises once more to a wooded hill beyond.

She has no idea why Edward drives his truck when everywhere worth traveling to is within walking distance. Cool canyons with roaring rivers, green meadows where the deer bed down at night, forests so dense, sunlight never touches the earth. If she walks all night, she'll reach the stand of river willows, perhaps even climb to the forest of firs on the next ridge. Her soles will turn from brown to black as all the manmade clicks and ticks and hums give way to rustling leaves.

She brushes her fingers across the jigsaw puzzle bark of the ponderosa before starting down the far slope. She still stumbles occasionally, and on the steepest descents she has to resort to a crouching slide that causes her to shriek with a mixture of terror and joy. The moon lights her way. She tells how far she's gone by habitat—by dawn she's ranged from meadowlands to wetlands to pine forests, then fir. When she can no longer keep her eyes open, she lies down on a bed of needles and falls asleep to the music of her woods.

Just after dawn, she awakens to a young woman kneeling beside her, prodding her shoulder with a stick. The woman's skin looks like a chickadee egg—smooth, pale and speckled. Her curly red hair falls around her face as she breaks into a wide grin.

"Oh, thank goodness!" the woman says. "You're alive!"

✦

"I walk this way every morning," the chickadee woman chirps, "and I just found you here! I had to summon the courage to even come over. I've been reading about those murders in California and you can't be too careful these days!"

May has no idea what she's saying, but she loves the quick tempo of her voice. The girl barely pauses for a breath before speaking again.

"What are you doing out here? Don't you have shoes? I'm sorry to tell you your hair could use a good combing. You're like some lost fairy I found in the woods!"

May smiles as she sits up. The fact that she has yet to say anything doesn't seem to bother the woman at all.

"Wait until I tell Bill," the woman continues. "He's always saying he knows everyone in this town, but somehow I don't think he's met you. Bill's my fiancé. I'm Francie, by the way."

She clasps May's hand between both her own. Her palms are soft; her fingers about the same length as May's. When May remains silent, the chickadee woman cocks her head.

"Why are you sleeping in the woods? Did you have some kind of accident? Are you running away from something?"

The woman studies her a moment longer, then suddenly laughs. "Listen to me go on," she says. "We can figure this all out later. The important thing is that I found you!"

Her voice is lovely, as quick and high pitched as birdsong. May can't stop smiling at her.

"Maybe you. . . I have a cousin who doesn't talk much either, but he's just the sweetest thing."

She extracts her hands and places one on her chest. "Francie," she says. "My. Name. Is. Francie."

May has played this game before. Blue jays are the best mimics, impersonating everything from a hawk's cry to a snake's rattle, but May studies the woman's mouth and responds with a fair-sounding imitation.

"Fran-see," she says and the woman nods delightedly. May puts her own hand on her chest and says, "May."

"May!" Francie says. "There we go! May and Francie. Let me help you up."

The woman rises from her knees and extends a hand to help May to her feet. Francie wrinkles her nose at the baggy pants and flannel shirt May wears.

"Those are men's clothes," Francie says. "I still can't believe you're out here without shoes! What happened to you? Are you sure you're not hurt? What are you, seventeen? Eighteen at the most, I bet. My dad's a policeman. I think you should come home with me. We can sort this all out."

She slips a hand around May's elbow and guides her firmly through the trees to a narrow, well-traveled trail. In the darkness last night, May hadn't seen the path, but even if she had she probably wouldn't have taken it. The trail leads back the way she came, not toward everything she has yet to see.

Still, for now, she lets Francie lead her. The woman looks like a chickadee but her voice is far more melodic. Instead of the bird's simple "fee-bee," Francie produces trills, gurgles and whistles, always with a rising note or laugh at the end of each verse.

"I'm getting married in July," Francie says. "I still can't believe it! I'd just graduated from high school and was studying accounting—not that I ever wanted to be an accountant or anything, but I did enjoy working with numbers. Then out of the blue, I met Bill. He's a lawyer. Have you heard of him? Bill Greene? He's obviously way older than me, but I love that about him. He's already established, you know? And smart and sophisticated. We met at the courthouse. My dad was testifying on some case and Bill was in court. I wouldn't say it was love at first sight, but . . ."

"Bill" is Francie's favorite word. Whenever she says it, she squeals. For the next hour, as they descend through pine forests to the wetlands and meadows on the valley floor, Francie squeals almost constantly. With an established trail to follow, they make far better time than May did bushwhacking in the dark. May even spots the distant rooflines of houses as they pass knee high grasses and spring flowers in shades of yellow, white and blue.

". . . so then Bill finally proposed," Francie continues, "and, oh my God, you have to see this ring." She stops abruptly and holds out her left hand, which is adorned with a glistening rock.

"Gorgeous, right?" Francie says. "Over two carats! And we're having the wedding at his club. I never thought I'd have the chance to live this kind of life."

She drops her hand and sighs. "I know this will sound crazy, but I worry that his friends won't accept me. I'm so much younger. And even though Bill was the one who wanted me to drop out of college, it makes it look like I'm just after him for his money, you know? And I'm not! I swear I would love him even if he wasn't successful! Even my parents were a little worried at first. I'm not sure they really like him."

Her cheeks flush red and she suddenly goes silent. The moment it's gone, May misses the chirp of the woman's voice.

"Fran-see?" she says.

Francie smiles and waves a hand. "It's okay. Of course it's okay! Bill loves me and that's all that matters."

A few minutes later, Francie leads them off the main trail. An overgrown path winds toward a cluster of well-maintained homes with blooming fruit trees and brick-lined garden beds in the large backyards.

"We're going to Italy for our honeymoon!" Francie says. "Can you believe that? I've never even been out of Idaho and now I'm going to Rome! It will be ama—"

She screams as she falls, gripping her leg. May drops to her knees as the brown and gray snake lowers its rattle and slithers away into the tall grass. Francie's shrieks scare the crows from the fruit trees while May looks around the meadow, then at one of the garden beds bursting with vibrant purple flowers. She leaps to her feet and wills her still weak legs to run.

"Don't go!" Francie cries. "Please, May, don't leave me!"

May charges across the meadow, reaching the yard in ten long strides. She doesn't even stop to admire how nimble and quick she's become before scooping up one of the garden bricks.

Francie's wailing echoes up the mountain as May kneels in the garden. The flowers are lush and beautiful, carefully tended, but what May needs are the roots. Using the sharp corner of the brick like a trowel, she digs and digs, shoving earth aside until she reaches moist, loamy soil. Quickly but carefully, she wriggles her fingers through the dirt and grasps the cluster of tender roots, wrenching them from the ground.

Discarding the stems and flowers, she shakes off as much dirt as she can, then chews on the roots to soften them. They have a spicy, tingly bite, one that will help nullify the effects of the snake venom.

Roots in hand, she races back to Francie's side. Prying the girl's hands from her leg, May finds the puncture wound surrounded by angry red swelling and presses the roots to the bite.

Francie shrieks and tries to wriggle away, but May merely holds on tighter and increases the pressure. It's a few minutes before the plant stimulates Francie's anti-venom antibodies. May knows it's working when Francie stops squirming and takes a breath between sobs. It may not be the best or fastest cure, but it's the only one May knows.

"H-how did you k-know what to do?" Francie asks.

May keeps the roots pressed firmly to Francie's leg. Geese instinctively use the sun and stars to navigate across continents; spiders spin webs right after hatching. Even human babies are born with protective instincts, crying at strangers to keep themselves safe from harm. There are things you just know. Trees exist for the benefit of all living things, and in return know all their secrets—how nettles sting but are also a tonic after childbirth; how usnea lichen stops bleeding when applied to an open wound. Motherwort strengthens the heart while poison hemlock attacks it, masquerading as the edible biscuitroot so that you'll be tempted to take that one little taste that will kill you.

May had to leave the grove, though, to learn one more secret: The world she's stepped into is a whole lot bigger than one man's house.

Francie's sobs have tapered off; even her tears are drying. When she lifts the clump of soggy roots from her leg, the redness has faded to pink.

"Is that the purple coneflower from my dad's garden?" she asks.

May cocks her head.

"Coneflower?" Francie repeats. "Echinacea?"

"Eck-ee—"

"Echinacea," Francie says. "Ech-i-na-cea."

May repeats the word, getting an approving nod from Francie. Then she wiggles her hand along the ground toward Francie.

"Ugh," Francie says. "Rattlesnake."

"Rat-snake," May repeats.

The plant Francie calls echinacea has anti-inflammatory and analgesic properties. May returns to the garden to gather more roots, applying another poultice while they wait for Francie to feel well enough to walk. In the meadow, May points to different plants and repeats every word Francie tells her. Sagebrush, arrowleaf balsamroot, willow, blue camas. Huckleberry, bitterbrush, and, when May points toward the mountaintop, larch.

"Larch," May says. *Larch.*

Francie cocks her head. "I almost don't feel the sting anymore," she says. "Are you some kind of witch?"

May looks at the mountains and knows the secrets of her sisters—how their massive trunks and canopies are only a fraction of who they are. Their unseen roots are their true lifeblood, absorbing the nutrients they need and sharing them with the neighboring firs through their mycorrhizal network, just as the fir shares with the pine. Down the mountain they go—a vast underground chain of living beings. Pine to willow to sage to echinacea, which May presses to Francie's leg. And she realizes she hasn't really left them at all.

She turns back to Francie and smiles widely. "Witch," she says.

✦

As May is helping Francie up the porch steps, the front door bursts open. An older woman with the same red hair and speckles as Francie rushes out and pulls Francie into her arms.

"Where have you been? I've been so worried! Oh my goodness, Francie, what's wrong with your leg?"

It turns out that not everyone broods silently in the dark. A few of the windows in Francie's house actually stand open and more words are exchanged in an hour than

Edward and his father will speak all year. May understands little except the gratitude of the older woman who goes from fussing over Francie's wound to squeezing May's hands.

"Francie was so lucky to find you! I can't even imagine what would have happened if . . . You're an angel, that's what you are."

The older woman helps Francie to a chair and brings them each a cup of steaming liquid. May smiles at the minty aroma, but has learned to take small sips that won't burn her tongue.

"I'm calling the doctor," the older woman says. She picks up the phone and talks to a long-winded man until her shoulders finally sag in relief. After hanging up, she gives Francie a hug.

"He's coming right over."

"See?" Francie says. "Everything is going to be okay. I'm already feeling much better, Mom."

"Mom," May repeats, which makes Francie laugh.

Francie gestures to the older woman and says, "Angela."

"Angel," May says, and the older woman smiles.

"Bless your heart."

The doctor arrives with a medicine bag and a scowl when he sees May's dirty poultice. He gives Francie an injection of anti-venom and tosses the echinacea roots in the trash.

"Call me if the pain or swelling worsens," he says brusquely before leaving. He never looks May in the eye at all.

Angel bustles around the kitchen, preparing such a wide array of delectable dishes that May wonders if Edward's noodles and canned sauce can be considered food at all. Francie tells her the name of each dish, but May is too busy eating to remember them. There are creamy things, crunchy things, things that make her mouth water when she smells them. She moans in pleasure with every bite. When she cleans her plate and looks up hopefully, Angel laughs and feeds her more.

Francie and Angel speak the same joyful language, laughing almost as much as they talk. Francie keeps her leg up and admires her snake bite from time to time.

"Bill's going to think I'm some kind of snake charmer," she says.

It's the one time that Angel doesn't laugh.

As darkness falls, a large, balding man walks through the front door and Angel hurries to greet him.

"Oh my goodness, Vern!" she says as he takes off his jacket. "You're not going to believe what's happened."

"Dad, I got bit by a snake!"

While Francie talks at length again, May sneaks the rest of the crunchy, creamy things onto her plate. She hears her name often, but, oddly, when the man pins her with his hawk-like gaze, she feels no threat. He's tall and broad-chested, but after the three of them finally fall silent, he crosses the room to sit beside her.

"Thank you for what you did today," he says. "Francie says you were sleeping in the woods. I hope you know that you can stay here. You're safe."

She likes the sound of his voice—deep and calm—and the surprisingly gentle way he pats her hand. Francie and Angel never say "Stay," but they make up a bed for May with even softer sheets than the ones at Edward's. Francie touches her arm.

"You're sleeping here tonight, May," she says. "My dad will look into the missing person reports tomorrow. There's got to be someone looking for you."

Francie brings May a slippery bit of pink fabric she calls a "nightgown." May rolls the silk between her fingers, then strokes it against her cheek. Without a hint of Edward's awkwardness, Francie helps May out of Edward's clothes and into the nightgown. Every time May twists, the pink skirt flutters.

"Rest now," Francie says, kissing May softly on the cheek. "Our home is your home."

That night, May lies in the soft bed thinking of Edward. In the end, she didn't "stay." She hates the thought that she disappointed him, but an even worse possibility is that he always expected her to leave. Unkindness is, perhaps, all he knows. Even with her extremely limited vocabulary, she's figured out that there are words to avoid, and others worth repeating. She's not sure that anyone has ever whispered the words Edward is looking for.

She closes her eyes and smiles, imagining that she will be the first.

Until then, she stays with Francie, Angel, and the man who answers with a smile whether May calls him Vern or Dad. She sleeps between sheets that smell of lavender and wakes to people who seem quite delighted to offer her a seat at their breakfast table. No one drinks alone in the darkness; Angel gets up early every morning and opens the curtains before making a big pot of hot bitter liquid that May hates at first, but day by day begins to crave.

They call their home her home, but even better, they teach her how to live in it. How to light the stove without burning herself, how to wash dirty dishes and where to put them when they're clean, how to cut with a knife, how to string her first sentence together.

"Thank you, Angel," May says when Angel fills her plate with what she now knows are scrambled eggs, bacon and her favorite—iced cinnamon rolls.

"You're welcome! But once again my name is . . . You know what? Angel is great."

May learns to put a napkin on her lap and not to gobble up all the food before others have had their share. She wakes not to the sun, but to the shrieking of the alarm clock in Vern and Angel's bedroom. Five days in a row, Vern wears a suit and leaves after a breakfast of coffee and toast, not to return until just before dinner. But there are two days when the alarm clock stays silent and Vern never goes farther than his garden bed or the chair in front of the box he calls a "TV." May likes those days best. Everyone seems happier and Angel always bakes a pie.

Many nights, Vern talks into what she now knows is a telephone, then comes to sit by May.

"I'm sorry," he always says. "That was another dead end. It's like you came out of thin air."

"I am May," she says, smiling proudly at all the words she strings together, and he pats her hand gently.

"I know you are, honey. I know."

The next morning, the spring chill has been replaced by the first warm wind of the season. May eats a stack of pancakes with syrup and two cinnamon buns, then points to the back door.

"Go walk," she says.

Angel shakes her head, but still smiles. "I want to go for a walk."

It seems like a lot of unnecessary syllables, but May appeases her.

"I want to . . . go for a walk."

Angel claps her hands and calls for Francie.

Healed from her rattlesnake bite, Francie walks with May every day—though always on the ugly pavement and never through the meadows or woods where a snake could be hiding again. The young woman fits May with a pair of her old hiking boots—marvelous, cushiony, leather wrapped things that not only protect her soles from rocks and goat heads, but give May the support she needs to walk for miles.

Today, as every day, Francie spends their entire walk discussing her upcoming wedding. May has learned many things since leaving her grove, but Francie has made it clear that nothing is more important than making sure the reception dinner is plated and not a tacky buffet. May is amazed at the complexity of the upcoming nuptials. There will be 12 bridesmaids and they will all wear pink tulle no matter what the Maid of Honor says. The bar will be open, the mother of the groom will be avoided, as she is a nightmare, the signature drink must be a classic gin and tonic, even though no one but Bill drinks gin. Bill also deplores music, but if they must have it, only a live band will do.

May learns the words "cummerbunds," "rehearsal dinner," "gift registry," and "honeymoon." And she knows now why Francie smiles so much.

"You love Bill," May says.

Francie stops walking and takes her arm. "Oh, I do! I honestly do."

They make a loop through town, Francie rattling off street names—Main, Broadway, 26th, Clover. May wonders who's in charge of making them all up. An hour later, after Cartwright, 9th Avenue, Hickory, and Grant, Francie launches into a tale about the "caterer from hell." They turn up Francie's street—Sycamore Lane, even though there are no sycamore trees in sight. Vern is on his knees in the garden, ripping out the spiny weeds that have overtaken his spring peas.

"And then he wanted to double the price of the beef medallions!" Francie says and throws up her hands.

May pats Francie's arm in sympathy, then walks over to Vern and picks up one of the weeds. Carefully, she tears away the leaf's spine, then pops the remainder into her mouth. Vern looks horrified, as if she's swallowed poison instead of wild lettuce.

"Sald," she says.

Vern looks up at Francie, who is the best at translating May's jargon.

"You mean salad?" Francie asks.

May nods enthusiastically and removes the spines of the rest of the weeds. Vern looks dubious, but puts the greens in the basket alongside his freshly picked peas. The salad, May knows, will be bitter, but the plant contains calming and pain-relieving properties that will make it taste far better than it is.

That night, they eat wild lettuce salad, fresh peas, and the next best dish Angel creates. First it was roasted beef with whipped potatoes, then delectable fried chicken and biscuits, followed by lasagna, tomatoes on toast, and tonight, the most delicious of all, something called "hot dogs" with mustard and baked beans. Afterwards, they sit in front of the TV, watching the adventures of a cat and mouse that look nothing like they do in real life. Halfway through the program, Angel brings out her homemade rhubarb pie and a tub of whipped cream. May waits for everyone to finish their first slice before she asks for another, then guzzles down a black fizzy drink that tickles her throat.

When the show is over, Vern turns off the television and retrieves a deck of what May now knows are playing cards. They have been teaching her games—silly sounding things like Go Fish and Gin Rummy—where the purpose is sometimes to gain cards, sometimes to get rid of them, but always to laugh and shout playfully in victory or defeat. It is right after May cheers at finally winning her first hand of Gin Rummy that she feels the hairs rise on the back of her neck. Anyone else might check for a draft of cold air, but she recognizes the feel of her sisters.

She hadn't expected to ever receive another warning from them. For a moment, it's almost as if she's back in the grove, receiving a jolt of pheromones as a wildfire draws near. She lowers the fist she raised in an instinctively human show of victory and the tingle along her spine slowly fades. She looks around: Francie is dealing the next round of cards, Angel brings steaming mugs of hot cocoa, Vern pats her hand and says, "Everything okay, May?"

She nods and squeezes his hand. The threat, she realizes, is that she could be happy here. And happy people move forward, not back.

After the game, May sits on the sofa, staring out the window toward the woods while Francie, Angel and Vern talk softly. She hears her name often, but doesn't try to understand more. There is worry in Angel's voice and caution in Vern's. Perhaps they're making up theories about where she came from. They never look where she looks, toward green hills that rise to a mountain covered in larches.

Only Francie's voice remains firm. "I know how strange it is, but I don't care," she says. "She's the first person on this planet who's needed me. I'm not letting her go."

They talk so long, May falls asleep on the couch. She wakes to Francie's hand on her shoulder.

"Let's get some rest, May," she says. "Tomorrow we're deciding on boutonnieres!"

When May finally meets Francie's fiancé, Bill, she knows at once that he's never stepped foot in her woods. He arrives late in the evening, wearing a gray suit with a white pocket square that smells of stuffy, windowless rooms. She's quite certain she has more dirt beneath her fingernails than he tracks in with his shiny black shoes. Francie tells her he's been out of town on a case.

"He's defending the senator's son," she says. "You know the one. Bill got him off with nothing worse than time spent. Bill's half the age of everyone else at the firm, but they're already talking about making him partner."

Whatever that means, it delights her. Bill removes his jacket and hesitates before extending a stiff hand to May. He is tall, with shrewd eyes and dark hair that's nearly as slick and shiny as his shoes. Vern taught May the custom of shaking hands, but Bill doesn't seem to care much for the feel of hers. He barely grazes her palm before pulling away.

"You must be exhausted," Francie says. "You want a soda, honey?"

"Whiskey," he says without acknowledging the blue dress Francie put on to please him, saying it was his favorite. He claims the middle of the couch and launches into a long-winded story about "that stupid airline" that only Francie cares to listen to.

" . . . even though I booked first class," he says. "And then this family of four boards, and I couldn't get the stewardess's attention to change seats. . ."

He sips the whiskey Francie brings him and picks at the tiniest bit of lint on his cuff, continuing to complain about "people who shouldn't be allowed to fly." Vern leans toward May and whispers into her ear.

"I don't like him much either."

Angel and Francie perch on the chairs, so May and Vern take the ends of the sofa. Bill turns his back to May and speaks only to Vern.

"I know you don't always agree with my tactics," he says, "but even you'll have to admit I put on one hell of a show."

Bill launches into another monologue, this time using complicated words May has no hope of making out. She's not sure how much Angel and Francie understand either, but it hardly matters because Bill never glances their way. It's obvious that Bill knows all there is to know about "subpoenas" and "countersuits," but very little about being interesting. May can't help but glance at the philodendron in a pot in the corner, the leaves of which would cause swelling of the lips, tongue, and throat if, perhaps, it was slipped into a drink.

"Fascinating," Vern says, and May tilts her head, sensing the lie. "We had some excitement here too. Francie was bit by a rattler, and May found a plant in the garden to save her."

Bill looks across the coffee table at Francie, then slowly shifts his body toward May. He's no predator like Edward's father, but she still squares her shoulders at his cold appraisal. He wrinkles his brow slightly, as if he can't quite believe his future in-laws let her into the house.

"Is that so?"

"It was amazing," Francie jumps in. "May ran straight for our purple coneflowers. I guess there's something in the roots that helps pull out poison. And since then—"

"That sounds dangerous," Bill interrupts. "Don't you know you're supposed to go straight to a hospital with a snake bite? What were you thinking? These so-called natural remedies can be far worse than what they're trying to cure."

Francie leans back in her chair, and May is saddened to see the joy dissolve from her face.

"Well, in this case," Angel says softly, reaching over to squeeze her daughter's hand, "the remedy was exactly what Francie needed."

Bill shakes his head, as if no one's words but his own can be trusted. It's strange that he's older than Francie because he has far less laugh lines around his eyes. He smells funny too, like the forest if Angel decided to mop it. When he turns back to her, May can't find a single errant whisker on his face.

"Forgive me," he says, his nostrils flaring, "but I'm not really clear who you are."

There is a moment's silence, then everyone starts talking at once. May is used to hearing her name, but she doesn't care for the way they all sneak nervous glances at her before uttering a barrage of new words—"foreigner," "illiterate," and "helpless," to name a few. She feels as if she's brought a whole mountain full of dirt and strangeness into the room.

Lifting her chin, she says, "I am May."

"This is insane," Bill replies. "You don't know anything about her! You could have brought a lunatic into your home."

Francie stands abruptly. "It's not like that. The thing you have to understand about May is—"

A loud pounding on the door silences her. It's late, an unlikely hour for visitors, and Vern gestures for everyone to stay put while he peers through the living room window. When he stiffens and opens the door, May gets to her feet.

Edward's father is there, wearing jeans and a flannel shirt that even May knows has been buttoned incorrectly,—one side hanging lower than the other. He's a head shorter than Vern, and fifty pounds lighter, but Vern rests a hand on the holster he always wears just the same.

"Cameron," Vern says. "Kind of late, isn't it? What can I do for you?"

The older man has already spotted her, and May steps out from behind Vern even after she hears Francie mutter, *May, don't.* Her heart is racing as she waits for Edward to appear behind him, but that hope quickly fades. Edward's father has parked his truck askew on Vern's lawn, and he's swaying. May can smell the alcohol on him, yet his finger is steady as he points it right at her.

"You," he says. "Pit bull. What'd you do to my son?"

When he tries to cross the threshold, Vern bars the door. "May didn't do anything, Cam. She's staying with us now."

Edward's father squints at May as if she's a little blurry. "Yeah, word got out that you took in the stray," he says. "You know anything about her, Vern? Where she comes from? If you're not gonna use your head, at least use your eyes. You really gonna trust some halfbreed walking around naked in the woods?"

Whatever that means, it makes Angel gasp behind them, but Vern merely squares his massive shoulders. "May is welcome in our house for as long as she wants. She saved Francie's life. We're lucky to have her."

Edward's father shakes his head. "Don't say I didn't warn you. She sure as hell did a number on Edward. Turned him into some kind of lovesick puppy who did everything for her. He's been worthless since she slithered off in the night."

May can make out more of his words now, but only one of them matters.

"Edward," she says.

Even with Vern standing between them, May feels as if it's only her and Edward's father in the room. His gaze is as mean as ever, but the way he juts out his chest makes her smirk. She was a 150-foot larch tree; this little man they call Cameron is nothing to her.

"You stay away from him," Cameron says.

Vern moves slightly, blocking Cameron's path to May, but she merely touches Vern's back gently and steps around him. It's human nature to be afraid of things you don't understand, but perhaps she's not all human yet.

May senses her sisters again, not due to any distress signal but simply because they're there. A chain of living beings that still reaches her.

"I love Edward," she says.

This time, it's Cameron who shakes his head and smirks.

"Well that's too bad for you, pit bull," he says, "because you're never going to see that boy again."

Seven

Western Red Cedar
(Thuja plicata)

There's a giant Western Red Cedar in northern Idaho that is over 3000 years old. At nearly 200 feet tall and more than 18 feet in diameter, she's considered the champion tree of the state. Too bad she's all alone. Though the champion is surrounded by a grove of sister cedars, the tree lives in isolation near a small stream, claiming the water source as her own. She's a celebrity; people hurry past her younger, more beautiful sisters to gaze up at her graying bark and drooping scale-like leaves. Everyone loves a spectacle—in this case a tree that chose notoriety over companionship and beauty.

✦

When May left Edward, it took her all night to scale one mountain. But on one of their daily walks, Francie shows her a road that leads back to him in less than an hour.

May makes the pilgrimage every day, but she never knocks on his door. Whenever Francie accompanies her, the young woman insists that they stand across the street, just in case Edward's father comes out.

"You need to be careful around Cameron, May," Francie always says. "There are stories about him that would make your skin crawl."

Francie fidgets and continually tugs at May's sleeve. The two of them never stay long—but nights are a different story.

Late every evening, after everyone falls asleep, May slips out her bedroom window and walks the dark, quiet road alone. She likes the town better at night, when people and cars are silent and owls hoot from the trees. When she reaches Edward's house, she settles herself on the soft earth beneath the elm tree and watches.

He never comes out. His demon truck sits in the driveway like always. The lights inside the house blaze most of the night. Sometimes May hears Cameron's raised voice, followed by a thumping that makes her stomach lurch. Then it goes eerily quiet. No one calls for help or storms out.

The woman May has become itches to pound on the door and use whatever means necessary to drag Edward to safety. But she's spent far more time as the creature she was before, the one who stands and waits. A witness to the creatures who give up and perish, and to those who find a way to fight to save themselves.

In the next two weeks, as the weather warms, she stays longer and longer, sometimes even until the first wood lark sings. But she makes sure she's always back in time for Angel's cinnamon rolls and waffles with maple syrup. One morning, as she adds a dollop of whipped cream to her third waffle, Francie clears the rest of the dishes to make room for a mismatch of fancy table settings.

One set has gold rimmed plates and fluted glasses, another wooden chargers, copper spoons and brown bowls. The last is blue floral china with silver goblets. Francie launches into an excited description of each "tablescape," but fifteen minutes later, she's in tears.

"I honestly have no idea which to choose! The gold and blue designs are classic, but are they forgettable? Is the wood and copper too much? What do you think, May? Everything in this wedding has to be perfect!"

What May thinks is that none of the "tablescapes" look appealing without waffles piled on them, but she has memorized the words that Francie needs to hear.

"It will be . . . beautiful. You will be a perfect bride."

After which Francie squeezes her and says, "Oh, May, I'm so glad you're here!"

That evening, Bill comes for dinner, but fails to comment on the blue floral china and silver goblets that Francie finally chose and left on display. Francie's face falls as he walks straight past the set-up without a flicker of interest.

"It will be beautiful," May says and Francie manages a tentative smile.

Angel prepares corn on the cob, coleslaw, fried chicken and mashed potatoes. And gravy! She even brings out a second gravy boat so that May can have her own. Once more, Bill talks only to Vern, telling him about his latest client, an out of state real estate firm that wants to restrict public access to its forest lands. Vern looks almost relieved when someone knocks on the door.

This time, instead of Edward's father standing drunkenly on the porch, it's a young woman on her knees.

Angel leaps from her chair and pushes past Vern. "Oh, Grace," she says. "Is it time?"

Angel helps the woman to her feet and May sees the bulge in her stomach. The woman's eyes are panicky with pain.

"I'll call 9-1-1," Vern says.

The woman, who could only moan until now, grabs Vern by the wrist.

"No," she grunts. Then she doubles over in pain again and lets out something between a moan and a scream. Vern looks to Angel, who shakes her head.

"You remember last time," she says quietly. "All the doctors and machines and still the baby didn't. . . She doesn't trust . . . Her husband just got deployed again. She doesn't have anyone else."

Vern takes a step back. "You're not suggesting—"

"I told her to come when it was time," Angel says. "You're trained in childbirth, Vern."

"Angela, that was 20 years ago, and thankfully I never delivered a single baby when I was on patrol."

Angel waves a hand at him as if he's just being modest, then turns to May. "And I thought maybe you could help too."

May looks at the young woman trying to breathe through the pain, unsure what Angel is asking of her. Every creature that gave birth in the grove did so alone. When elk cows sense the arrival of their calves, they choose a spot with the thickest vegetation to keep themselves and their newborns safe from predators. But sometimes labor is so difficult or lengthy, none of them survive anyway. There is no herbal cure to conquer fate.

On the other hand, black cohosh will relax the uterus and stimulate contractions, while raspberry tea helps to slow bleeding and expel the placenta. Or maybe what the young woman needs most is simply someone who isn't afraid.

So May nods and crosses the room, placing a hand on the young woman's hot, firm belly. When the woman looks in her eyes, May smiles comfortingly.

"I will help," she says.

The woman's sigh of relief turns abruptly to tears as another contraction builds. May squeezes her hand until the pain passes, then leads her outside. Step by step, they cross the road and continue into the tall weeds of the empty lot across the street. No one has dared to build on the lot due to the ditch running through the property, along with the mammoth purple ash tree they'd either have to cut down or build around. Unkempt and overgrown with stinging nettle and clover, it's May's favorite place on the block.

Bill mutters as he and the others follow, but May pays him no mind. She leads the woman—Grace, Angel calls her—to the base of the towering purple ash. Ash trees are odd creatures, more likely to stand alone than in a grove. Their wood provides straight and valuable timber, but if left alive, they offer so much more. Ash leaves stop itching; their seeds improve libido; ash bark creates a stunning yellow dye and is a tonic to relieve stomach cramps. But none of these attributes are why May leads them here.

A long time ago, an errant ash sprouted in the larch grove. There's no telling how it got there—seeds carried in the wind or animal droppings, perhaps, or caught on a wolf's shaggy fur. It grew in the only place it could, away from the shade cast by May and her sisters, in an unwelcoming patch of rocky earth. It never amounted to much. Stunted by loneliness and barren soil, it topped out at twenty feet before dying a quick death one winter. Yet even when it became nothing but a skeletal roost for spotted owls and ravens, elk cows and fox vixens chose to give birth in the tall grasses around its trunk. Perhaps it was just coincidence, but not a single one of them or their newborns ever died.

May eases Grace into a sitting position against the trunk of the ash, her knees pulled up to her chest. The men keep their distance across the street; even Francie stands in the shadows, as if pain and potential heartache are contagious. Only Angel dares to approach them and wipe the sweat from Grace's brow.

When the young woman gasps in pain once more, May kneels beside her.

"Breathe," she says.

May inhales deeply through her nose and Grace tries to mimic her. But when the pain becomes too intense, the woman merely cries. May turns to Angel and points at the red raspberry bushes that line her fence across the street.

"Leaf tea," May says, and Angel gives a quick nod before darting across the street. Then May motions toward Francie, pretending to dab a cloth to Grace's forehead.

"Oh!" Francie says. "A washcloth, right? And clean towels? I'll get them."

Vern offers to help, following Francie back to the house. Then only Bill remains, watching them dispassionately even when Grace's cries become screams. It isn't until neighbors emerge to see what's happening that he crosses the street, wrinkling his nose when he reaches the overgrown lot.

Bill tiptoes through the nettle and clover, as if trying to avoid raw earth. He stops just short of them, standing outside the boughs of the ash tree, a shrewd move in May's opinion. She's living proof that you can never be sure of what a tree will do.

He clears his throat. "I don't know w—"

Another contraction, accompanied by Grace's scream, cuts him off. He purses his lips in annoyance, and the corners of May's mouth twitch.

When Grace finally quiets into hoarse, labored breathing, Bill starts again.

"I don't know where you came from, but around here a woman doesn't give birth under a tree like some animal. You could go to jail for this. If things go wrong."

His words are gibberish, as usual, but she doesn't have to speak his language to understand him. Everything from his curled lip to the way his gaze wanders when anyone else is talking tells her that he has yet to meet anyone who is up to his standards. She imagines Francie, with all her decorating ideas and joyful chatter, waking up every morning to the disdainful stare that May receives now. A man like this doesn't deserve a blue and silver tablescape or a girl who overlooks his ridiculous snobbery because she sees something worthy inside him that no one else can. What he deserves, May thinks, is a little dirt on his shiny shoes.

Bill smirks as May scoops up a handful of soil, probably thinking it's another of her unorthodox remedies. She's not sure if it's arrogance or stupidity that makes him stand directly in her line of fire, but either way, she flings the dirt at his ankles and shoes.

Bill jumps backwards, but too late. "What do you think you're doing?" he cries, swatting at the mess on his shoes.

May is delighted to see dirt clods sticking stubbornly to his socks. He tries shaking one foot then the other, appalled that he can't get them off.

He glares at her, but seems reluctant to come any closer. "In all my years I've never . . ." He shakes his head, for once stumped for words. May turns back to Grace, who grips her arm tightly during another long contraction.

"Don't turn away from me, young lady," Bill says from behind her. "You do realize I'm an—"

"Asshole," May interjects without turning around. It's a word Francie uses to describe every wedding guest who has yet to mail back their RSVP. May has grown quite fond of the sound of it.

"Asshole," she says again. "Go . . . away."

She doesn't turn back to see what he'll do. Grace is digging her fingers into May's arm.

"Something's wrong again," Grace says through clenched teeth.

May slides up Grace's skirt to reveal legs soaked with amniotic fluid and blood. Whatever Bill sees over May's shoulder makes him finally go quiet, then flee to safety across the street. Angel passes him by the curb, carrying a mug of steaming raspberry tea. May doesn't mention that, at this point, it won't do any good. What matters more is thinking that it will.

"Drink," May says to Grace. "Everything will be fine."

She helps the woman sit up to take a sip. They are surrounded by plants that could help with pain—salicylic acid, nature's aspirin, in the bark and leaves of poplar and willow trees, flavanoids in feverfew to reduce inflammation. But May merely smiles at Grace and encourages her to finish the tea. Sometimes, it's the pain that you need. Pain that you shouldn't be able to endure but do, pain that does so much damage tearing through you, scar tissue grows over your weak spots—leaving you less shiny and soft, but tougher to break.

So they sit beneath the purple ash, serenaded not by mockingbirds but by Grace's whimpers and screams. Francie and Angel bring more tea and blankets. Bill and Vern, along with the neighbors, stare from across the street with pale, terrified faces while the moon rises then falls. The hours may seem endless to the rest of them, but this is the kind of time women in labor and May understand. Not minutes, but hours, maybe days. Time enough for everything to change.

Just before dawn, a few of the bravest neighbors come over to see if they can help, only to have Grace hiss at them to go away. The baby's head crowns an hour later, when the pink morning light causes the growing crowd to murmur about indecency. Exhausted and nearly incoherent, Grace barely responds when May urges her to keep pushing. Sirens sound in the distance.

"May, we have to hurry," Angel says. "They'll take her to the hospital for sure."

May studies Grace's pale face. Her hair is limp, her skin drenched with sweat. May watches her belly tighten with each contraction, but Grace does little more than moan. What's the point of trying if you already expect the worst?

The sirens grow louder as May sits beside her, resting a shoulder against the trunk of the purple ash. Once, on one of their morning walks, Francie told her that she'd found a wedding dress she was sure Bill would love. Then Francie grimaced and ran to the nearest tree—a rather forlorn looking cypress trying to grow outside its natural habitat—knocking three times on its trunk.

"I hope I didn't jinx it!" she said.

Francie laughed about silly superstitions, but she was closer to the truth than she knew. Trees have no nervous systems, but when a woodpecker pecks, they release tannins and terpenes to protect themselves. When a person "knocks on wood," trees emit a stream of chemicals like ethylene gas to alert nearby trees that they're not alone. They all know you're there.

So May holds the ash with one arm and Grace with the other.

"Push," she says. "It's time."

Grace raises her head slowly. Maybe she feels the comfort of the tree, maybe not. Two police cars and an ambulance turn the corner, lights flashing, as Grace holds her breath and bears down. May presses on Grace's stomach as a baby boy emerges, still and slightly blue, the cord wrapped tightly around his neck. May untangles the cord quickly, but the newborn is silent. She massages the infant's back, rubbing up and down to stimulate his breathing as men in uniforms run their way.

"Please breathe, baby!" Grace cries, looking down at the quiet thing between her legs.

Angel strokes the hair plastered to Grace's face and glances nervously toward May.

"Is he…"

May rubs the baby's back harder and faster, until the skin beneath her hand finally warms and fluid leaks from the infant's lips. She pinches open the baby's mouth, using her pinkie to scoop out the mucus, and finally a piercing cry fills the air. Grace wails in relief as May wraps the crying newborn in a blanket and places him gently on Grace's chest.

The EMTs tend to Grace while policemen approach May, looking far too surly for the happy occasion. She wonders if they've ever seen a newborn baby before.

"Are you a midwife?" one of them asks. "You have a license?"

May cocks her head at the unfamiliar words as another one says, "It's public indecency, at the very least."

Angel starts to argue, but by then they've hauled May up by her elbows and twisted her hands behind her back. Vern is crossing the street, saying, "Larry, Tom, come on. This is all a big misunder—"

"We can sort that out at the station, Vern," the biggest of the two men says. "For now, you know we gotta take her in."

Then they clamp her wrists together with something sharp and cold, and launch into a speech about "rights" that she doesn't care for. Angel, Francie and Vern are all talking at once, so May has to lean toward the largest officer to make sure he hears her.

"Asshole," she says and, when he squeezes her elbow painfully, she grins.

May smiles until they open the door of the police car and try to push her in. There's no way she's getting back inside an automobile. She jerks out of the policeman's grip, but it's only a momentary getaway. Before she can fling herself at Francie, who is biting her lip and crying, two more officers manhandle her into the backseat of the car.

"It'll be okay, May!" Francie shouts as they slam the door. May throws herself across the seat, trying to get out the other side, but even if her hands weren't shackled behind her, there are no handles. No matter how hard she slams her shoulder against the glass, it doesn't break.

The policemen get into the front seat. One of them looks over his shoulder to bark words at her, but all she hears is the gunning of the engine. Then they're off, whizzing past trees and buildings; every car, house and storefront is a blur.

The worst part of having her hands bound is that she can't brace herself for every bump and turn. The men in the car pay no attention to her whimpering; if anything, they drive faster the louder she gets. When they speed onto a four lane highway, May curls forward and squeezes her eyes shut. She pictures her sisters and counts them in her mind, from the newest, slender sapling to the oldest and most gnarled, forty six of them in all. She imagines them right now, swaying but not falling, their roots intertwined and entrenched in the earth. And maybe she still has the ability to send out distress signals because all at once she smells the citrusy scent of their needles. The sound of the engine and speeding cars is replaced by the wind through their branches. The car continues to vibrate and jolt, but she is somehow secure, nestled in the grove in her mind.

When they finally reach the squat, gray building that houses the police station, May is queasy but resolute: She will never enter another automobile. Nor will she burden Francie and her family any longer. They've been amazingly kind, but she doesn't belong with them. Myths, with all their dark and complicated creatures, are born of pain, not happiness. Edward is the only reason she's here.

Francie, Bill, Angel and Vern jump out of a car right behind them, and the shouting begins at once. Francie and Angel are the loudest, but even Vern raises his voice in a way that would terrify May, if she hadn't heard him whispering endearments in Angel's ear. Whatever he says must carry some weight, because one of the policemen removes May's handcuffs.

"Practicing midwifery without a license is only a misdemeanor on the first offense," Vern continues.

With a little dirt still on his shoes, Bill chimes in, "That's true, Vern, but it can still mean a fine and up to six months in jail."

"You can't blame May!" Angel cries. "I was the one who told Grace to come if she needed help. May had no idea . . ."

A policeman still grips May's arm, but Vern takes the other one—gently.

"It's going to be okay," he says to her. "The others will have to stay out here, but I'll be with you the whole time."

They escort her inside the stark building, into a small room that no one else seems to realize has no windows. A new, older policeman arrives and barrages her with questions she doesn't understand.

"I am May," she replies each time. "I want . . . to go for a walk."

Vern shakes his head. "This isn't an act, Keith," he says. "She doesn't remember much except her name."

For the next two hours, Vern answers all the questions that she cannot.

"We have no idea where . . . I've been combing through missing person reports . . . didn't even know the simplest things . . . good with plants . . . wasn't her fault . . . someone had to help . . ."

May imagines the needles on her sisters turning a bright golden green, and the cacophony of hoots and chirps in the grove that are still, somehow, quieter than the men in this room. They take her picture and stain her fingers with ink, and all the while Vern talks in one voice to his colleagues and in another, softer murmur to her. He brings her a glass of water and when one of the men jabs a pen and some papers at her, Vern takes them himself.

"Let me show her," he says.

He positions the pen between his thumb and forefinger—the same way Edward taught her to hold a fork—and draws a few squiggly lines.

"May," he says, pointing to the squiggles. "This says May."

He shows her how to curl her hand into a claw and hold the pen above the paper. He keeps hold of her hand, guiding her until they produce a decent copy of his squiggles. She laughs and tries to write it again on her own, but without Vern, her movements are wild and jerky.

One of the men in the room shifts nervously in his chair. "Is she, you know, retarded or something?"

Vern ignores him and grabs a second pen.

"M," he says, drawing only the first part of the squiggle. "Up, down, up, down."

He smiles kindly and May makes multiple attempts to copy his motion, producing a passable drawing on her seventh try.

"Em?" she says.

He nods. "Yes, that's the letter M. Now add an A, then a Y."

May studies his motions, then puts her head down, ignoring the grumbles of the policemen who have begun to pace around the room. Once she learns the symbols, Vern shows her how to loop them together to form a single word. She stares at the letters as if they're her first real roots in this world.

"May," she says, tapping the letters, then herself, then looking up at Vern. She's never seen him smile so widely.

"Yes, honey," he says. "You wrote your name."

✦

The sun is high in the sky by the time they emerge from the station. Francie and Angel run to them, their eyes red from crying, while Bill hands out his business card to a haggard-looking woman and the sullen teenager she drags behind her.

"Goldman and Lane," he says. "Criminal law. Call anytime."

Angel pulls May into a tight embrace. "Oh, May," she says, "I'm so sorry for all this. I was just trying to help. I can't believe they arrested you!"

After Angel makes sure that May is unharmed, she puts her hands on her hips and turns to Vern.

"I can't believe you let this happen!"

Vern takes a step back. "Don't blame me! There are certain rules law enforcement has to follow. My bet is it'll only be a small fine." When Angel still glares at him, he adds, "I'm not saying I like it."

The policemen made sure May learned the word "rules" today, which is pointless because she doesn't plan on following any of them. She takes Angel's hand and squeezes.

"I'm okay," she says, smiling. "I'm May."

Angel covers May's hand with her own while Francie drapes a sweater over her shoulders. May loves how they form a circle around her, almost like her sisters in the grove, but the one thing she doesn't care for is how much they talk. First about unjust laws and which nosy neighbors likely called the police, then on to Grace and how thankful they were that May was there to help her. On and on, often repeating themselves, with hardly a breath between syllables. May admires their eloquence, but wonders if there's such a thing as too many words. She looks toward the linden trees that line the street, but there's no chance of hearing the rustling of their leaves over the ceaseless chatter. There is only one man who is silent enough to soothe her.

"I . . . want Edward," she says.

They all go silent, which is a delight. Riding in that police car, May lost all sense of direction, but now that she's on solid ground she realizes how far they traveled. Back at Francie's, Battlecreek Peak stood just north of them, but from here it lies far to the east. The ugly gray buildings in this neighborhood are useless as landmarks. She needs a pine forest where the firs grow above and willows below, or a tiny stream that starts at a distant peak and ends in a raging river that leads to the ocean, if you follow it long enough.

Angel squeezes her arm. "I don't think that's such a good idea, May. Remember his dad told you to stay away from him?"

More words that don't matter. Edward's father doesn't matter. She wants Edward.

"I'm going," she says, heading down the stairs. She will walk toward Battlecreek Peak and find her way from there. It doesn't matter how long it takes her.

Bill shakes his head and says, "She doesn't know what she's saying."

"I think she does," Vern says. "She's going to Edward no matter what we say. Let me go inside and try to get a hold of him. I'll meet you at the car."

While Vern returns to the station, May turns east toward Battlecreek Peak. Angel tugs her arm in the opposite direction.

"Come on, honey," Angel says. "Our car's over there."

May wriggles free and keeps walking toward the mountain. She hears Bill scoff, but Francie hurries after her.

"May?" she says. "We've got to drive. It's too far to walk."

May merely points at the mountain and keeps walking. Past the police station, the road slopes slightly uphill. The air stinks of smoke and gasoline from the nonstop traffic, but at least there are tiny garden beds in front of the storefronts. Francie stays on her heels, pleading with her to come back to the car. At the first intersection, May stops at one of the red lights she doesn't care for, even though Francie has told her repeatedly that they are there to keep her safe.

"May, please," Francie says.

May turns around just enough to squeeze Francie's hand.

"Thank you . . . for everything."

At the first break in traffic, May crosses the road despite the red light, keeping Battlecreek Peak in her sights.

Francie shouts to the others to follow them in the car, then races to keep up with her. At the next intersection, May turns right, stepping into the road just as the green light turns red, and smiling at the drivers who honk at her.

She goes three more blocks before Vern's car pulls up beside her and everyone gets out. Francie comes hurrying up the sidewalk, breathing hard but already talking. Vern shushes her as he turns to May.

"I got a hold of Edward," he says. "He doesn't want you to come, May. I'm sorry."

His voice is so kind. In the forest, he'd be an ancient willow, with long green leaves that lull you to sleep.

"I want Edward," she says again.

"I understand that," Vern replies gently. "The trouble is that I don't think he wants you."

Francie gasps, but May merely cocks her head. Vern is kind, but misguided. Edward could go anywhere but he stays in the one place he hates. He doesn't know what he wants.

"I will go to him," May says and walks again.

"May, it's twenty miles!" Angel calls after her. "It will take all day!"

They all start talking again, but May has already turned the corner. A minute later, Angel catches up to her and loops an arm through hers.

"They're going to follow in the car," she says. "We want to make sure you stay safe."

For the next hour, Vern drives at a snail's pace, waving irritated drivers around them while Angel points out the town's landmarks.

"The Laramie Hotel used to be a brothel," she says. "The building beside it was a gold refinery before it became City Hall."

May is less interested in the town's buildings than she is in its dying trees. The lindens are healthy, but the tops of the red oaks planted around City Hall are wilted and browning, probably from oak wilt, which could kill them within a few weeks. Someone also made the unfortunate decision to line the building with hedges of tropical bamboo, which is barely clinging to life in the arid Idaho air. Though she's eager to reach Edward, May pauses to brush her fingers over the bamboo's limp, yellowed leaves.

"Vern took me to Japan right after we were first married," Angel says. "They had this bamboo forest that was too beautiful to be believed! And everyone had these little gardens. I'd see the older women out every morning, sweeping their dirt walks. It was almost like an art form, the way they took care of things."

She strokes the bamboo, too, the car idling in the street beside them. Bill leans his head out the back window.

"Ladies, are we moving or what?"

"Wait!" Francie says. "I'll walk too!"

Bill mutters something unintelligible from the back seat as May, Angel, and Francie walk past the last of the downtown buildings into a neighborhood of well-kept, turn-of-the-century homes. Francie keeps up a steady stream of chatter about the differences between Craftsman and Colonial designs and which houses need renovation work. The trees here aren't native either, but the towering maples and catalpas are thriving anyway, creating a cool canopy of green.

Beyond the old homes, the creek and foothills start their long journey toward Battlecreek Peak. Angel and Francie keep trying to steer May toward town, but she's already spotted her first larch on the ridge. If she's going to walk all day, she might as well do it in the woods.

The paved streets give way to gravel, then to a dirt road that hugs the cottonwood-lined stream. Even Angel and Francie go quiet once in a while to listen to the rustling of the leaves. They stop only once to drink from the spring-fed stream, despite Bill's insistence that it's likely contaminated. May forages up a lunch of miner's lettuce, oyster root and huckleberries, which Bill refuses to eat.

Hours pass. Angel and Francie eventually tire out, getting back in the car while May walks alone. She doesn't mind the solitude. Despite the constant rumble of the car inching along behind her, it's quiet enough to hear a distant waterfall and the squealing "wee-EEE" of a young hawk. Cottonwoods give way to conifers, a dark green swath of pines, spruce and fir. She can just make out the citrusy scent of the larches above her.

Bill never leaves the car. He takes over the driving in the late afternoon, grumbling every time he has to pull over to let a logging truck through. Vern walks beside May now, nearly as silent as she is. He looks at her from time to time, but the sun sets before he speaks.

"You're comfortable here."

May nods, but doesn't meet his probing gaze. "Yes."

"You know where you're going."

May's shoulders stiffen as she turns to him. "I do."

He squints at her, then looks up the mountain. She can almost see him putting the dots together. He may not know exactly what she was, but he knows what she wasn't. He was never going to find her on a missing persons report. She came from here, from this mountain, where nobody lives.

May doesn't realize she's holding her breath until his chuckle releases it. He takes her hand and squeezes it.

"You're something special, May," he says, and asks nothing more.

May's face warms with pleasure. The lights of Laramie have begun to twinkle in the distance. She knows exactly how far she's come. She followed Edward out of the grove and never once considered that it might be other things, other people, who would make her happy here.

After darkness falls, Bill complains of hunger pains while the rest of them feast on fireweed and wild strawberries. Angel and Francie join their walking party again as they leave the last pine behind and wind back toward Laramie's suburbs. They did this for her, walked with her; unlike trees, people get to choose where to put down roots.

"Thank you," May says quietly.

Francie slips an arm around May's waist. "Thank *you*, May. I never knew I could walk this far!"

They stop to watch a great horned owl take flight from a cottonwood tree until Bill honks the horn.

"Let's go!"

It's only a few minutes later when a car heads toward them, headlights ablaze. Bill pulls to the side of the road once more, but the car merely stops and kills the lights. Then May realizes it's not a car at all, but Edward's truck.

May leaps forward as the door opens and Edward steps from the cab. Francie grabs her hand as if to say, *Now wait a minute. Think this through*. But there's nothing to think about. It's too dark to see the look on Edward's face, so May simply extricates herself from Francie's grip and runs. When she's close enough, it's almost second nature to push off on her remarkable feet and leap into the air, knowing he'll catch her.

"Edward," she says as she's flying. "You . . . came."

Eight

Western Juniper
(Juniperus Occidentalis)

People who hate gardening plant junipers. Even if they never give the shrub or small tree a drop of water, it will still become a healthy, dusty, spiderweb-infested specimen in their yard. The Western Juniper launched its invasion of California, Oregon, Nevada and Idaho in 1870, and by the 20th century had increased its range threefold. Adaptable, rugged, and nearly indestructible, in some wild western landscapes junipers are the only trees for miles. Distillers and imbibers love them, as juniper berries are used to make gin.

✦

Edward catches May as she leaps, but sets her down immediately. He stiffens when she speaks his name.

The others hurry toward them as he untangles May's limbs from his body. Bill has gotten out of the car and holds Francie's hand tightly. Nobody speaks until Vern clears his throat.

"You found us," he says.

Edward nods. "I had to work late and I didn't want . . . My dad is at the house."

May cocks her head. Something has changed. His voice is clipped and flat, and he won't look at her. He stands stiffly, careful not to touch her, and something inside her thinks, *He's gone*.

But that's ridiculous. She knows who he is. She knows what's inside him, even if he has forgotten.

"Edward," she says, and takes his hand.

There are new scabs on his wrist, along with a round burn mark below his thumb that looks like it came from a lit cigarette. Even in the darkness, she sees the purple bruise beneath his eye, and when she leapt into his arms, he winced. She squeezes his fingers, but he pulls his hand away.

"Edward?" she says.

She had debated whether he felt disappointment or relief when he found her gone; she had never imagined that he might have been hurt. She'd *hurt* him. He'd taken a risk bringing her home that day, and she'd repaid him by leaving without a word. The realization brings a flush of heat to her face, and there it is again: Shame. She not only left him; she left him *there,* where he'll never be safe. He believes he's all alone, and she still doesn't have the words to tell him that he's not.

So she takes both his hands this time and squeezes hard, until he has no choice but to acknowledge her.

"Jesus, May," he says. "Stop."

She smiles and thinks, *There he is*. She softens her grip.

"I . . . miss you," she says.

He looks at her as if her words are a foreign language, but at least he looks at her. Francie releases Bill's hand and steps up beside them.

"You know your dad came to our house, right?" she says to Edward. "He pretty much ordered May to stay away from you. That man—"

"We've been caring for her," Vern breaks in. "For May. She had a little run-in with the police last night. Everything's fine, but it was frightening for her. She asked for you."

Edward's gaze drifts to May's thumb, which she slides across his wrist. Everyone is looking at her, expecting her to say something, but May is content just to be touching him.

"What am I supposed to do here?" Edward asks. "I don't have any idea who she really is. She just turned up in the woods, you know? I was trying to do the right thing, help her somehow. I know it's not comfortable staying in that house with my dad, but I did all I could to keep her safe. When she left . . ."

Edward tries to pull away from her, but May is quicker and links her arm through his. He shakes his head.

"My dad's giving me one more chance to prove myself. He put me in charge of the logging up Battlecreek Peak. If I don't come through this time. . . "

Vern steps forward. "No one's asking you to do anything, son."

"She is," Edward says, lifting his chin. "May asked for me. She came for *me*."

The others glance at each other, but May can't take her eyes off Edward.

"I'm not trying to be unkind," Vern says. "But you're a young man, still living with his father. You're in no position to care for someone like May."

There are too many words to decipher, but after Vern speaks there's a shift in Edward's posture, a straightening of his spine. A man isn't all that different from a larch, really—both start soft and harden over time. A tree's flexible inner bark passes food from roots to crown, but only lives for a short time. After it dies, it turns to cork and joins the tree's protective outer wall.

"May came for me," Edward says again.

In the silence that follows, May is the only one who realizes that Edward is trembling. She squeezes his arm and is pleasantly surprised when he leans into her.

"Well," Vern replies at last, "I'm not sure where we go from here."

May releases Edward's arm so can slip her hand around his waist. She pulls him even closer and has no idea why everyone gasps.

"Edward," she says. "And me."

The others shuffle nervously, but Edward's tremors finally subside. He looks down at her as if she might be the person to say everything he's ever wanted to hear, if she could only learn the words.

She raises her palm to his cheek and says, "I will."

Once again, there's a lot of pointless talking.

Bill uses the biggest words, which is a shame because no one listens to him. Angel and Francie beg May to "talk this over," while Vern recites a list of reasons why Edward won't be able to care for her.

"You have to consider May's memory loss, Edward," Vern says. "The obvious language barrier. Her naïveté when it comes to the real world. Not to mention all she needs to learn. How to read and write. Why she's supposed to walk on the sidewalk and not in the middle of traffic. How to toast bread and comb her hair and—"

"I know all that," Edward snaps. May is happy to see that his back is still straight. "I know the things that May needs. I'm not a fool."

"Aren't you?" Bill asks.

The man steps around Vern, a smug look on his face. They're all listening to him now.

"What is your father going to do when you bring her home with you?" Bill continues. "Give her a black eye to match yours?"

Everyone but May flinches.

"Bill, please," Francie says.

"Well, it's true, isn't it?" Bill doesn't look at anyone but Edward. "It's no secret what kind of man your father is. And, to be frank, I've seen no evidence that you're any different."

May isn't sure what the sudden hush is about, and it doesn't matter. She knows what she has to say; she even forms the words into a complete sentence to please Angel.

"I will go with Edward," she says.

Bill turns to her, his face no longer smug, but scornful. "Then you deserve whatever you get," he says before he walks back to the car.

His footsteps sound inordinately loud as Vern and Angel shuffle uncomfortably.

"Oh, May," Francie says, "I apologize for Bill. He can come across a little harsh sometimes, but he's got a good heart, I swear."

May shrugs. She doesn't care what Bill says or what type of heart he has if he can't be the kind of man that Francie deserves.

"Bill did make a fair point about bringing May back to your father's house," Vern says. "I doubt very much that Cameron will welcome her with open arms."

Edward shakes his head. "I'm not going back to my dad's," he says, his voice wavering for just a moment before he steadies it. "I'm still working for him, but I can't . . . I won't live there. I know a place where May—where both of us will be safe."

Whatever all his words mean, May can see that Vern and Angel are reluctant to believe him. They look at each other, then at May, until finally Vern squeezes his wife's arm and says, "May's a grown woman. She can do what she wants."

"Dad!" Francie cries, but Angel nods, her eyes moist as she walks to May's side and kisses her cheek the same way she kisses Francie's every night before bed.

"We are always here for you," she says. "Day or night."

Vern squeezes May's shoulder. "You'll do fine, kiddo," he says. "If you need anything—"

Francie throws herself into May's arms, cutting him off.

"What am I going to do without you?" she wails. "You have to promise to call. Use. The. Phone."

The three of them linger, fussing over her, until Vern gives Edward one final, stern look. Francie is crying as they return to the car, but finally Vern gets behind the wheel and starts the engine.

Francie leans her head out the back window. "You take good care of her!" she shouts as they drive back toward town. When the rumble of their car finally fades in the distance, May takes a deep breath. The air tastes of mint and poplar leaves. Only the crickets and stars are out.

Edward shakes his head. "I must be crazy."

He walks back to his truck and, for a moment, May thinks he's going to abandon her the same way she abandoned him. But he merely retrieves a flashlight from the glove compartment and returns to her side. With one last glance toward town, Edward takes May's hand and shines the light toward the mountains—not in the direction of the grove, which is due north, but farther west, up an adjacent ridge. May's legs are throbbing and she has blisters on her feet, but when he heads toward the woods, she matches his long stride.

It's a relief to say nothing. Despite his size, Edward treads lightly through the forest, keeping to rocks and hard-packed soil, never breaking a single twig beneath his boots. Even the nighthawks relax, croaking their distinctive "auk auk auk" call instead of flying for cover as they pass.

Edward holds her hand and no longer trembles, as if he's changed something basic, something at the heart of himself, too. So when they reach the first pine grove, she doesn't tell him what she feels.

The warning prickles the hairs on the back of her neck. It's a miracle, really, that she can still feel it—through a network of roots and fungi, the woods recognize her as one of their own. And tell her to be afraid.

The trees recognize it as easily as if Edward were a beaver sinking its teeth into their trunks. He is the danger. He can hurt them; he *has* hurt them. And he can and probably will hurt May, too. It's only human nature. May might have gained the ability to walk away from him, but what does it matter if she's never going to do it? Freedom is wasted on anyone in love.

And just as she thinks that, the warning fades. The goosebumps across her body retreat; there's only the sound of the crickets and the lack of the slightest whisper from the trees. To save the forest, trees let their weakest sisters fall. May touches the brown scales on one of the pine's trunks.

"Stay," she says, and Edward twitches as if she's a nightbird who startled him. But just for this moment, she rests her cheek against the tree and doesn't look at him. *Stay*, she thinks.

But they don't.

✦

May ignores the blisters on her feet and the stitch in her side as lodgepole pines turn to spruce and fir. She and Edward follow a steep, rocky path to an old logging site, then keep climbing past a small creek until they reach the summit. The crescent moon disappears behind Battlecreek Peak to the east just as a dilapidated cabin appears in the darkness.

It can't be more than one room, with a single window obscured by bindweed vines and dust. The roof might have been wood once, but at some point it sprouted a moss garden, while the rotting gray walls lean precariously to the left.

It's the best house she's ever seen.

Edward gestures for May to wait outside while he opens the door and shines his flashlight into the cabin. She sees the light reflect off the dirty window, then hears the thud of his boots as he crosses a wooden floor. A match is struck, casting a warm, golden glow over the threshold. Edward reappears in the doorway and beckons her inside.

May glances back toward Battlecreek Peak and the grove that she knows lies just beyond. As the crow flies, she's less than two miles from her sisters, yet she's never felt further away. No warning signals reach her, and even if she were to find a path down the steep cliffside and across the rugged canyon that divides them, they wouldn't welcome her back. She fell in love with the most dangerous thing in the forest. That makes her a dangerous creature of her own.

She walks to the door of the cabin and peers inside. As she'd thought, it's a single room, with a pair of dirty cots, two wooden chairs beside a rough hewn table, and in the corner a rusted wood stove. Cobwebs envelop the rafters; the dim light comes from a single oil lantern on the stove.

"Hunters use this place during elk season," Edward says. "But otherwise no one comes up here. I get that it's pretty rough. If you hate it, we'll try somewhere else."

He stuffs his hands in his pockets and looks away, and May's not sure how other humans stand it—this swelling of the heart. Even in an oxygen-rich forest, it's difficult to breathe.

It comforts her that he doesn't breathe right either, that he might feel this thing, this connection, between them too. He has no idea how much he's given her, bringing her to this house that is more outside than in.

"May," he whispers, though in the tiny cabin it sounds like he's shouting. "I'm sorry about my dad. I'm not making any excuses for him, but after my mom died, it was like he couldn't stand softness anymore. Not in himself, or in anyone else."

She cocks her head, trying to understand him.

"I never should have brought you there," Edward continues. "I knew what it was like. I knew it wasn't . . . safe."

May rises up on her delightfully strong tiptoes and kisses him. He hesitates a moment before slipping his arms around her and pulling her close. The oil lamp hisses as his lips part and he flicks his tongue against her teeth. May feels such a shiver of pleasure, she barely notices the field mouse that scampers across her foot and out the door.

Edward is the one to pull away. He looks almost as frightened as he did as a child, as if being with her could do far more damage than his father ever could. There's the thinnest band of green ringing his heartwood-colored eyes, like a tree that's not done growing yet, and his lashes are obscenely long. This close to him, she can make out a few freckles hiding between his whiskers and scars. Every moment of his life is a bruise written on him somewhere, but she will never tell him that.

They will move forward, not back. This will be their starting line, so that nothing in his past taints him, and she will never shock or repel him with who she was. Perhaps this isn't the way it ought to be, but it is how it must be for them. She takes his hand and leads him to the table, a cloud of dust rising as they sit. And in a cabin in the woods, they begin.

✦

Perched on the mountaintop, the walls of the hunting cabin rattle in the relentless wind. A dozen spindly fir trees eke out an existence on the blustery summit, all of them leaning precariously downwind.

They've been talking for hours. Or, rather, Edward has been trying to explain to May how difficult it is to survive this deep in the woods, even if they have a warm, snug cabin to shelter in. He keeps saying the same words over and over: Water. Food. Heat. Shelter.

"No, May," Edward says, when she heads toward the door and the tantalizing storm. He grabs her hand and leads her back to the table. "It's not safe out there."

May cocks her head. Despite how much he knows, he's wrong about the most important things. His bruises prove that the most dangerous place anyone can be isn't alone in the woods, but inside, with someone else in the room.

"It's important that you understand what's happening here," he continues. "I'll have to bring food in after work every day. There's no refrigerator to keep things cold, and all we've got to cook on is the wood stove. We don't even have plates or utensils yet."

May understands about plates and utensils from Francie's tablescapes, and the refrigerator was the most rewarding thing in her friend's whole house, always stocked with the soda pop May loves. While it will certainly be harder to find food in the woods than in Francie's kitchen, everything they need to survive is right outside the door. Fallen logs for firewood, fresh water from the creek a quarter mile away, and a forest full of delicacies—everything from nutty chanterelle mushrooms to the delicious miner's lettuce that grows rampant under poplar trees. Where the trees give way to sunny meadows, they'll find wild mustard, the edible leaves and seeds of plantain, primrose root and field mint, while the river banks offer wild raspberries, twisted stalk, cattail roots that can be pounded into flour, and peppery, Vitamin C-rich birch bark for tea. You can't take a step into the forest without finding something that will feed, heal, or soothe you.

She smiles across the table at him and tries to find the right words.

"Easy there," she says. "Better here."

The wind on the mountaintop rages all night. When May grows sleepy, Edward stands guard by the window, flinching every time a fir branch slaps the glass, while she stretches out happily on one of the cots. The gale storm is a lullaby; she falls asleep within seconds and doesn't wake until dawn.

When she opens her eyes, Edward is sitting up on the cot beside her. A single, dull ray of sunlight penetrates the dirty window to fall across his cheek.

"The storm broke just before dawn," he says.

His eyes are bloodshot; she doubts if he slept at all. May gets up and sits on the cot beside him. For a long time, they don't say anything at all. He takes her hand and strokes each of her fingers, as if he's as stunned by the intricacy of her bones as she is.

"I feel like I might not be able . . . " He stops speaking and looks away from her. "I wanted to go to Stanford, study chemistry or physics, but I've worked for my dad since I was 15 and I didn't have the grades. Nobody around here goes to college. Or if they do, they're not welcomed back here when they're done. So now I'm stuck. I could leave, but go where? Do what? I worry that I'm not going to be able to do this right. Take care of you the way I should."

He slumps in exhaustion. It's the most he's ever said at one time. Most of it sounds like gibberish, but May understands enough to know he's wrong about at least one thing.

She hurries out the door before he can tell her it's not safe. It's the kind of morning she understands—frost-dusted trees topped by a brilliant blue sky, a pair of robins headlining the morning chorus. The pine-scented air is still after last night's storm, but May knows the wind will return by mid-afternoon, as it always does this high on the mountain. When Edward emerges from the cabin behind her, she grins at him before hurrying to the closest Douglas fir.

Despite the brutal winds, the tree has managed to produce a bit of spring growth. The soft, new fir tips, which taste surprisingly like citrus, are packed with electrolytes and Vitamin C to help ward off colds. May could use the needles in sauces or infuse them in teas and syrups, but for now she just snaps off the bright green tips and pops them, whole, into her mouth.

Within 30 feet of her, May can see half a dozen things they could eat. Everything from dandelion leaves and chiming bells to elderberry blossoms, lichen and a cluster of scrumptious white puffballs. She walks toward the cluster of chiming bells, their dangling trumpet flowers blooming in shades of blue and pink. The lance shaped leaves are edible, but May only eats a few. With their oyster-like flavor, deer sometimes graze on the plant for days, then die suddenly from the plant's toxic alkaloids. The secret in the forest, and probably anywhere, is to know when enough is enough.

She gathers puffballs, dandelion leaves and more of the fir tips, then brings her harvest back to Edward. In quantity and flavor, none of it will compare to Angel's glorious lasagna and garlic bread, but what she wants him to understand is that she doesn't need him to take care of her. She can keep them both alive.

Edward offered her the most words he's ever spoken so she tries to do the same. She speaks haltingly, but he never takes his gaze from her face.

"I will stay here . . . with you," she says. "We will be fine. I'm . . . sorry I left you. You are . . . why I'm here."

May holds up her bounty and Edward picks up a fir tip. She mimics chewing the way he once did, and he laughs as he pops the fir tip into his mouth. It's not easy to chew. Nothing in the forest comes easy or quick. The wood's always wet, the path too steep, the blackberries surrounded by thorns. You can spend all day just trying to start a lowly campfire, but that night, when you lie down beside even the smallest flames, you'll have the best sleep of your life.

"It's almost sour," Edward says. "Like a tangerine."

May smiles as she brings her offerings inside the cabin. They eat all of it, no matter how tough, then sit on the dusty chairs.

"I still have to go to work," he says. "I'll hike down today and come back tonight with the truck and supplies. Blankets, clothes, food. There's a logging road nearby where I can park. You'll be okay here on your own until then?"

She smiles and waves her hand at the forest around them. Edward shakes his head, but the corner of his mouth twitches.

"Of course you will," he says. "You are May."

✦

After Edward disappears down the mountain, May explores the forest around the cabin. Just below the summit, the firs sport blackened trunks from an old ground fire, but their upper branches still thrive. Fir trees are a shifty bunch, hogging sunlight and burying any plants that dare to get too close to them under mounds of acidic needles. Normally, fir and larch trees grow quite amicably together, but back in the grove, when the first firs started sucking the nutrients from the soil, May and her sisters pooled their resources and grew so intertwined, the invading firs were dead within a year.

May tilts her head back to look at the tops of the trees. If the firs have any lingering animosity toward her, she doesn't feel it. In fact, she doesn't sense anything from the forest at all. She touches one of the gnarled trunks, imagining her toes extending into lateral roots that tunnel beneath the soil while a deep taproot anchors her feet to the earth. It's a comforting vision, but it doesn't last. Her leg itches; she thinks of Edward; she has more forest to explore. It's been only a month since she left the grove, but already it's getting hard to imagine anyone, or anything, standing still all day.

So she gathers cones. First the young, green fir cones she can use to make syrups, then the egg-shaped ones that have dropped from the slender, lodgepole pines. Lodgepole pines are clever, sealing their cones with so much resin and woody tissue, the only way to release the seeds inside is with intense heat—usually a wildfire. The very thing that devastates most trees is the only reason lodgepoles survive. And the cones make perfect firestarters.

There is no clear path across the mountain, so May climbs and descends, gathering cones and knocking on the trunks of fir, pine, and larch. She gets no answers. Even when she sits with her back to one of the larch trees, she feels nothing except the scrape of its bark. Trees speak their own secret language; they're a social, but cliquey bunch, and she's on the outside looking in now. The only lonely things here are people.

Yet, as she gets to her feet, she doesn't feel lonely, and she wonders if she ever will. She's a woman, yes, but with a tree's sensibilities. She knows not to rush things. Focus on roots first; cones and branches will come later. Savor the storms; in the end, they're what nourish you and make you stronger. Be the reason that others survive.

May spots one of the larch's winged seeds on the ground and takes it with her, along with a clump of morel mushrooms she harvests from a downed log. Luckily, the pockets in Edward's jacket are deep enough to hold all her treasures, including large handfuls of purple salsify, whose roots taste like oysters.

If she could make it down the cliff to the riverbank, she'd likely find enough edible plants and berries to last them for days. But the near vertical drop and sheer walls of granite stop her. Instead, she aims for the smaller, spring-fed creek she and Edward passed last night.

Edward had crossed the slow-moving stream without even glancing at the treasure trove of cattails along its banks, but after retracing their steps, May heads straight to the tall, slender reeds. Every part of a cattail is edible, from its flowers, seeds and shoots all the way down to its roots. May sits beside the creek and pulls a stalk out of the water, peeling away the tough outer layer before devouring the delicious raw shoot inside. With a moan of pleasure, she grabs another stalk and chews more slowly, savoring the cucumber-like flavor and the gentle, tinkling sound of the stream. It's so peaceful, it takes her a moment to realize that everything else in the forest has gone silent.

With a prickle along the back of her neck, she looks upstream and spots him lumbering toward the water. Her heart races at the sight of the scar tissue where his left ear used to be and how much weight he's put on since he was last in the grove. The one-eared bear is now a menacing, full grown grizzly, with three-inch long claws, a large shoulder hump and thick, dark brown fur. He claims the far bank by scratching his back against a river birch and ripping out every cattail in sight.

May tries to still her breathing. Even with only one ear, a grizzly has twice the hearing range of humans. He swipes at another cattail with his long, curved claws and comes away with the whole plant, roots and all. As he settles down to eat, he makes a disarming purring noise, yet he's easily five times the size of her, capable of battling, and besting, a 700 pound moose.

Trees can't run from danger, and there are times when humans would be crazy to try. Grizzlies are more than content to feast on roots and berries until something bigger and tastier moves. Once you flee, you're prey, and a grizzly can outrun you, so May keeps low to the ground and slides backwards soundlessly. But the one-eared bear still lifts his head.

He stares right at her, a cattail shoot protruding from his mouth. For what feels like forever, they stare at each other until the grizzly huffs once, then goes back to eating, ignoring her as if she's still just another tree in the woods.

May doesn't move again. She sits quietly, barely breathing, while the bear finishes his midday meal. Being still isn't as easy as it used to be. There's an itchy spot on her neck, one foot goes numb, flies land on her and it's all she can do to not swat them away. But eventually the one-eared bear tramps back into the woods and she drops her tense, aching shoulders. She waits another few minutes just to be sure, then heads back to the cabin, leaving the rest of the cattails for the bear's next meal.

She puts her salsify and mushrooms on the table, and her cones and seeds on the dusty window sill. She has no idea how to light a fire inside the rusty cast iron stove, and even if she did she'd never set a flame to wood. When she gets hungry, she eats half the salsify roots, and later, when darkness falls, she eats the rest. With her stomach still rumbling, she eyes the morel mushrooms, but knows she'll get a stomachache if she eats them raw. She considers heading outside to pick dandelion leaves or even going back to the stream for more cattails, but she doesn't like the idea of stumbling upon a grizzly at night.

So she sits at the wooden table in the dark. Edward didn't show her how to light the oil lamp, and the flashlight he left behind flickers briefly before going out. When the wind picks up and blows a cloud of ash out of the wood stove, May doesn't have a clue how to clean it up. And though Edward might show her how to sweep and light a lamp, she's not certain she'll ever do any of that. It's not the darkness or soot on the floor that bothers her; it's the waiting. For the first time in her life, she wishes that the wind was a little quieter so she could hear if a car is coming. The cabin was more than big enough this morning, but once she starts pacing, it feels like a cage.

Flinging open the door, May hurries outside into the howling wind. She'd rather run into a grizzly than spend one more minute waiting for someone who might not come back. The other thing she hasn't been taught is how to choose the right person to love. Someone steadier and more communicative, perhaps. Someone who can teach her more than words and practicalities; a person who has known joy in addition to sorrow.

But that's not who she loves. Sense has nothing to do with it. She loves the boy in the man, the person Edward could be, might be, if she stays.

May gathers a handful of dandelion leaves and sits beneath the rising moon to eat them. Every hour that passes, she discards another thing she might do if Edward doesn't return. She could go back to Francie's, but she doesn't want to burden their loving family any longer. She'll always consider the grove her home, but that doesn't make her welcome there, or protect her from exposure and hypothermia. Her best bet would be to stay in this cabin, surviving on fir tips and cattails, but even here a hunter will eventually come along to kick her out. She doesn't regret stepping out of her bear wound to save her sister; her only mistake was not tallying up the price she'd have to pay.

The moon reaches its apex and starts falling again before May finally hears a distant engine. The wind has let up, allowing a touch of frost to coat the grass, but that's not why her hands shake. As she strains to hear if the car is coming closer, she realizes that love feels an awful lot like fear. She's not yet sure that it's worth it.

Finally, a distant light flickers across the mountain, weaving slowly in and out of the trees. Her heart raced when she saw the one-eared bear, but now it pounds against her chest. She watches the headlights for half an hour, until they disappear below the summit and don't come again. Then she gets to her feet and walks to the nearest fir tree, knocking on wood until her knuckles are raw.

It doesn't matter if the tree is silent; she needs to not feel alone. And maybe her years in the grove were even more magical than she realized because suddenly she hears someone thumping up the mountain. Running. Edward races onto the summit, out of breath, and bruised.

"May," he says, dropping a stuffed backpack at his feet. The skin around both his eyes is purple and swollen. "I'm sorry," he says. "I tried to come hours ago. He . . . "

May loves the boy in the man. She rushes to his side and wraps her arms around him gently, afraid of other wounds she can't see. But he pulls her to him and buries his face in her hair. All this time, she's been trying to fit into his world; it never occurred to her that he might be trying to fit into it too. Maybe everyone struggles a bit at being human.

"It's only this bad when I fight back," he says.

She wants to know if he at least got in a few good punches, but she doesn't know how to form the words. Wolves, particularly the males, will kill each other for dominance and territory, and their aggression only increases with age. The grayer the coat, the more likely a wolf is to target his own pack, taking out any males who dare to challenge him.

"I don't know what to do," Edward says.

May pulls away to look at him. "Leave? Be . . . different."

His bruised face contorts in anguish. "That's not possible here. People in this town are loggers. And they're tough. That's all we know."

When a tree weakens significantly, the surrounding grove will decrease the amount of nutrients they share with it, focusing instead on their own survival. But May is no longer a tree.

In all her years in the grove, she was never struck by lightening, but she imagines that the fury coursing through her body feels much the same. Her skin is on fire; she hears her own heartbeat in her ears. She itches to race down the mountain and confront Edward's father, preferably with a rock or sharp branch in her hands. She's not sure she's entirely in control of her own actions, yet it's the most alive she's felt so far.

Edward may not know what to do, but she does. She loves who she loves. This is his battle, but she was born so that others could live. She can't send him warning signals, but now that she's here with him, she can fight.

"He is," she says, "asshole."

There's moisture in his swollen eyes, but the side of his mouth twitches. She raises a hand to touch his bruised cheek.

"Stay with me," she continues.

The moisture finally spills from his eyes as he says, "I will."

That night, after Edward shows her the supplies he's brought—a coffee pot and frying pan, paper plates and utensils, matches, batteries, blankets, clothes, a jug of water and enough food to last them for days—May pushes the two cots together so she can lie beside him. Edward is exhausted and falls asleep almost instantly, while she lies awake watching him, counting the scars that his father will have to atone for: Two black eyes, a cut by his lip, pink welts across his neck, the old burn mark that has never healed.

By morning, the swelling around Edward's eyes has gone down, but the bruises have turned deep blue. He grimaces as he puts his shoes back on, while May sits on the cot beside him, waiting for him to look at her. He avoids her gaze as he slips on his jacket, then walks to the table.

"These are beans," he says, showing her a tin can. "You use this to open it."

He picks up a metal gadget and twists it around the rim of the can to slice off the lid. Inside is a heap of slimy brown pellets that remind May of elk droppings.

"You can eat them cold, though they'll be better when we get that wood stove going."

She eyes the contents dubiously, quite sure that she'll never swallow a single bite.

"We're prepping the Battlecreek site today," he tells her. "I'll bring something hot for dinner when I get off work."

Then he heads for the door. He'd been so different last night, so vulnerable. Reachable. He'd said that he'd stay.

"You . . . can't go," she says. "He will . . . hurt you."

He doesn't look at her. Doesn't dare pause as he steps outside and thumps across the summit.

May doesn't move for a long time. It's no surprise that words can't be trusted. Language is a far less accurate means of communication than a shot of hormones through your roots. What does startle her, though, is the realization that people are more treelike than trees. Bound to the earth, a larch will at least stretch for the sky. People, on the other hand, have the freedom to go anywhere, choose anything, yet so many of them stay in the same holes they were born and raised in, digging themselves in deeper and deeper every day.

She shakes her head, then puts on the boots Francie gave her. She's already spent centuries in one spot; perhaps it's time to see just how far she can go.

When she steps outside, the wind is calm again, the sun just beginning to rise over Battlecreek Peak. May knows the cliff is too steep to head east, so she braves the trail back to the creek where she spotted the one-eared bear. There's no sign of him by the cattails this morning, but she still hurries past without gathering any shoots.

Beyond the stream, the terrain quickly turns steep and rocky. May's legs are getting stronger, but her muscles still burn as she makes the forty minute climb to the next ridge. She bends over at the summit to catch her breath, then looks out over a spectacular range of forested slopes and distant white-capped mountains. She knows the wilderness doesn't go on forever, but it's nice to imagine, for a moment, that it does.

Descending into the next canyon, she tells how far she's gone by the trees she passes—hemlock, western red cedar, river birch and alder, juniper, grand fir, spruce. She collects seeds and cones, and grazes on the mountainside's delicious blue violets. By a river bed, she drinks crystal clear water and harvests the watery, cucumber-flavored red berries of twisted stalk. On the mountainsides, she eats red clover blossoms and pineapple weed until her stomach is full.

The shadows cast by the towering silver pines have grown long and dark by the time May sits against one of their prickly trunks. She rubs her throbbing legs, plucks thistle thorns from her socks, and smiles. Even if her sisters don't acknowledge her, she's still a part of the forest. Another creature sitting on the earth. She takes a long, deep breath, watching the moths flutter to the tops of the pines and wishing Edward was with her. Turns out the only limit to how far she can go is her desire to go home to him.

Darkness swallows the last shadows as she heads back. By the time she climbs over the ridge and down to the cattail-lined creek, a deep purple sky fades to black. She hears snuffling as she crosses the stream, but keeps walking. Now that she's found her place in the forest again, not even a grizzly scares her much. By the time she climbs the last ridge to the cabin, Edward is already there. He stands in silhouette in the doorway, the flickering lantern on the table behind him.

"I thought you'd gone again," he says, his voice flat. Hurt.

She crosses the summit and wraps her arms around his waist. In the darkness, she can't check for new bruises, but he doesn't flinch at her touch. She rests her head against his chest.

"I walked," she replies.

He stands stiffly for a moment, then finally exhales and slips his arms around her.

"I was worried," he says softly. "You need to be careful up here, May. This is grizzly country."

It's because of grizzly country, and a certain one-eared bear with a taste for larch wood, that she's even here.

Edward leads her back into the cabin, which smells far different than when she left. She can't identify the scent, but it makes her mouth water. There's a new mound of food and supplies on the table, along with a cardboard box.

"I stopped at Francie's," Edward says. "She gave me more clothes for you. And I got us a pizza."

He opens the cardboard box. The gooey disk inside looks strange, but smells intoxicating. Edward shows her how to pick up one of the triangular slices, then bite into the pointy end. He picks up another triangle and lifts it to her mouth.

"Go on," he says. "Trust me."

May takes a hesitant bite, then opens her eyes wide, grabbing Edward's arm in delight. He laughs as she snatches the triangle from him and sits down to savor each bite. While she eats, he takes the two green lumps he calls "sleeping bags" from the table and rolls them out on their cots.

"My dad and I used to camp," he says. "It was a long time ago."

He reaches into his jacket pocket and hands May a piece of paper.

"From Francie," he says.

She looks at the squiggles on the paper, including the three shapes Vern taught her to write.

"May!" she exclaims.

Edward smiles. "Yes, she wrote your name. It's a letter to you."

She stares at the note again. The "a" in May is in other places on the page, a secret code she needs to crack.

"Teach," she says, looking up at Edward. "Please?"

She holds out the note to him and, when he takes it, promptly sits on the cot. Edward sighs and sits beside her.

"Reading isn't easy, and I'm no teacher. I'm happy to help you, but it's going to take time to learn."

May ignores him and points to the squiggles that come after her name.

"That word is 'How,'" he tells her. "It starts with an H. You say it like huh. The O and the W go together—ow. Huh—ow. How."

She cocks her head. He barely opens his mouth to make the 'Huh' sound, but stretches it a little wider to add 'ow.'

"Huh—ow,," she says.

He smiles. "Yes. The next word's tricky. The A and R go together, but the E is silent. Don't ask me why."

They stay up late, eating pizza and practicing sounds. It takes hours just to work through the first three sentences of Francie's note.

May,

How are you doing up there? I hope the cabin isn't too rustic and horrible! I can't imagine! These are some clothes I thought you could use. I sure miss seeing your smiling face every day!

Reading is, by far, the most difficult thing she's had to learn, with silent letters and vowels that change their sounds depending upon where you put them. But it's also the most rewarding; one precious note and it's almost as if Francie has walked right into the room.

"It's late," Edward says. "We can go through more of the letter tomorrow."

May carefully refolds the letter and sticks it in her pocket before slipping inside the cocoon-like sleeping bag. When Edward turns off the lantern, she serenades him with the letters she knows.

"Muh, huh duh, oh, ow, oo."

Edward chuckles as he slips into his sleeping bag and she wriggles closer to rest her head on his shoulder. The bed at Francie's house is softer, but May has never felt as safe or comfortable as she does now.

They're silent for a long time, until his breathing evens out and she dares to whisper, "Did he . . . hurt you again?"

When he doesn't answer, she assumes he fell asleep. Then he pulls her close and kisses her forehead.

"Just a little," he says.

By the time May wakes in the morning, Edward has already taken a newspaper out of his backpack and crumpled up a few of its thin pages.

"It's Saturday," he says. "Time to teach you how to light the wood stove."

They put on their boots and head outside to collect broken sticks and dried fir needles for kindling. It's not until they head to the stack of firewood behind the cabin that May steps back. The split logs are a mix of fir, pine and larch, still wet and golden, recently felled. Edward grabs the pine logs—the fastest burners—then heads back inside. May hears the clunk of each log as he sets them in the firebox.

"May? Come inside. I want to show you."

But she doesn't come.

He reemerges a minute later. She hasn't left the wood pile in the back.

"Are you okay?" he asks. "What is it?"

It takes a pine tree fifty years to grow a trunk thick enough to be chopped up for firewood, and even longer for a trip to the lumber mill. Some lumberjacks won't bother sharpening their saws for anything less than a century-old giant.

But humans are also creatures on this earth. And some of them won't even make it to fifty. It might comfort them to be sitting beside a crackling fire at the end.

So May closes her eyes just for a moment before saying, "Nothing. I'm coming in."

Edward explains how he stacked the wood like a teepee over a bed of crumpled newspaper. Making a fire, it turns out, is easy: Simply forget that every log was once a living being and strike a match. Maybe trees are the lucky ones—every part of them contributes to the safety and comfort of someone else. But May still twitches when the wood sends up sparks.

She makes herself stand there the whole time it burns.

Edward is delighted with the stove. He puts a skillet on top of it and brews May a delicious cup of coffee. He even heats up his beans. Once the fire simmers down to embers, May sits beside him at the table, where they work through the remainder of Francie's letter.

. . . face every day! Bill wants to delay our wedding until Christmas time. Now I have to come up with a whole new winter tablescape! I hope to see you soon. Edward better be taking good care of you!
Love, Francie

May and Edward go through the letter dozens of times until she has it memorized. The next day dawns warm enough that, instead of using the newspaper to start a fire, Edward gives it to May to read.

"It's a comic strip. Brenda Starr Reporter," he says, pointing to an illustration of an attractive red-headed woman talking on the phone. "I think you'll like it."

Painstakingly sounding out each word, May slowly discovers that Brenda Starr is a glamorous reporter who is secretly in love with a mysterious man who wears an eye patch and drinks black orchid serum to keep from dying—a fact which would have made May fall in love with him too. On Monday morning, when Edward puts on his boots to head to work, May holds up the newspaper and says, "More? And pizza?"

Edward laughs as he walks to the door, but by the time he steps outside, the smile is gone. For a week, though, he comes home with only the daily newspaper. No new bruises. The skin around his eyes fades from black to green. He never speaks of his father, or of the job they're doing together, but his eyes grow a little brighter when he gets an idea of what to do next.

"Some of my dad's crew go out to the logging camps each year," he says. "They say it's pretty rough conditions, but it pays better than anywhere else. I'd have to live there though, for a few months at a time."

May looks at him. "Stay," she says.

Edward doesn't hold her stare. "We'll see."

While Edward's at work, May reads the newspaper, circling every word she doesn't recognize—at first, nearly every one. Edward brings home pizzas and the daily paper, while she offers him a salad of miner's lettuce and twisted stalk berries. They stay up late sounding out words until Edward nearly falls over from exhaustion. Lying side by side in their twin sleeping bags, Edward closes his eyes while May serenades him with the words she knows.

"I love you," she says. "You're a good man. I will never leave."

He doesn't open his eyes, but his face looks pained, like he can't bear the words. So she repeats them, louder.

"I love you. You're a good man. I will never leave."

Finally, he opens his eyes and May says, "I win."

Edward always falls asleep before she does. May waits until his first deep sigh before shimmying closer and laying her head in the crook of his neck.

Whenever she wakes during the night, he is on his side, holding her close. One night, when he cries out in his sleep, May crawls out of her sleeping bag and slides into his. The tight squeeze wakes him, and he goes as still as a deer in the brush. Then he places a tentative hand on her waist and she presses her body closer.

But a few days later, when she presses her knee between his leg and touches him, he stops her.

"May," he says, "I don't know if you understand. I don't want to hurt you."

She scoffs and tosses his hand aside. The only way he hurts her is by keeping her away. Perhaps she doesn't understand everything, but she can find her way across his body with her fingers, then with her lips. Sometimes he lets out such a long breath of air, she wonders how long he's been holding it.

Each night, they explore a new part of each other. He marvels over the curve of her breast; she kisses each muscle and rib. She seems to be as much of a wonder to him as he is to her. Some nights the only word he speaks is "May."

May used to tell time in seasons, but now there is only the time she's with Edward, and the long hours when he's away. She counts down the minutes they have together, and when he wastes too many precious ones still talking about the things she doesn't know, she says, "Then show me."

He hovers, naked, above her, his weight on his elbows to keep from crushing her.—though she doesn't think she'd mind it if he did. Her heart races as he spreads her legs, but his gaze never leaves hers as he slips inside her. It does hurt, but as he grasps her hands and lets her guide them, it quickly becomes bliss. This, then, is the real difference between trees and people. A tree gives all that is has indiscriminately, while humans are stingier, offering themselves only to the ones they choose. Both are gifts, but only one is love.

After work, Edward brings home mason jars for May's cones and seeds, and she stops flinching whenever he lights a fire. For another week, they read and laugh and make love every night, so May doesn't mention that she no longer sleeps. At first, she chalks it up to not wanting to miss a moment of her time with Edward, but then she notices the way her hands shake. One afternoon while carrying home a basket of chickweed, an earthquake rumbles through her, knocking the basket from her hands and taking her to her knees. It's a while before she can get back on her feet, and her head snaps straight toward the grove.

This is no warning. It's a goodbye. When Edward gets home, May wants to ask him what he did at work that day, but she can't bear to hear the answer.

The next morning, Edward leaves for work before the sun has even risen.

"Stay in bed," he whispers. "I'll see you tonight."

May listens to his receding footsteps and, later, the distant sound of his truck. She doesn't tremble, but her heart is racing. She wriggles out of the sleeping bag and sits on her cot eating the toast Edward left for her. The sound of her own chewing is deafening in her ears.

When she finally stands, pain rockets up from the soles of her feet. Her skull feels as if it's rattling around inside her head and she cries out, reaching for the edge of the table. Almost blind from the pain, she thrashes around the cabin for her jacket and steps into her boots. Flinging open the cabin door, she looks across the mountain, in the direction of the grove. Her head clears the moment she hears the saws.

Nine

Douglas Fir
(Pseudotsuga menziesii)

The Douglas Fir is a liar. It's not a true fir at all. The tree is named after two men—David Douglas, a Scottish naturalist who declared himself the first to cultivate the species in 1827, and Archibald Menzies, who actually beat him to the punch by documenting the tree in 1791. In addition to discovering this "pseudo fir," Menzies and Douglas were the first and second men to reach the summit of the Mauna Loa volcano in Hawaii—though only Archibald Menzies returned. David Douglas fell into a pit trap and was mauled to death by a bull someone had placed inside it. Though Archibald Menzies never admitted to luring his nemesis there, the man enjoyed an uncommonly successful career afterwards, gathering more than 400 botanical species hitherto unknown to science.

✦

The truth is that May never wanted to know what Edward did when he left her every day. She noticed the wood chips on his jacket and didn't complain when he came home smelling of gasoline. A creature of the forest, she trusted his silence more than his words.

The woods are no longer silent. Through a web of roots and fungi, the whole forest knows when May's first sister falls. Edward and his father have brought heavy machinery that echoes for miles. The kind that can fell and remove a whole grove in mere days.

Every morning, it takes Edward 20 minutes to hike to his truck, plus another hour to drive the winding, dirt road to the grove. Walking the whole route, May doubts that she would reach her sisters by nightfall. Her only option is the most direct one—straight down the cliff at the edge of the summit, then back up and over Battlecreek Peak.

But when she takes her first step toward the cliff, a jolt of pain drops her to her knees. Her second sister has fallen; May's whole body shudders as the 200-year-old trunk hits the earth. The only thing they'll share with her, it seems, is the end.

She struggles to her feet, even as her third sister cracks. Tearing through a thicket of bunchberries to reach the summit's edge, May eyes the cliff's obstacle course of boulders, shorn granite, and hazard trees below. Without hesitation, she crouches low to the ground and steps off the edge.

It's more of a free fall than a descent. For the first few feet, she doesn't even touch the earth, then a bed of nails rises to greet her. Despite Edward's jacket, she cries out as the jagged spine of the mountain cuts into her back. The fall feels endless. Down, down, down, scraping over granite, ricocheting off boulders, until she finally slams into the trunk of a pine and comes to a stop.

The impact breaks her fall, but also takes the wind from her lungs. It's the first time her tender skin bleeds.

It's a moment before she regains enough air to realize she's stuck. Below her is a sheer wall of granite; above a vertical cliff she can't climb. She clutches the tree trunk in terror and closes her eyes.

She has no idea how long she clings to the pine tree, frozen in fear, but at some point she realizes she can no longer hear the echoes of saws or heavy machinery. This deep in the canyon, there is only the roar of the river below, accompanied by her own shallow breathing. She tries to still herself, take a deep breath, then another. The pine is steady in her hands, the rough bark a comfort. She taps the tree once, then opens her eyes.

There is no choice. While going on is merely terrifying, turning back is impossible. She doesn't have the strength to climb a near-vertical mountain, but she can find the courage to let go.

The drop beneath her is at least twenty feet, ending in a ledge of gray scree. Certainly, it's going to hurt, but so does standing there while another of her sisters is slaughtered. If you care about anything, pain is a given.

So she releases the tree and falls, a small landslide of pebbles coming with her. It all happens so fast, she doesn't even think to scream. Her jacket rides up, the mountain scraping her skin raw before she comes to a sudden, painful halt in the heap of sharp rock.

The scree is four feet deep, the work of decades of erosion and landslides. May struggles to find her footing atop the rubble, every inch of her either aching or bleeding, yet when she looks ahead, she breathes a sigh of relief. The path to the river is still steep, but it's navigable. She picks her way carefully across the scree field, then leans into the cliffside, slowly sidestepping her way down.

When she finally reaches the riverbank, she tries not to panic. What looked like a narrow, passable creek from the mountaintop is actually a wide, fast-moving blockade of whitewater. There's a bridge somewhere that Edward drives across each day, but she has no idea where it is. Nor does she have the time to find it. All she can do is choose the narrowest crossing and step right into the water.

The cold is shocking. This is no underground spring or misty forest rain. The icy current pummels her; one wrong step and she'll be bowled over. May's waterlogged boots weigh her down as she wades into a waist-high rapid. The cold is numbing. *Go*, she thinks. *Faster.* But the whitewater only grows stronger, and with her next step, a wave easily sweeps her off her feet.

There is nothing to hold but white froth. A fallen larch tree might have gotten hung up on the rocks, but a woman is little more than a wad of debris the river toys with for a bit before drowning. The current slams May into the rocky bottom and holds her there. She struggles to break free, but the weight of the water is like a mountain on top of her. Her chest tightens painfully, her body pinned to the rocks. When she searches for the surface, all she sees are stars.

Then, one by one, the stars twinkle out. It's calmer, at least, the darkness.

She hardly notices when an errant wave flings her upward, but all of a sudden she's gasping at the sudden shock of air. She's swept into a rocky channel near the far shore, as weightless as a cork, banging into one obstacle after another until, at last, the river grows bored and discards her into a slow-moving eddy.

May's feet finally touch the river bottom, though it's a few minutes before she can gather the will and strength to stand. She stumbles onto dry land, collapsing on the bank, her body shaking uncontrollably. For some reason, she can't bear to look at the sky. She squeezes her eyes shut tightly, and presses herself into the earth.

She gives herself a moment—just one—to remember a life without pain. Decades, centuries even, spent without physical discomfort or sorrow, but also without joy. If she was offered the chance to go back, she wouldn't take it. There's nothing to do but go on.

She shivers beneath her heavy, wet clothes and eyes the climb ahead. Though not as steep as the mountain she just tumbled down, Battlecreek Peak is more wooded. She maps out a course that will avoid an ominous cliff face and the worst of the raspberry thickets. There are a few rocky outcroppings she'll have to maneuver around, but even crawling uphill is better than falling. And this is the mountain she knows.

May threads her way through the river willows, grateful for their steadying branches whenever she feels another of her sisters fall. Soon the slope grows steeper, and she climbs steadily, trunk by trunk. Pine, fir, the occasional cedar and hemlock—she gives each a squeeze and hoists herself up. She gets hung up by a rock slide, but quickly finds an alternate route. When she passes the first larch, she quickens her pace. It smells like home now. And gasoline.

The grove is tucked into a small bowl on the other side of the summit, but even from here, the screaming of the saws is deafening. Her legs burn as she struggles toward the summit—a narrow, sun-baked crest of cheat grass and wind-bent firs. She doesn't pause for breath when she reaches the top, but runs straight across the ridge. Down the eastern slope, she finally spots the feathery crowns of her sisters. The rest of the forest is still, but their boughs tremble as an army of machines cuts them down.

There's only one more obstacle between them—a rocky talus field that doesn't faze May at all. She boulder hops across it and keeps running. When she enters the grove at last, she's so stunned by the quantity of men and machines, she can't cry out, not even when one of her sisters falls right at her feet. Dozens of men are already limbing the downed larches. And there is Edward, directing them all.

She would go to him first, but the man driving a feller buncher is closer. He shouts as she steps between his machine and the group of her youngest sisters, who he's picking off one by one.

"Lady!" he says, cutting the engine. "What the f—"

The scream erupts from her suddenly. She didn't even know she could make the sound, but it's loud enough to stop every engine and saw. Edward suddenly appears beside her, grabbing her roughly by the arm. He has that face again, the one she doesn't recognize. The one that isn't him.

"May!" he shouts. "What are you doing?"

She can't stop screaming. Once the saws stop, all she sees is carnage. Her beautiful, long-lived sisters hacked into pieces. Gone.

Edward shakes her. "May, stop."

It's his fingers digging into her skin, the pain he's causing her, that finally quiets her. She takes him in, every bit of him, and narrows her eyes.

"You stop," she says.

He looks at his hand on her arm and releases her, but the red imprint of his fingers remains.

"I didn't mean . . . You can't jump in front of heavy equipment like that. You could have been killed. What are you doing here?"

The machines are quiet now and all the men have gathered. May looks past them to count her fallen sisters. One, two, three of the youngest, plus the five largest whose boughs once rose above them all, shading them from the harsh summer sun.

She takes a sudden, angry step toward the men. Two of them retreat, but most just laugh. The driver of the feller buncher throws up his hands and says, "Another one of those."

May looks at Edward, tears forming at the corners of her eyes.

"You stop," she says again.

Edward takes her arm, gently this time, and leads her away from the men. He doesn't seem to notice that they stop at the base of the tree she came from, the place he once ran to for comfort. The larch grows on indifferently without her, but May knows that she's home.

"I'm not sure what you hope to accomplish here," Edward says quietly. "The deal is done. We've got a couple hundred trees to take out. You can't beat larch wood for shingles and fencing."

Fencing. They'll use her tree and her sisters to block the view and keep out the wild. She thinks of all the words she's learned, but none of them will stop him—not when he's looking at her with his father's eyes. So she does the only thing she can think of, and steps inside her old bear wound.

"May," he says, annoyed. "Don't be ridiculous."

She inhales deeply, breathing in the scent of the wood. The center of a tree trunk is dead tissue, serving only to support the weight of everything else, and with a half turn, she fits perfectly inside of it, the wound wood taking the shape of her own body, every inch of her held tight.

May looks out at her grove, and the man trying to destroy it. "You will have to . . . cut me down too," she says.

There's panic in Edward's eyes, and fear. If he stops the logging, his father will come. She knows that. She knows exactly how brave she's asking him to be. It's possible, though, that he's no different than a larch tree, and what was best and deepest inside of him has died too.

The men drift off to smoke cigarettes while Edward stares warily at her inside the bear wound, then glances at the root that startled him once by pushing its way up through the soil. May has no idea how much he's willing to believe. He was there when she first stirred; he's had to teach her things any human girl should know. But his world runs on industry, not magic. All she really needs him to know is that he's the only reason she's here.

But all he says is, "I'll take you home."

She shakes her head. "No."

"May—"

"You will stop this."

He runs his fingers through his hair. "I won't. I can't. It's my dad's company. This is the biggest deal he's ever had."

She stares at him a moment longer, then crosses her arms. The men laugh again; one of them calls out, "It's your dime, Eddie." For people who cut down trees for a living, they're awfully cavalier about a larch's—or a woman's—ability to outlast them.

Edward balls his hands into fists, which doesn't scare May much. He's not his father, no matter how hard he tries to prove otherwise. She motions for him to come closer, and though one of the men says, "For crying out loud," Edward steps forward and kneels atop her old roots.

"May," he says softly, so that only she will hear. "You can ask anything of me but this."

May merely looks at him. The men are rumbling now, complaining, but they don't matter. It's always been just the two of them. Her and Edward.

"It's not right," she says, "what you're doing." And though of course she means clearcutting the grove, they both know it's so much more. It's not right to let someone else's cruelty define you. Not right to not even try to scab over your own wounds. Scars and bear wounds arise from horrors, but they're also the things that change you the most.

She understands how much she's asking of him—not only to stop cutting, but to lose face with men he wants so badly to impress. To disappoint, perhaps even enrage, his father. To ruin his own life.

No, not ruin it. Start it again.

She doesn't go to him. She can't change him. Only he can do that.

"Decide what's right," she says. "I'll be here."

✦

Men shout like warring crows, and May has never liked those birds much. She sits inside her bear wound, trying to tune them out. It isn't until one of them dares to rev up a chainsaw that she emerges, walking calmly past Edward to stand between the lumberjack and the tree he's about to cut.

The crows squawk louder. A squabble begins about private property and tree huggers, until Edward tells the men that it might be best if they sort this out later and call it a day. The crew grumbles as they pack up and leave, but Edward walks out of the grove without looking back.

When their trucks finally rumble off and the forest settles into silence, May takes a long, deep breath. She sits in the battlefield beside her fallen sisters. There's not a breath of wind.

"I'm sorry," she says.

Sorry for what the men did. Sorry for leaving them. Sorry for how the world beyond the grove works. Her sisters are born with everything they need, while everyone else resorts to stealing. Robins pluck out larch needles for their nests, humans seek board feet for shelter, even May herself has sat beside a crackling fire, fueled by this very forest. It's impossible to live without hurting others.

Unless you're a tree.

The final piece of May's transformation from tree to woman is the sorrow she learns to carry. Humans have only two choices: Either define their lives by the heartaches and tragedies they've suffered, or look to the future and soldier on. May grieves as she touches her sisters' carcasses, but she also finds comfort in knowing that she can survive it.

She expects Edward to return to the grove with his crew and perhaps even his father, but no one comes that night, or the next day. May sleeps on a bed of larch needles, surviving on miner's lettuce, fireweed stalks, and the cool water from a nearby spring. She knocks on her remaining sisters' trunks, cherishing the time they still have. She was lucky to have lived here. Her sisters are lucky. But luck runs out.

Two days later, May is sitting in her bear wound when Edward finally returns. She looks past him, expecting to do battle with his father, but he walks toward her alone. His face is fierce, but not angry. He stares right at her, at what he must know she is, deep down. He touches her tree first, lightly tapping its trunk, then kneels beside her.

"I cancelled the logging," he says. "You're all safe."

And though she lived her first two centuries feeling nothing, May puts her face in her hands and weeps.

Ten

Bur Oak
(Quercus macrocarpa)

There's nothing frilly about the Bur Oak except its golfball-sized acorns, which are adorned with elaborately fringed caps. Bur Oaks stand like giant sentinels where woodlands give way to tall grasses, resisting the flames of prairie fires and the heat and drought of long, rainless summers. Midwest pioneers loved these shady oases—probably too much since the Bur Oak savannas went from 32 million acres to just 6400 in 85 years. Still, the Bur Oak holds no grudges. It will happily adapt to the harshest urban environment, resisting air pollution and car exhausts.

✦

Two hours after May and Edward return to their cabin, they hear a truck skid to a halt on the forest road below. There's only one man who's coming for them, and Edward juts out his chest, telling May he'll handle it. A gallant move, but May still slips two knives into her pant pockets.

They're waiting on the porch when Cameron Cousins strides across the summit, not yet reeking of alcohol which means the redness in his face is pure rage.

"You want to tell me what the hell is going on?"

May stands close enough to Edward to feel his trembling, but his voice is surprisingly strong.

"I had a chat with the Olsens about their Battlecreek Peak site," he says. "They had a right to know the remoteness of the site would limit their profits significantly, especially compared to, say, grazing land. Tom Huckabee's been wanting to retire and swap his pastures for private hunting grounds. I helped the two of them strike a deal."

For a moment, it seems as if everything will be all right. Edward's father looks past them toward the cabin, taking in Edward's boots on the stoop, the home his son is trying to make for himself.

Then his lip curls, turning him as ugly as the larches who fall prey to bleeding cankers and needle blight. Some creatures can be given all the sunlight and nutrients in the world, yet still rot from the inside out.

By the time Cameron comes at them, May has both knives in her hands. But Edward steps in front of her and, without a word, levels his father with one hard blow to the cheek. Cameron falls to the ground as unceremoniously as the deer he once shot. Out cold.

May nudges the man's ribs with her boot, then beams up at Edward.

"Good," she says.

Edward's grin is a little more shaky. It's a while before his trembling subsides.

"Now what?" he asks.

When Cameron starts to come to, May is standing over him, knives in hand. He blinks, trying to bring her into focus, then scoffs. His voice is satisfying weak when he says, "You can't be serious."

May shrugs. She imagines she's capable of a lot more than Cameron Cousins can imagine. Edward steps up to her side.

"You need to go, Dad. We're done here."

As Cameron gets slowly to his feet, May grips the knives tighter. But he merely takes a cigarette out of his shirt pocket and lights it, then blows the smoke in May's face.

"She's a witch, you know," he says to Edward. "She'll be the death of you."

Edward shakes his head, but May feels a prickle along her spine, the same way she does when her sisters send a warning. Cameron looks right at her and smirks, as if he's learned the secrets of every tree he's cut.

"Don't bother coming back to work," he says to Edward. "You're the one who's done."

He saunters across the summit and disappears down the path to his truck. All is quiet except for the wind through the trees. Edward takes a long, deep breath.

"I made a decent commission on that land swap," he says. "We'll be okay."

May slips her knives back into her pockets and puts her arms around him. But the prickle down her spine remains.

While Edward heads to town each day to look for work, May gathers fallen branches. He changed for her, so she will do the same. She stacks the wood by the cabin door and, once, on a chilly night, even lights the wood stove herself before he comes home.

There is no work. Even if his father didn't hold sway over every logger in town, Edward killed a deal that would have paid his crew's rent through winter. No one in Laramie will hire him; many won't even take his calls. So he accepts a job as a store clerk in a neighboring town and doesn't come home each night until May is asleep. They make love every morning and she clings to him.

"Don't go."

He holds her close, but only until the sun rises. "I have to, May. We need the money. This is the way the world works."

May wrinkles her nose. She's not sold on the ways of the world. Certainly, finding food, water, and shelter are essential and even rewarding, but everything else seems made up.

Edward, however, works not only his normal 40 hours a week, but any side jobs he can get. Some days, he leaves the cabin before the sun rises and doesn't get home until well after midnight. While he's gone, May discovers that if she follows the logging road, she can reach the grove in about five hours, far less time than she'd thought and without falling down the mountain or nearly drowning. She visits her sisters every few days and naps in her bear wound. No matter how long she sleeps, she never dreams, and when she wakes, she's not hungry. A few stalks of fireweed are all she needs to feel satiated. Now that May's sisters are free from danger, their signals are mere whispers, the comforting brush of soft needles along her cheek. She saved them. She chose them. Her sisters have accepted her back.

May sleeps so late in the grove one day that her entire walk home is in darkness. The shy new moon lets the stars dazzle, and she has to sit for half an hour just to take them all in. She passes Edward's truck as she follows his well worn path to the summit. Smoke curls from the chimney.

When Edward hears her coming, he steps out the door and falls to one knee.

May rushes to him, afraid that his father has hurt him again, but although he looks fearful, there are no bruises on his face. He takes a small box from his breast pocket and opens it. There's another star inside.

"May," he says, "will you marry me?"

She takes a step back, horrified that he wants cummerbunds and fancy tablescapes. She doesn't even know what pink tulle is. But he continues to kneel, so she slips to one knee beside him.

"Like Francie and Bill?" she asks.

Edward pulls her onto his lap. She moans in contentment, stretching out her aching legs.

"No," he says. "Not like Francie and Bill. Marriage is when you vow to be with someone forever. You do have a ceremony, but I thought we could have ours in your grove."

She leans back to look at him. They've never said it out loud—who she is, where she came from. But then words aren't her native language, and she's not sure they're his either. He wants to be with her; he's promising to never leave.

She feels the warning from her sisters at the same moment she kisses him. She doesn't stop until the prickles fade.

"Marry me," she says, and Edward smiles. He opens the box again and puts the ring on her finger.

"I will."

✦

They marry in the grove. It's private hunting grounds now, but even Vern steps around the No Trespassing sign and doesn't say a word.

Francie's family, Bill, and May's sisters are the only witnesses. Vern tries to explains to May that, since she has no traceable identity or social security number, the marriage isn't legally binding.

"You won't get tax benefits," he says. "Health insurance might be more expensive. Even to open a savings account you'll need—"

May stops him with a hand on his arm. "I'm May."

He sighs as he says, "That you are." Then he takes his place between her sisters.

May wears a lacy, floor-length sheath—one of Francie's castoffs now that she and Bill are switching to a "winter wonderland theme"—that picks up larch needles with every step. The fabric reminds May of the delicate, white moths that float dreamily through the grove all summer. Edward apologized for not being able to afford a tuxedo, whatever that is, but all May notices is him standing beside Vern, where he'll vow to love her for the rest of his life.

Francie explained the wedding rules. There must be flowers—May picks a small cluster of yellow goldenrod right before the ceremony—and an officiant. The only time May has ever seen Vern cry is when she asked if he would marry her and Edward. There will be vows, the exchanging of rings, then at last a kiss. Rather than personal vows, traditional ones are a safer bet, Francie told her. Who knows what a man might blurt out on his own?

May walks alone down an aisle formed by two of her fallen sisters, who are already shelter for snakes and mice. Vern asks them to repeat promises to love and honor each other, and afterwards he brings out the rings—her beautiful star and a secondhand band for Edward that, for some reason, makes Bill scoff. They slide them onto each other's fingers, marking their union the way a broad tree ring indicates a particularly bountiful year.

Edward stares solemnly down at their hands. May squeezes his fingers, harder and harder until he finally looks up. The smile he gives her then takes her breath away. Her only regret since leaving the grove is that she'll only have a fleeting human lifetime to see it.

"And now," Vern says, "I pronounce you husband and wife. Edward, you may kiss—"

Before Vern can finish, Edward scoops May up in his arms and kisses her so deeply, Bill says from somewhere far off, "I can guarantee you I won't act like that on our wedding day, Francie."

To which Francie replies, "Well, I don't see why not."

Despite Bill's grumbling, Francie insists that their wedding gift will be a place for Edward and May to honeymoon. Francie wanted to fly them to Hawaii, but since May won't get in a car and looks appalled when Francie explains how airplanes work, they settle on Bill's cabin on neighboring Lost Lake.

May and Edward set out at dawn for the 20 mile hike. Bill's "cabin" is a three story Tudor mansion on a lake ringed by equally grand second homes. Despite the beauty of the landscape—a mirror-like lake hugged by a shoreline thick with pine, spruce and fir, there's not a soul around when they arrive, hungry and tired, in the late afternoon. They use the key Bill gave them after he made it clear that his wine cellar is off limits, and let themselves into the house. The entry has a curving marble staircase and bronze statues of ferocious-looking dogs that May doesn't care for at all.

They wander from the blinding white kitchen to a dining room with an ornate mahogany table set for twelve, their footsteps echoing down long, sterile hallways. Upstairs, they find the master bedroom, where Francie has left rose petals on the bed that she must have plucked from a perfectly happy bush. They're already crinkling at the edges, devoid of perfume. But the view from the balcony is lovely. Bill's house is situated in a small inlet, with thick evergreens on either side and a view out to the turquoise lake.

Edward drops his backpack onto the bed while May steps onto the balcony. She's never seen a lake before, but after her encounter in the river, she's grateful that Bill's house is set well back on dry land. Edward emerges a moment later, with a bottle and two skinny glasses in his hand.

"Champagne," he says. "Francie left it for us."

The bottle makes a popping sound when he opens it. He pours two glass of the foaming liquid, but after one sip, May sets the glass aside.

"Pepsi?" she asks. "And pizza?"

Edward laughs as he heads inside and fumbles for the two cans of Pepsi and the box of cold pizza he slipped into his backpack.

May devours half the pizza and guzzles the delicious soda she would drink for every meal, if she could. A lone boater appears across the lake, gliding soundlessly in a small, white sailboat. May and Edward sit side by side, watching the setting sun cast long, lean shadows across the water.

She loves Edward's gentle breathing and quietude; being with him feels like she never really left the forest at all. It could take hours for either of them to speak, which is wonderful because the ripples the sailboat creates on the water are like a living thing; one trick of the light and they become tentacles and shimmering blue scales.

As dusk falls, the sailboat turns back. By the time he reaches the far shore, the lake is lost to darkness. Edward walks inside and returns with a blanket he drapes over May's shoulders and a small, white box in his hands.

She frowns. The star on her finger is perfect; she doesn't need or want anything more. But when Edward opens the box, she sees that it's filled with larch cones—red, purple, and, in the case of the mature ones, light brown. As the cones slowly dry and open, each will reveal beautiful, winged seeds. He holds the beginnings of another grove in his hand.

"I collected these from the trees we . . ." He clears his throat. "I can't be anything more than who I am, May. And I can't guarantee the future of your grove or of anything else. But I'll do everything I can to be worthy of you."

She picks up one of the brown cones, its seeds nearly jumping out, eager to be planted. She will sow them where no one expects anything to grow—along the desolate highway and in cracks in concrete sidewalks. In the perfectly manicured lawn in front of the mayor's house and out by the trailer park, where people might welcome a little foliage and shade. Most won't germinate, and the few that do will likely be ripped from the ground. Still, the rare ones that survive will be showstoppers. Things of beauty nobody expected to see.

She carefully puts the cone and its precious seeds back into the box and stands beside her husband. Edward wraps his arms around her, and they stare out a lake they can't see.

"You are worthy," she says, and he squeezes her tight.

May and Edward spend three days at Bill's cabin, exploring the lake, hardly talking, and making love. When they finally make the trek back to the hunter's cabin, they find an official Forest Service note taped to the door.

Camping in any one area (campground or designated Forest Service cabin) is limited to a total of 14 days during any 30 day period. Camps must be relocated at least 5 miles away (road miles) from the original site to qualify for a new 14 day period.

It sounds like gobbledygook to May, but the paper will make great kindling for the wood stove. Edward stares at the note a long time before snatching it from the door.

"I'll bet my dad told them we were here," he says. "The Forest Service almost never comes up this way."

He looks around the summit, as if his father might be stalking them, lurking behind a tree. May touches his arm, and he shakes his head, crumpling the note.

"I'll go in and talk to them tomorrow," he says. "See if I can work this out. We'll be okay."

The next day, Edward returns home at noon. May is gathering a fresh crop of morels when he walks toward her. Before she can get to her feet, he says, "I'm sorry, May. The store let me go."

The words are wonderful—he can go. Spend more time with her. But his face is grim.

"My boss was trying to get his son a job on my dad's logging crew. The only way my dad would agree to it was if he cut ties with me."

His words are still a jumble, but May understands enough to know that Cameron Cousins is never going to forget that one punch. She walks to Edward's side and puts her arms around him.

"We'll be okay," she says, repeating his words.

He nods, but steps out of her embrace. "I convinced the Forest Service to give us a 30 day extension, so at least we won't be homeless for a while."

May cocks her head; sometimes he just talks nonsense. They could lie down in the clover and call it home as long as they're together.

"We'll be okay," she says again.

But in the days that follow, she wonders. The weather mimics Edward's mood, turning cold and blustery. Winter is a bully in the mountains, often obliterating fall and frosting the ground in July. May quickly harvests frozen elderberries and hangs the last of the summer burdock from the rafters while Edward fishes the river that almost drowned her, bringing home strings of salmon and rainbow trout. May preserves the fish by smoking them over a campfire. Sometimes she even lights the fire herself.

Edward doesn't go into town to look for work. Instead, he chops firewood for hours, bowing to May's wishes to buck up nothing but downed trees. Their firewood stack grows eight feet high and still he doesn't stop chopping. The constant thunking of his axe sends May back into the forest, where she gathers the last of the edible greens in peace.

The colder it gets, the earlier Edward rises. His search for downed trees takes him clear to the river, where he chops and chops, then climbs up and down the mountain, hauling firewood to their door. When the 30 day extension with the Forest Service is up, he chops wood in the morning, then finally heads back to town. When he returns that evening, he falls into his chair by the wood stove.

"The Forest Service won't give us another extension. They said we have to be out of here within the week."

May looks at the window that is now blocked by a monstrous pile of firewood they were never going to use. Most nights, Edward falls asleep the moment his head hits the pillow, too tired to hold her, let alone make love. If he'd known this day was coming, why did he waste all the days before?

She raises her chin. "We will stay."

Edward shakes his head. "We can't. They'll come up here and kick us out. They don't want anyone here when the snow flies. It's too remote in case anything happens."

May sniggers. How can anywhere be too remote?

Edward takes her hands. "Maybe this is a good thing. It's time I join that winter logging camp up near Priest River. The pay's really good. A few months there and I can get us back on our feet. Get us a real home. But I can't take you with me. I need you to go back to Francie's until the spring."

May sits back in her chair. Edward's fishing pole is propped against the wall, her herbs hanging from the rafters, two sleeping bags zipped together. She doesn't understand why he was so slow to escape the place he hated, yet so quick to leave the one he loves. Leave *her.*

"Stay?" she asks, almost wishing she was still silent. The word comes out like a plea.

Edward scoops her up and carries her to their cots. This time, he holds her, making love to her with such intensity and tenderness it can mean only one thing: He's going.

The fire in the wood stove burns down to embers, but she won't let him leave their bed long enough to stoke it. She pulls him close and he buries his face in her hair.

"This is my only option," he says, his voice breaking.

She clings to him, not trusting herself to speak. He kisses the tears on her cheeks.

"I don't want to leave you, May. Please tell me you'll stay with Francie while I'm gone."

She pulls away. Steadies herself. *I am May*, she thinks, and kisses him. To keep him here with her. To keep from answering.

The next morning, they don't speak as Edward packs his bags. As always, the silence doesn't bother her, but her hands shake as Edward erases himself from the cabin. She turns to the window, where there's nothing to see but stacked wood.

When he's done, Edward stands by the door. "So there's nothing I can say to convince you to go to Francie's?"

She wants to ask him the same thing—if there's anything she can say to make him stay. But they both know the answer.

"No."

She keeps her back to him, afraid that if she watches him leave, whatever's at the core of her now—heart or heart wood—will shatter. But then he's there, turning her toward him and taking her face in his hands.

"It's just a season," he says. "We can weather it."

May blinks back tears as he kisses her gently, then turns and walks out the door.

Wind and woodpeckers drown out his footsteps. A pair of chipmunks scrabble across the cabin roof just as Edward starts up his truck. May glares at the ceiling, wanting the one thing the woods won't give her. Pity. She wants to scream, cry, sit in her chair and not move for days, but there's already a fat spider there, spinning her web.

I am May.

She swipes at her tears and takes a deep breath. Then another. She remembers who she was and straightens.

It's just a season. She can weather it.

Two nights after Edward leaves, the snow starts. Five inches the first night, seven the next. Storms come one after the other, building up eight-foot drifts and making foraging impossible. May steadily empties the woodpile, getting back her view out the window only to find it blocked once again, this time by snow. But the truth is, she doesn't mind it. Her sisters depend on the winter snowpack for their survival. As the snow builds up around their trunks, it creates air pockets that hold in heat and prevent the soil, and their roots, from freezing.

The cabin is no different. Snow piles up on the roof and foundation, blocking the frigid wind and making it easy for May to keep the temperature inside a toasty 65 degrees. She taps on the wood of each log she sets in the wood stove and painstakingly rereads the newspapers Edward left behind. She makes cattail root soup and dried fish for dinner; dessert is a cup of willow tea sweetened with rose hip syrup. Once, she sees headlights in the distance—most likely the Forest Service—but after half an hour stuck in a snowbank, whoever was trying to get to her gives up and turns back.

May busies herself with winter's tasks—digging out the snowfall by the door; hauling in firewood; melting snow into a surprisingly minuscule amount of water; searching—usually in vain—under sheltered tree trunks for any roots and frozen greens she can find. She works all day and falls asleep the moment her head hits the pillow. She dreams of trees that turn their starches to sugar to keep from freezing and women who only grow stronger in the dark.

She misses Edward, but with every day that passes, she grows more confident that she doesn't need him. It doesn't feel like a bad thing—to love someone, yet know you'll survive without them—but she can't help remembering how many times Francie told her she would die if Bill wasn't in her life. A statement that becomes more alarming when Vern knocks on May's cabin door early one morning.

"Bill is threatening to call off the wedding," he says.

Without a word, May closes up the cabin and follows Vern to a snowmobile he's managed to maneuver through snowdrifts from the road to her door.

"No," she says, taking a step back.

Vern squeezes her arm. "Francie needs you. It would take days to trudge through this much snow. I'll go as slowly as you like."

May eyes the snowmobile, with its open air seating and skis for wheels. It certainly looks less terrifying than a car, but she makes Vern drive it alone first to prove he can move at a snail's pace before she agrees to climb up behind him.

May grips Vern tightly around the waist and buries her head in his jacket, even though they're moving barely faster than her walking pace. After half an hour, she dares to look up. The snowflakes are as large as quarters now and cling to her eyelashes. She eases her grip on Vern's waist just a bit. She doesn't care for the loud whining of the engine, but being carried through the forest isn't the worst thing in the world.

It takes them two hours to reach Vern's car and snowmobile trailer parked near the highway, but Vern is well aware that she won't step foot inside the automobile. The highway is always well plowed, but many of the smaller streets are snow-covered and navigable by snowmobile. Thirty minutes later, after taking a circuitous route through the snowy suburbs, they finally pull up at Francie's house. Angel waits for them in the living room, her eyes red from crying. But it's Francie's wailing from the back bedroom that fills the air.

"She won't come out," Angel says. "She's pregnant, May."

May squeezes Angel's arm and walks down the hall. The house no longer smells of Angel's delicious cooking, but of something that burnt in the oven, as if no one was paying it any mind. After the ride through the snow, the heat inside the house is almost unbearable. May pushes open Francie's door to find her friend lying on her side in bed, knees pulled up around her still thin belly. May walks to the window and opens the sash, welcoming a rush of cold air into the room.

"Hello, Francie," she says.

Francie looks up through bloodshot eyes. "Did they tell you? I'm pregnant! I don't know how this happened. I used my diaphragm like always. I swear it! Bill has always said he doesn't want kids and now he . . ."

She dissolves into sobs, unable to get out the rest of the words. The wailing is deafening in such a small room, as if four walls aren't enough to hold all of Francie's sorrow.

"Francie," May says, but the woman only cries harder. She's like the birch trees that ooze sap for months after an minor injury, just to prove how badly they've been hurt.

May could go to her, but there's no point in comforting someone who is doing all they can to not feel better. So, instead, May sticks her hand out the window, where the large flakes stick to her skin. It's this kind of heavy, wet snow that snaps tree limbs, but May is less breakable now. Humans are far less fragile than they'd have you believe.

She turns from the window. "You cry too much," she says.

The words are harsh, but sometimes they have to be. At least Francie stops crying long enough to look up.

"H-how can you say that? I've lost—"

"You have . . . lost nothing," May says. "You will be a great . . . mother."

Francie's bottom lip quivers. "You don't understand. Bill thinks I did this on purpose to . . . snare him. He's not sure if he wants to marry me anymore. He said—"

May waves a hand, cutting her off. She doesn't care much what Bill said.

"Sit up," she says, walking to the side of the bed.

May expects more wailing but, surprisingly, Francie does as she asks. Her sobs even die down a bit, as if even she can run out of tears over a man like Bill.

For a moment, it's quiet enough for May to hear the grandfather clock ticking in the living room. Then Francie suddenly squeezes May's hand.

"There's something you can do, right?" she says. "You must know of some herb I can take."

May had known the question was coming. There are herbs, of course, as well as reasons for taking them—none of which involve placating some man.

"Is that what you want?"

Francie abruptly lets go of May's hand. The tears come again, but silently this time. There's the slightest bulge—unnoticeable to most—to Francie's stomach. She must have known she was pregnant for weeks now. She didn't tell Bill until there was only one decision left to make.

“I want the baby,” she whispers. “But I want Bill too, and he’s not ready to be a father.”

May narrows her eyes because, truth be told, Bill doesn’t seem ready for much. And maybe, deep down, Francie knows this too because suddenly she laughs. Not her usual schoolgirl giggle, but something deeper, fuller. The laugh of a young woman who now has more than one person to love.

May laughs alongside her, and Angel must hear them because pots start clanking merrily in the kitchen. Soon, the intoxicating smell of sizzling bacon wafts beneath the door.

“I’m so hungry,” Francie says.

They get to their feet, but before Francie opens the door, she takes May’s hand and places it on her belly.

“Can you tell if it’s—”

“A boy,” May says, and Francie’s face lights up.

“I thought so,” she replies. “I’m going to name him Paul.”

Eleven

Common Yew
(Taxus beccata)

Yew trees can live to 3000 years old, which is terrifying considering how quickly they'll kill you. Except for the red flesh of its berries, the entire tree is poisonous to humans and animals. The consumption of even a few needles results in death by cardiogenic shock. Yew trees are associated with churchyards, and it is thought that they were planted on the graves of plague victims to purify and protect the dead. Why anyone plants them in their yards today is a mystery, as they are globally considered to be an omen of doom.

✦

Francie gets her appetite back, but still cries every time the phone rings and it's not Bill on the other end. May sleeps in the bed beside her, missing the cabin but determined to stay until her friend can get through a day without tears. Days pass, then a week, then two. When Francie's heartbreak is coupled with her first bout of morning sickness, May brews her a cup of peppermint ginger tea and waits for her to fall asleep before slipping out the bedroom window.

The deep snow blankets her footsteps as she crosses the yard and turns east, away from the home Edward once shared with his father. She's no longer interested in anything Cameron Cousins says or does. Tonight's target lives five blocks in the other direction, in the fancy, gated neighborhood known as "Laramie Heights."

The wrought iron gate that protects the enclave is impressive but useless; May slips around it easily and finds Bill's elegant, but surprisingly understated ranch house halfway down the block. White clapboard, brick chimney, a a welcoming front porch with Bill's boots and a snow shovel piled stacked neatly by the door. May has no intention of knocking. Instead, she picks a spot in the middle of the yard and uses the knife she always carries to dig through six inches of snow and another two of frozen soil. Then she takes one of the priceless larch seeds Edward gave her from her pocket and tucks it into the ground.

One seed starts a forest, but even if it doesn't sprout, this spring Attorney Bill Greene will have an unsightly patch of bare earth in his otherwise perfect lawn that will drive him mad. May smiles as she turns to leave, then abruptly goes still.

The heavy October snowfalls could have forced the one-eared bear into an early hibernation, but instead he sits on the edge of Bill's snowy lawn, eating the heap of roots, grasses and berries that someone has left on a stump. May might have thought she was dreaming if not for the fact that Bill has come out onto his porch stoop in his robe and slippers to stare fondly at the 500 pound grizzly.

"I set out one meal a year for him," he says softly, without taking his eyes off the bear. "Just to plump him up a bit before winter. I started it a few years back and now he's decided it's a tradition."

The one-eared bear ignores them both as he devours his yearly treat. Then, with a satisfied snuffle, he turns and lumbers back up the hill. Once the grizzly settles into his den, he won't emerge until March or April, by which time Bill will be the father of an infant son named Paul. The man's done everything he can to make people think he won't rise to the occasion, but now May wonders if that's just another of his courtroom tricks.

"Francie's worth ten of you," she says.

She expects one of his long-winded, lawyerly arguments, but the man merely stares at the spot where the bear disappeared then, without a word, retreats back into his house.

Just after dawn, Bill arrives on Francie's doorstep with his head bowed and a baby bonnet in hand. May expects Francie to throw herself into his arms, but is pleased when she merely puts her hands on her hips and asks questions.

"You're going to marry me?"

"Yes, of course," Bill says. "I'm sorry—"

"*And* welcome our baby?"

Bill nods. "Yes. You have to understand—"

"If you ever hurt me like that again, I'll leave you and never come back."

May is standing beside Angel in the hallway, so she hears the woman's intake of breath. Bill tenderly tucks the bonnet into his jacket pocket, then takes Francie's hand.

"You're worth ten of me," he says. "I'll never disappoint you again. I swear it."

A month later, Francie stands at the altar in an empire-style wedding gown that hides her baby bump and she and Bill honeymoon in Italy for three weeks.

✦

May returns to the hunter's cabin with extra blankets and three of Angel's decadent three cheese casseroles. Vern snowmobiles in every week, bringing her fresh fruit, Angel's pie of the week, and Pepsi. This week, he also drops off the letter Edward sent to their house, along with her husband's first paycheck. May has no idea what to do with it other than stash it away in a drawer.

Edward must enjoy the feel of a pen and paper because he writes far more words than he speaks. May stays up all night sounding out his words.

I'm hoping this letter reaches you. Mail depends on whether or not the postman can make it through the pass. I heard last season the snow was so deep no one got a letter out until April.

You would love this forest, May. So green and thick, light never touches the ground—not that there's much daylight this time of year.

Living conditions are pretty rough. Canvas tents. Twelve hour work days. A lot of gambling and drinking at night so we forget how sore and tired we are. But they pay us well. Just a few months of this and I should have enough to buy us a property somewhere. I miss you. I can't wait to come home to you.

He encloses seeds from the trees he fells. Winged larch, pine, fir, spruce, each a tiny apology. Perhaps, one day, he will learn how to garden—to sow instead of fell.

One day, after gathering birch bark from the riverbank, May finds tire tracks along the road and fresh footsteps that lead straight to her cabin door. Another notice has been taped there, with words only Bill would understand.

Pursuant to 16 USC 551, persons or organizations may not camp, store equipment at, or otherwise occupy any single location within the Forest for more than 14 days within a 30 day period. This is hereby a notice to vacate these premises by January 31st.

As she has no idea what day it is, she tosses the paper into the firebox. But two weeks later, as she drags home a heavy fir branch that broke under the weight of the snow, she finds two men in green coats and funny round hats standing at her door.

"Time to go, lady," the older one says. "Squatting time's over."

They made it in on snowmobiles this time. Edward told her that if men from the Forest Service show up, she shouldn't let them into the cabin. But they have already been inside; her clothes and canned goods have been stuffed into garbage bags by the door.

May runs past her belongings into the cabin—not to barricade herself inside, but to slip Edward's letter and seeds into her pocket. The men enter behind her, the younger one grabbing her sleeping bag and Edward's fishing pole while the older one rips her drying herbs off the ceiling. When there's nothing left inside but the cabin's original cots and table, the men escort her out.

May stands on the porch while the men pack her things onto their snowmobiles. The younger ranger heads back into the cabin for one more check, returning a couple minutes later with Edward's paycheck, which she'd forgotten about.

"I'm thinking you're going to want this," he says.

She puts the check into her pocket with the seeds as the man takes off his hat. His eyes are a darker brown than Edward's, and his small smile is kind.

"We'll give you a ride back to town," he tells her. "Where should we take you?"

May watches the older man padlock the cabin door. She might still be able to break in through the window, but then what? All her things are gone, and the men will only come back to evict her again.

Still, she shakes her head. Even if she can't enter the cabin, she's not going anywhere with these men. The young man sighs and puts his hat back on.

"Ma'am," he says, "if you stay out here, you'll freeze to death. And if you break into that cabin, you'll end up in jail."

May remembers her terrifying ride in the police car, but plants her feet and says nothing.

The older man scoffs. "Come on, Sam," he says. "We're done here."

The younger man glances at May one more time before climbing onto his snowmobile.

"Your things will be at the ranger st—"

His last word is drowned out by the roar of his partner's snowmobile. The young man nods goodbye, and a few seconds later the two of them disappear across the summit. May listens to the whining of their engines as they zigzag down the mountain, waiting for the forest to become still again before she drops her shoulders.

Edward is gone; Francie is off with Bill now; she won't burden Angel and Vern any more than she already has. May sags against the padlocked door, realizing she might have been a little harsh with Francie. Sometimes you just have to cry it out, or look up to the tops of the trees and scream.

May shouts until she's hoarse, chasing every last starling from the pines. Then she scoops a little snow into her mouth to soothe her burning throat and comes up with another option. When you're lost in the woods, you can either turn back the way you came or walk deeper into the forest.

She walks.

She may no longer have roots and fungi to communicate her distress, but every creature in the forest hears her footsteps thumping through the snow. At first, she follows the snowmobile tracks, scattering Edward's seeds along the way. The forest rangers think they're done with her, but they'll get a spring surprise—pine, fir, and larch seedlings where a road ought to be. A few more trespassers for the men to evict. She continues sowing until the snowmobile tracks turn toward town, then she heads over the bridge across the river. Her path is pristine—a blanket of untouched snow—and deep. She sinks to her knees with every step and puts her head down for the long, uphill climb.

It takes most of the day and all of her strength to clamber up the mountain. The sun is already setting when she finally stumbles into the grove.

May makes a racquet clunking through the snow, but her sisters are hushed. Trees never know loneliness, while May stands beside her old bear wound, alone. She bows her head, waiting for some signal—a chill, a breeze, anything. But in the way of trees, all that comes is an even deeper, enveloping silence—the kind that penetrates skin and bone and holds the world at bay.

Darkness falls as May slips inside her bear wound and closes her eyes. She falls asleep on her feet, her exhaustion inducing the sweetest dreams—a rush of sugary nutrients flooding into her body and lowering her freezing point, her heart and lungs slowing to conserve energy through the long, dark winter. The starlings return to alight on her branches. As her dreams fade and she stills, her sisters rustle, talking amongst themselves, watching over her.

She doesn't wake for 40 days.

✦

When May opens her eyes, it's early spring. She's still standing; her skin, along with the wound wood around her, steams with warmth from the rising sun. She blinks a few times, taking in the sodden earth and last patches of snow peppered with tiny pitchfork-shaped tracks. Her sisters' limbs are swollen with buds that hopefully won't burst until April, after the last of the damaging spring frosts have passed.

She closes her eyes against the brightness, hoping to slip back into winter's comforting sleep, but her shoulder itches. There's a knot of wood protruding against her hip bone that makes her fidget. She has far more room to wriggle in her bear wound than she ever had before.

She's hungry. Famished, actually. She puts a hand to her shrunken torso, feeling the curve of each rib. The chipmunks have emerged from their winter torpor and are making a racquet, chip-chipping as they scramble up her tree's trunk. With a sigh of frustration, May opens her eyes again, fully awake.

A matted tendril of her dark hair falls past her eye; she brushes it away with fingernails far longer and more lustrous than they were before. She's lost weight, but she's been nourished. Kept warm. Kept alive. She's never questioned the magic of the woods, or been more grateful for it. She nods to her sisters and steps from the tree.

Her body is nearly as stiff and unwieldy as it was the first time she left her bear wound, but at least now she knows how to walk. One ungainly step, then another, until her legs find their rhythm again. Edward should have come home by now, wherever their home will be. But even as she smiles at the thought of their reunion, the connection to her sisters snaps. The forest keeps the world at bay, until you bring a woodcutter in.

Still, May touches every one of their trunks as she crosses the grove. She bows to them once more before leaving the grove.

The combination of stiffness and gnawing hunger slows her dramatically. She stumbles like a toddler, forcing herself to not devour every shriveled rose hip she can find. Even the few she does eat make her stomach roil. For a long time, she sticks to handfuls of crystallized snow, which never quite quenches her thirst.

There is only one place to go. Down the mountain, back toward town, to an angel. Even before she can knock on the front door, it flies open and Angel is there, her eyes full of tears.

"May!"

Angel throws her arms around her, while May inhales the scent of some kind of heavenly pie.

"I can't believe it," Angel says. "We thought you might be . . . Vern talked to the Forest Service. We've looked everywhere! Francie is beside herself. The pregnancy . . . She worked herself into such a state, she's on bedrest."

May's smile fades. She hurt Francie. Trees are constantly receiving signals of how their sisters are faring, but humans live blind. When someone walks out the door, they worry. May should have spent less time learning to read and more learning how to be kind.

"I am sorry," she says.

Angel shakes her head. "I'm just glad you're okay. There was no other way to contact Edward, so we sent a letter. We haven't heard back."

The air rushes out of May's lungs. He's not here. Even after all this time. They told him she was missing and he still did not come back.

But Angel is here, tucking May's tangled hair behind her ear, squeezing her arm to make sure she's real. May takes Angel's hands and squeezes them tightly.

"I am sorry I . . . worried you," she says.

Angel smiles and leads her inside to the kitchen, which not only smells of pie, but of chicken soup.

"You've lost so much weight," Angel says, sitting May at the table and bringing her a bowl of soup. May's mouth waters, but she eats cautiously, forcing herself to set down her spoon after every bite until the food settles. When Angel calls Francie to tell her May is safe, May can hear Francie's cry of relief and flurry of questions from across the room.

"I don't know," Angel answers. "I wondered that, too. She hasn't said."

As May's hunger pains subside, she asks for another helping of soup. And pie. Angel gets a pen and paper and writes a second letter to Edward, letting him know that May is home and staying at their house.

When Vern's car pulls into the driveway, May stands. He, Angel, Francie, and even stodgy Bill deserve more than an apology; she owes them the truth. Yet when Vern walks into the kitchen and stops cold at the sight of her, May can't bring herself to speak. He knows her secret and has never revealed it. Or perhaps he never really believed her at all.

"May!" he says.

May starts crying the moment he hugs her. His arms are as strong and protective as wound wood.

"Honey, don't cry," Vern says.

But May buries her face in his jacket. Once upon a time, all she had to do was grow. But this . . . this doing and thinking and feeling and deciding. She wonders if anyone else ever feels that it's too much to ask.

"Come on now," Vern continues. "Everything is okay. Let's have dinner, then we can talk about where you've been. Something smells amazing."

May nods and swats at her tears. Vern and Angel eat dinner, while she makes room for another slice of pie. After she's cleaned her plate, she takes a deep breath.

"I went to the woods," she says.

Angel looks at her husband, but Vern keeps his face blank.

"You didn't tell us you have a cabin somewhere," Angel replies. "That's lovely. Where is it?"

May shakes her head. "There's no cabin."

"A house then," Angel says. "Maybe one of those condominiums over in Harrisburg?"

May glances at Vern, but stays silent.

"Now, dear, it's freezing out," Angel continues. "How could you possibly have—"

Vern touches his wife's arm, stopping her. "We're just relieved you had a place to go," he says to May. "Maybe you can take us there someday."

May feels a flutter from her sisters, as if they wouldn't mind it. Vern and Angel have lived in a house beside the woods for decades and never cut down a single tree.

"Yes," May says, "I would like that."

Later that night, Angel puts fresh sheets on the bed in Francie's old room and doesn't say another word about where May has been. Instead, she takes a wooden apothecary chest off the dresser.

"I got this for you when you were gone," she says, handing May the box. "It helped me think you were okay somewhere, and you'd come back to us."

Angel shows her how to open the tiny, labeled drawers, each of which holds different, exotic seeds. May runs her finger over seeds she'd never find in her forest—turmeric, ginseng and fever root. Gingko, blue snakeweed, witch-hazel, ashwagandha.

"You have such a gift with plants and healing," Angel goes on. "I didn't know what you would be able to use, so I got a little of everything. Some might be useless, I suppose."

May tucks the amazing box to her chest and beams.

"You like it then," Angel says, smiling. "I also bought potting soil and converted the garage into a greenhouse. I may have gone a little crazy."

She turns to go, but May quickly sets the box aside and hugs her.

"Thank you," May says. "You are . . . an angel."

Angel laughs as she pulls away. "Tell that to Vern when he wants to put his car back in the garage."

Angel turns off the light on her way out, but a few minutes later, May turns it back on. She sits up in bed, opening each of the drawers in the apothecary chest, marveling at the treasures inside. Medicinal and culinary seeds, ginger and lily rhizomes, acorns and bulbs and bare roots wrapped in moist newspaper. She could create her own botanical garden with what she holds in her hands. It's the nicest thing anyone has ever done for her.

An hour later, May finally turns off the light. She's sleepy, but Angel and Vern are not. She hears them talking in their bedroom on the other side of the wall.

" . . . something you're not telling me," Angel is saying.

Vern sighs. "There is, but I don't have all the facts."

"Don't give me that detective routine, Vern. You've never kept anything from me before."

When they go silent, May's cheeks burn, thinking she's caused an argument. But after a moment Vern softly replies, "What I think is pretty outlandish. And it's not my story to tell."

May goes very still. *Outlandish.* Bill once used the word to describe his opposing attorney's arguments. Outlandish, laughable, not even worthy of a response.

"Vern," Angel says, "you don't think . . ."

"Think what?" Vern asks.

This time, their silence is even longer. "Nothing," Angel says at last. "I'm just letting my imagination run away with me."

When the two of them finally go quiet, May closes her eyes. It's a long time before she sleeps, and when she does, she suffers her first nightmare. In it, Edward returns, completely transformed. His hair is pure white, his fingernails two-inch long daggers. Instead of giving her seeds, he offers her the trunks of the trees he's cut, each one more mutilated than the one before.

May comes awake abruptly, her body covered in sweat. It's dark outside, but the light from the living room spills in under the door. She's not the only one who can't sleep.

✦

Angel teaches May how to read a calendar. It's easy enough to memorize the names of the days and months, but harder to grasp why March 21st is considered the first day of spring when the peonies are already blooming and the snow has been gone for weeks.

May stands at Vern and Angel's front window, watching a robin build her nest in their yew tree—a daring decision, considering most parts of the yew are toxic. It's spring, but Edward hasn't come. Angel has been trying to lure May to the kitchen with her decadent cinnamon rolls and bacon, but for once she's not hungry. If the calendar says winter is over, then Edward should be home.

Angel pads out from the kitchen, holding a plate piled high with bacon. "Eat," she says. "I fried it crisp, the way you like it."

May humors her by picking up a piece, then quickly turns back to the window. A truck rumbles in the distance, then fades away.

"Honey," Angel says, "you can't stand here forever. We really don't have any idea when or—when Edward will come home."

If. Angel was going to say when or if Edward will come home. She puts a hand on May's shoulder.

"People don't always live up to our expectations," she says gently.

May doesn't reply. Human beings disappoint each other every day, and usually manage to forgive each other. Her problem is not living up to her *own* expectations. May understands why Edward had to leave; she wishes she was good enough to come home to.

"I will wait for him," she says.

She finally eats her bacon, and later takes a few quick bites of lunch and dinner so she can return to the window and stand watch. After dark, Vern brings out a pillow and sheets.

"If you won't go to your room," he says, "at least try to sleep on the couch. The window will be there tomorrow."

She looks down the empty road. "Do you think he'll come?" she asks without turning around.

She hears Vern fussing with the sheets, plumping the pillow. She makes a fist as the silence stretches out.

"I think he'd better," he says at last, "or he'll have to answer to me."

May listens to his footsteps down the hall, followed by the click of his bedroom door. Angel says something muffled, and May can tell by the tone of Vern's reply that he's telling her everything will be okay. May closes her eyes for a moment. The trouble with waiting for someone is that it makes you overlook the ones who are already there.

So she forces herself to turn away from the window, to slip between the sheets Vern laid out. Tomorrow, she will check to see if any of her new seeds have sprouted. She'll eat a whole meal at the kitchen table with Vern and Angel; she'll check on Francie, who is still on bedrest with three months until the baby is due..

She falls into an uneasy sleep, her dreams coming one after the other. The hall in Vern and Angel's house stretches for miles, with silent, empty rooms behind every door. Francie's baby turns out to be a girl instead of the boy May promised, and Bill sues her for emotional damages. She's back in the grove, a twin to her sisters, except that her bark has grown a layer of tender skin. A woodpecker hammers away at her, mindless of the blood that splatters.

May wakes abruptly, surprised by the morning light and the fact that the hammering isn't a woodpecker, but someone knocking on the front door. Vern is already crossing the room to answer it while Angel peeks out of the kitchen.

"Now don't get your hopes up," the woman says.

May owes Angel so much, she doesn't tell her that this is a perfectly ridiculous thing to say. Isn't the whole point of hope to swap out the world as it is with how you'd most like it to be?

When Vern opens the door to find Edward standing there, May gets to her feet. The problem with getting what you want is that you haven't given a thought to what you want next. She barely notices Vern's cautious greeting or Angel hesitating before welcoming Edward into the house. Edward has added a beard, but lost weight. When he scans the room and finds May, his heartwood eyes turn fierce. There's not an ounce of softness left in him.

He steps into the living room, never taking his gaze from May's face. She has yet to smile. She's not angry, but she's done waiting for the rest of her life to begin. The long silence doesn't bother her, even as Angel fidgets. Edward barely breathes until May holds out her hand.

With two long strides, he reaches her and pulls her into his arms.

"May," he says, burying his face in her neck, his whiskers as feathery as larch needles.

He kisses her forehead and the corners of each eye. She breathes in the scent of him, wondering if she's still dreaming. She has no idea when Vern and Angel disappear., but suddenly Edward scoops her off her feet. She wraps her arms around his neck as he carries her outside. She doesn't care where he takes her, as long as it's forward, not back.

They cross the street, where Edward sets her down gently beside the purple ash. Atop matted grass and the dead stalks of last year's mullein stands the weathered real estate sign that has been there for ages. Today, though, there's a SOLD banner on top of it.

"I got Vern's letter that you'd disappeared," Edward says.

May stiffens, but Edward merely shakes his head.

"I figured you'd gone to the woods," he says. "I don't worry about you there. I had to stay at camp a little longer than I'd planned so I could buy this."

He waves his hand at the purple ash and the land beyond. Sheep Creek cuts through the back of the property, expertly avoiding the ditch someone carved to reroute it. Beyond that, the forested flank of Battlecreek Peak blocks the rising sun.

"I put in an offer on the lot this morning," Edward continues. "I want to build us a house. I thought you'd like to be near Angela and Vern, and have a view of the woods. If you don't like it, I can always—"

May cuts him off by throwing her arms around his waist and holding him tight. She could tell him that it's perfect, but deep down he already knows.

Twelve

Prairiefire Crabapple

(Malus 'prairiefire')

The Prairiefire Crabapple is the perfect front yard tree. Compact and tidy, with stunning dark pink flowers in spring and tiny fruits birds feast on all winter, along with brilliant bronze leaves in the fall. The crabapple has long been associated with love and marriage, and it's said that if you throw its seeds—called pips—into the fire while saying the name of your true love, the love is true if the pips explode. Then again, you might not want to risk it, since in Chinese culture the blossoms are considered "heartbroken," and the tiny, tart fruits represent bitter love.

✦

Before Edward nails one board on their new house, May starts her garden. Vern walks across the street to coach her on the neighborhood soil.

"Our ph levels are low," he tells her. "Add lime and wood ash every spring, and fertilize with high nitrogen three times a year."

May thanks him for his advice, but has no intention of following it. She's not here to grow show pumpkins, or anything else that requires pampering. She doesn't know the first thing about fertilizer, but she does understand the way wild things grow: Exuberantly one day and listlessly the next. Unpredictably, crookedly, with beetle holes, maggots and mold.

Edward surrounds the garden with a wooden fence, while May carves the sign to hang on one of the posts.

WARNING! POTENT PLANTS AHEAD. ENTER AT YOUR OWN RISK.

The weeks that follow prove that hoping for the best sometimes leads to just that. Long warm days for May to plant rows of skullcap and valerian while Edward hand-mixes concrete for their house's foundation. Cool nights lying in sleeping bags where their house will be, making love under a blanket of stars. Angel and Vern graciously offer up their guest bedroom, but since the logging camp, Edward has taken to pacing nervously whenever he's inside while May is a wild thing herself. She'd be happy if they never had a roof at all.

At first she worries that Edward will go into the forest to fell the trees he needs, but then they receive a massive delivery of peeled, 12-feet long lodgepole pines. May sits next to the stripped trees Edward might have cut down himself while he worked in the logging camp. He stands before her, blocking the sun from her eyes.

"I'm sorry," he says.

May blinks back her tears. He doesn't have to apologize for the way his world works, but she's glad that he does.

He tells her he's building a full scribe cabin. Whatever that is, she's thankful to see him using his saw as something other than a weapon. Over the next few weeks, he stacks the log walls, carefully carving a lateral groove into the bottom of each to ensure that it will fit perfectly onto the one below it. Whenever he catches her watching him, he smiles, finally proud of the things he can do with wood.

"I didn't know you were a . . . builder," she says to him after he sets his last log into her kitchen wall.

He stares at his handiwork, a shadow crossing his face. "I learned from my dad," he says quietly. "He wasn't always a logger. He used to be a construction foreman and built a lot of the nicer homes in town. Before my mom got cancer."

He picks up his chisel and walks the length of the logs, looking for imperfections, anything he's done wrong.

"You never talk about her," May says.

Edward doesn't look at her. "It's not an easy subject. I was 11 when she died. It was very sudden; we had, maybe, six weeks with her after she got the diagnosis. She couldn't get out of bed, so she and I played cards—gin rummy was her favorite. Then one day she couldn't sit up to play anymore, so she gave me the deck of cards. Told me it helped her to think I'd find someone else to play with after she was gone."

In the grove, at least one tree is always dying. Sometimes quickly from lightning or wind, but more often than not wasting away slowly, invisibly, without a fuss. There's no drama about it; one tree falls so another can take its place.

"We should play," May says. "Angel and Vern taught me how."

Edward shakes his head and stands beside her. "I threw away the cards. I couldn't look at them without picturing her rotting away in that bed. My dad nearly skinned me alive when he found out. Said I was weak and my mom would be ashamed."

May leans against him. "Your father is the one who's not worthy."

Edward shrugs. "After the funeral, he stopped going to work and eventually lost the company. He couldn't build things, so he tore them down."

Edward may hate his father, but that doesn't stop Cameron Cousins from driving down their street most afternoons. If Edward notices him, he gives no sign except for a slight tightening of his jaw. One day, when Edward heads to Spokane for supplies, Cameron pulls right into their driveway, glaring at May and her roofless house through a cloud of cigarette smoke. He leaves the engine running, but rolls down his window just enough to chuck his lit cigarette into the weeds. As May runs toward the small fire that sparks in the grass, Cameron smirks and guns the engine, trampling her valerian on his way out.

May puts out the flames with her boot and doesn't tell Edward about his father's visit. Cameron Cousins isn't worth her dredging up the words. But that night, as she lays in Edward's arms, she offers him a little history of her own.

"I only have sisters."

One of Edward's arm twitches, while the rest of him goes still.

"Family is . . . tricky," May continues. "Sometimes you have to leave them behind."

When Edward finally speaks, it's only a whisper.

"What about your parents? Who raised you?"

It's the closest he's come to asking who she is. *What* she is. She wonders what he'd like to hear—that she's like every other woman, or that she's not.

"No one," she says. "It was always . . . just us."

She fears he'll pull away from her, so she nuzzles close enough to hear his racing heartbeat. The crescent moon rises, the nightjars sing, and her words change nothing. Not really. And, gradually, he must agree because his pounding heart slows, his breathing steadies.

In the morning, though, he starts on the roof.

It takes Edward a little over a week to install the log and tile roof, and May finds that she doesn't mind staring up at forest instead of sky. At the back of the house, Edward builds the wooden frame of a greenhouse, but the glass delivery keeps getting delayed. May's seedlings grow anyway, toughened up by the warm summer breezes.

Francie is nearing the end of her pregnancy and is still on bedrest, though her doctor did agree to let her leave the house on occasion, as long as someone drives her and she limits activity..

"I'm going crazy!" she says to May as she sits on May's front porch, sipping lemonade. "If I lie in that bed for one more second, I'll lose my mind."

May harrumphs from the back of her garden—Poison Alley, Edward calls it—where she grows the dogbane and jimsonweed she won't let anyone else touch. Both look innocuous enough, but one will cause cardiac arrhythmia and the other hallucinations, convulsions, and potentially death. Neither belong in a home garden, but in a medicinal one the plants can shrink tumors and cure vertigo. A misery for one person is a miracle for someone else.

"I don't see why I can't do more," Francie continues. "Yes, my blood pressure went through the roof while you were gone, but it's nearly back to normal now. Just the occasional blip when I get worked up."

"Like now?" May asks with a smile.

Francie laughs. "I suppose." She sets aside her lemonade and shifts positions, her large belly making it impossible for her to get comfortable. Jamming a pillow behind her, she sinks back into the chair.

"One good thing," she continues at last, "is that when people come to visit, all we do is sit and gossip. I can tell you, quite a few marriages are on the rocks around here. Oh, and you know what I heard about Edward's father? He's behind all the delays with your greenhouse windows. He and the supplier go way back. Word is they're planning to cancel your whole order so you won't be able to grow anything for next season."

May turns to the patch of pasqueflower, harvesting the giant pink flowers that bloom only when the sun is shining. Another plant that can cure or kill you, pasqueflower speeds childbirth and can be used as an antidepressant, but may also slow the heart.

"Is that so?"

"It's so petty," Francie says. "What kind of father does that? How is Edward ever going to get another job in this town if Cameron continues to sabotage him? It's amazing that your husband could build you your dream home, but he can't just putter around here forever."

May wraps her cuttings in newspaper and tucks them into a pouch on her tool belt, beside a hand shovel and trowel. Cameron continues to drive past their house every afternoon. It could be that he's trying to intimidate them, but May wonders if he simply has nowhere else to go.

"Edward's father doesn't scare us," she says, getting to her feet.

Francie looks dubious, but before she can say more she lurches forward and gasps for air. May runs for the porch, unsure if her friend is suffering a heart attack or going into labor.

"I'm okay!" Francie says, tapping at her chest. "Just . . . breathless. The doctor said it's usually normal in late pregnancy, but could also be a sign of a blood clot in the lungs. It's another reason he won't let me get up and about."

Francie's doctor, May thinks, would not be very fun at parties. She takes her friend's hand and squeezes.

"What's wrong with me, May?"

Since she asks, May places her other hand over Francie's racing heart. "You're afraid."

"Wouldn't you be? I'm going to have a baby and I'm getting weaker every day. Do you think it could be a blood clot? The doctor called it a pulmonary embolism. What if something happens and the baby—"

May stands, not listening to the rest. "Come with me," she says, pulling Francie to her feet.

"I'm lightheaded, May," Francie protests. "I'm not supposed to—"

May ignores that, too, and guides her friend gently but firmly to the glass-less greenhouse stuffed with a hodgepodge of flower starts, herb seedlings and saplings—the happy result of planting every seed and bulb Angel gave her. On the back shelf are the potted ginkgos, already grown to the length of her hand. Ginkgo trees can be either male or female, but May won't know their gender for 20 years. That's when the male trees stay tidy while the females drop mounds of foul smelling fruit. If cooked and eaten in moderation, the nuts inside the fruit are edible, but the flesh itself smells like rancid butter or vomit. May smiles at the seedlings that she rather hopes will be female—a beautiful, but malodorous wooden army.

"Take this and follow me," May says, handing Francie a sapling and gathering two more for herself.

"May, I can't plant anything right now. The doctor says I shouldn't be—"

May walks out of the greenhouse, unconcerned with whatever else the doctor said. "We're not waiting for Bill to pick you today," she calls back. "We're walking you home."

Francie waddles after her, her voice growing a little hysterical. "May, I can't! It's so hot and the doctor says walking is dangerous!"

May turns around as Francie catches up to her on the sidewalk. Her friend's face is so strained and full of fear, she hasn't even realized she's breathing fine.

"I would never do anything to hurt you," May says. "Do you believe me?"

A tear slides down Francie's cheek.. "I do, but—"

"But nothing. We walk."

It's not far, and they go at Francie's slow-footed pace, which means covering the five blocks takes an hour. Enough time for Francie to run out of reasons why she could die at any moment. Enough to find her rhythm and soak up some sun. To stop letting someone else call her fragile.

Since Francie and Bill's wedding, Bill's modest ranch house has expanded to include a new family room and master bathroom. Francie requested a beautiful white gazebo in the backyard. May is pleased to see that, despite all the construction, a certain larch seed has sprouted, its feathery stem lurking stealthily in the front lawn.

May takes the ginkgo seedling from Francie, who is sweating profusely, but hasn't tapped her chest in panic once.

"Your yard needs more trees," May says.

She sets the seedlings on the lawn and takes the shovel from her tool belt. Choosing a spot near Francie and Bill's bedroom window, May digs a trio of holes with enough space for each tree to receive full sunlight while still keeping their roots intertwined.

"One for you, one for Bill, one for your baby," she says, placing a seedling in each hole and tamping down the dirt. "Ginkgos are ancient. They've . . . survived over 200 million years."

Francie looks at the seedlings, but for once doesn't speak. May tucks away her shovel and stands beside her. The air smells of cut grass and late blooming wisteria. Francie leans her head against May's shoulder until the flush on her cheeks starts to fade.

"I'm not ready to be a mother," she says quietly.

The statement is so ridiculous that May laughs. Francie found a strange woman in the woods and gave her a home. She's already a mother.

"Paul will . . . adore you," May says.

Francie stares at the third, and smallest, ginkgo, then turns to May.

"Help me?" she says as she tries to lower herself to the ground. May grabs her by the elbows and lowers her gently onto the dirt. Francie touches the tiny seedling and smooths the soil around it. She's never had dirt beneath her fingernails before, but it suits her.

"What if it dies?" she asks quietly.

May cocks her head, not sure that she understands the question. Everything dies.

"Living comes first," she says.

Two weeks later, May walks to Francie's house in the evening to find her friend and Bill pulling weeds around their flourishing ginkgos. May is delighted to see that Francie's not wearing gloves.

Francie gives birth to a healthy, nine-pound baby boy. At Bill's insistence, this happens under sterile conditions in the hospital but, as soon as they come home, Francie starts calling the shots. She can't get enough of her good-natured, dark-haired baby and moves Paul's nursery into their bedroom. Her gazebo becomes a swing set, the front porch a dumping ground for strollers, rattles and tiny coats.

"Look at how tiny his fingers are," Francie says to May.

May has been invited to admire Paul's tiny fingers every day for weeks. She's already brought the wooden train set she asked Edward to make and cloths soaked in catnip tea for when Paul starts teething.

"He's perfect," May tells her, smiling.

"I've already had to clip his nails. It was terrifying!"

Except, as Francie stares adoringly at her son sleeping soundly in his bassinet, she looks far more radiant than fearful. Bill took a mere two days off for Paul's birth, but Francie's not particularly bothered by his absence. She even refused his offer to hire a nanny or housekeeper, telling May she doesn't want strangers in the house.

Today, what she does want is to talk about the massive layoff at Laramie Mill, the largest employer in town.

"It's going to hurt so many people," Francie says. "And poor Edward! Even without his dad trying to ruin him, he's really going to struggle finding a job now."

May can't argue. She's grateful that Edward is still finishing up the electrical and plumbing in their house rather than brooding over every employer who's rejected him. He sends out job applications every morning. There's nothing more she can ask him to do.

Francie picks up Paul the moment he fusses, and he quickly goes back to sleep in her arms.

"Maybe it's time *you* think about making some money," Francie says. May turns to her, but Francie only has eyes for her son.

"Remember Grace?" Francie continues, rocking slowly side to side. "The woman who nearly got you thrown in jail for helping her give birth? Her son, Oliver, is over a year now and has a really bad case of eczema. You know how Grace feels about doctors. She's willing to pay you if you can help her out."

May has no idea what to say. It costs her nothing but time to make her remedies; no one, she thinks, should have to pay for the medicine nature freely gives. But Francie takes her hand.

"You need money, May. At least until Edward can start bringing some in. You'd be surprised how many people are in pain and need you."

A few days later, Grace stands at May's front door, trying to contain the wriggling toddler in her arms. His skin is covered in a blistering, angry rash. Grace's skin is blotchy too—not from eczema, but from tears. The dark circles under her eyes suggest that Oliver has yet to sleep through the night.

"Is there anything you can do?" the young woman asks.

May nods, leading them around the house to the backyard. Edward is at a rare job interview, so he won't mind if Oliver sits in the grass, banging on his tool chest. May puts Grace to work picking the low-growing heal-all that's taking over the lawn. Part of the mint family, most people mistake the plant for a noxious weed, but heal-all is actually true to its name, curing everything from outbreaks of eczema to eye infections and diarrhea.

Once the two of them are settled, May heads to her garden. She started the beautiful but potentially toxic pasqueflower late, so it's just starting to bloom. Too much and ingesting the flower will be fatal, but in small doses the blossoms will give a worried mother the best nap of her life.

May quickly brews a cup of pasqueflower tea and offers Grace a cup. Like any mother with a toddler to look after, Grace fights the sleepiness that quickly comes over her until May says, "You're no good to him if you don't sleep. I promise you'll get a great few hours of rest and I won't leave Oliver's side."

With another glance at her son and a grateful nod, Grace allows May to scoop up Oliver. May leads the woman inside and tucks her into bed, then takes Oliver to the kitchen. Her heal-all salve is one of her staples. She opens a jar and spreads it over the toddler's fiery rash. He only cries for a moment, until the itching stops.

"Should we go play?" May asks.

They make mud puddles, which also helps Oliver's rash when he smears it onto his skin. By the time Edward gets home, the garden hose has turned the lawn into a swamp.

"What's all this?" Edward asks.

May can tell at once that he didn't get the job. He looks around the yard at the muddy mess, but never at her. She paints a stripe of mud on Oliver's forehead while Edward turns off the hose.

"Eczema," she says. "I made a salve."

When Edward turns his somber gaze on Oliver, the boy's grin fades. He scoots closer to May, until their muddy knees touch.

"It's late," Edward says. "We should go in and make dinner. You need to wash up."

May shakes her head. "We can't. Oliver's mom is asleep inside. She needed a nap so I made her tea."

She smiles proudly. Before Grace fell asleep, she insisted on paying May fifty dollars.

"Are you saying that I can't go inside my own house?" Edward says.

There's an edge to his voice that May hasn't heard before. Oliver crawls onto her lap and May wraps her arms around the boy.

"Yes," she says to Edward. "That's what I'm saying."

In the silence that follows, Oliver buries his face in her neck. The sweet smell of him makes her stomach tighten. She hasn't felt her sisters for months, but something else has taken root. A connection not only to Edward, but to this bit of land, this community. The more she's needed, the deeper it grows.

"It's been a long day," Edward says at last.

It's hard to learn a new language, but even harder to know which words not to say. *Every day is long for you now. I don't know how to help you. Is there any way for you to be happy?*

"Sit with us?" May asks, but Edward shakes his head.

"I found a secondhand sink for the kitchen," he says. "Just needs a little polishing. Let me know when I'm allowed inside."

He stomps off, disappearing into his work shed. May hears the rattling of tools, followed by a radio with the volume turned all the way up.

May rocks Oliver to sleep in her arms, trying to hear the wind through the trees over Edward's jarring music. Forty minutes later, Grace emerges from the house, clear-eyed and smiling.

"What was in that tea?" she asks. "I've never slept so hard in my life!"

May smiles. "Secret formula."

"Well, you should bottle it," Grace says, taking her mud-covered, sleeping son from May's arms. May follows them to Grace's car and hands the woman the jar of heal-all salve.

"You're saving my life," Grace says. "I'm going to send my sister to you. She's been trying to get pregnant for ages."

The sun is setting as Grace drives away, the shadow from the purple ash stretching all the way to the creek. May walks to the work shed, where Edward toils with his back to her, buffing the sink he purchased until it gleams. She turns off the radio and smiles at the pair they make—her caked in mud, him in sweat. When Edward finally looks at her, she pulls the $50 bill from her pocket.

"For the heal-all salve and a little tea," she says.

Instead of congratulating her, Edward turns back to the sink. Normally, she's comfortable with his long silences, but this time she raises her chin.

"I can work too," she says. "I can help people."

Edward keeps his back to her. "That's great, May. Good for you."

May doesn't know what kind of reaction she was expecting, but it certainly wasn't for him to lie. There's a tic in his jaw. He's not happy for her at all. She steps up next to him and drops the money into the kitchen sink.

"May," Edward says, but she's already walking away.

Grace's sister arrives that very night. Edward takes his dinner in the bedroom while May prepares an extract of chasteberry and red clover.

"Forty drops a day," she says, pouring the liquid into a brown glass dropper bottle. "It tastes like pepper but helps . . . regulate hormones."

The woman clutches the bottle to her chest. "You have no idea. We've been trying . . ."

She shakes her head, crying, and opens her purse. This time, it's two $50 bills instead of one.

"That's too much," May says at once.

The woman presses the cash into May's hand. "Nonsense. You're giving me a chance. I'd pay double if I could."

After she leaves, May sets the money on the kitchen table and eats her dinner alone. Edward may have built the table, but May chose the wood. She found the dead pine snag, riddled with knots and owl holes, halfway up Battlecreek Peak and asked Edward to fell it and bring it home. As she eats, she runs a finger over the gnarled tabletop; Edward often complains about the wood's imperfections, but the cracks and pockmarks are what she loves best.

Eventually, like always, Edward turns on the television in the bedroom. The noise keeps her awake at night, but somehow lulls him to sleep. She heads outside, thinking at first that she'll work in the greenhouse, but at the last minute deciding to climb the mountain instead.

There's no moon to guide her, but she can always find the way home. The hairs on her arms rise and fall with the fluttering of bat wings. She counts the hours by how many trees she touches, smelling her sisters long before she sees them—their familiar and pungent, citrusy scent.

They know she's coming; they awakened the moment she left Edward behind.

It's nearly dawn when she steps into her bear wound and falls asleep on her feet once more. She dreams she opens her eyes to find her sisters slinking across the grove, their roots trailing gracefully behind them lacy cathedral trains. They form a circle around her, keeping her safe from bears and the lone wolf who prowls the grove. Love, it seems, has set them free too. They twirl in the wind, a troupe of lithe, green dancers. But with the clunk of a heavy footstep, they return to their places, silent and still.

May's eyes remain open as Edward steps up to her bear wound.

"I'm sorry," he says.

If he finds it strange to find her standing inside a tree, he doesn't show it. May reaches for his hand.

"I know."

Thirteen

Shellbark Hickory
(Carya laciniosa)

Carya laciniosa, or Shellback Hickory, comes from the Greek word "karya," meaning walnut tree. "Carya" herself, the daughter of a king, took Dionysus, the god of wine, as her lover. Angered by Carya's jealous sisters, Dionysus turned them to stone and Carya into a walnut tree, to protect her from his lustful desires. Unfortunately for Carya, other men lusted after her tough, shock-resistant wood and used her to make gunstocks and ramrods. Few shellbark hickories remain.

✦

Determined to redeem himself, Edward installs the kitchen sink and cancels his doomed window order in favor of hunting down salvage glass from old barns and demolition sites. For two weeks, he works on May's greenhouse, piecemealing together a stunning mosaic of warped, tinted, and bubbled glass—a kaleidoscope of light. Beside the greenhouse shelves, he installs a propane stove where May can brew her often foul-smelling remedies. He gives her a tin box with a lock to store the money she makes, but he never asks for a cent of it. He manages, finally, to secure a temporary job with a road crew, laying hot asphalt from dawn until dusk.

May does a brisk business in potions and salves. Her acne cream is a big hit with teenagers, as is willow bark aspirin for their harried mothers. Women who've been suffering painful menstrual cramps come from all over not only for May's tincture of motherwort, ginger, and angelica root, but to escape the male doctors who tell them their discomfort is all in their heads.

May treats everything from sore throats (chokecherry and hedge nettle) to kidney infections (goldenrod, bearberry leaf and tansy). Her number one seller, however, isn't an herb at all, but a nap. Mothers, businessmen, parents who juggle work, children and home—it's amazing how many of them need a place to go where no one can find them. The mothers of young children often fall asleep before May can even brew her pasqueflower tea. She refuses the money they offer her; her fee is playing with their children. Shy babies who warm up to her once she carries them through the woods; five year olds whose eyes go wide when she tells them the legend of the larch tree who becomes a woman; teenagers who sit sullenly until she asks if they'd like to take a walk through Poison Alley.

One of those teenagers, a lanky 17-year-old boy named Gregory, glances at her scornfully when she tells him she has 26 plants that could kill him on the spot. His mother is inside, sleeping off a headache and what she calls his "rotten attitude."

"You're lying," he says.

"Hmmm," May replies as she walks into her garden.

She doesn't mind a skeptic or even a bristly teen. Plenty of young trees wilt dramatically at every breeze and change in temperature, yet eventually firm up and thrive. You just have to give them time.

"Belladonna," she says when she reaches the lush plant with bell-shaped purple flowers and green berries. "Some call it deadly nightshade. A single leaf could kill you."

She glances back in time to see Gregory's eyes light up before he blinks it away and crosses his arms.

"Water hemlock is worse," he tells her.

May smiles, delighted with him. "Oh, I know. I have that too."

When Gregory finally deigns to step into her garden, he walks straight to her most lethal plants.

"That's oleander," he says. "It'll either stop the heart or treat heart failure. And if that water hemlock over there doesn't kill you in the first 15 minutes, it will cure your migraine."

When May stares at him, his cheeks turn red.

"Plants are cool," he mumbles, jamming his hands into his pants pockets.

May smiles widely. "Indeed they are."

Gregory's mother emerges from her nap to find her son watering the plants in Poison Alley and talking animatedly. When Gregory shows her the water hemlock and asks if he can come back tomorrow, the woman turns to May.

"Just how long did I sleep?"

The next day, May shows Gregory her henbane, and the day after that the humble castor bean, which makes an amazing laxative but also contains ricin, one of the most lethal substances in the world. For a month, Gregory comes straight to her garden every day after school, notepad in hand, writing down everything she teaches him.

"What's with this kid?" Edward asks her the night Gregory helps May harvest her belladonna. "Is he suicidal? Or planning to poison someone? I just don't know if you should be telling a 17-year-old about this kind of stuff."

Gregory showed up with a rotten attitude and now sits in her garden with light in his eyes.

"He thinks plants are cool," she says. "This *stuff* is what makes him come alive."

After his job with the road crew ends, Edward finds occasional work as a framer and landscaper. By the end of summer, a local carpenter agrees to take him on as an apprentice—a low-paying position, but one that could lead to lucrative, full-time work. But only a week later, the carpenter loses two of his top clients and packs up for a better life in Seattle.

When Edward installs and paints the cabinets in their bathroom—his final project on the house—he celebrates with a glass of whiskey. As the weather turns colder and even the odd jobs disappear, one cocktail a night becomes three.

The women come in the daytime, while the men often slink onto May's doorstep at night. Middle-aged men, mostly, who lurk in the yard and offer ridiculously high sums for baldness remedies and May's maca-ginkgo blend that offers a boost in the bedroom.

Tonight, the man in the yard is older, in his seventies at least, and holding his hat in his hands. May steps onto her porch, already knowing that she can't help him. Tree or human, the outside goes a little gray when the inside rots.

"I'm sorry to bother you," he says, "but I was wondering if you might have something to help my son. Ease his suffering a bit. It's killing him, watching me die."

The old man wears a wool suit and tie, and smells of minty aftershave. She leads him through the door to her kitchen. Edward glances over from his chair in the living room, where he's topping off his whiskey, but doesn't say a word.

She looks into the man's milky eyes. "I can't keep you from dying," she says as gently as she can.

Surprisingly, the man smiles. "No one can, my dear. That's what I keep telling my son. I just want him to be at peace with it. It's a weight on my shoulders, trying to soothe him before I go."

It's not the first time someone has asked for a remedy not to heal a broken body, but to comfort an anguished soul. People want spells and amulets, a bubbling potion to make their dreams come true. They ask her for crabapple pips that are said to bring true love if they explode in a fire, and bay leaves they can pin to their pillow so they will dream of their future partner, and be married within the year. They want her best superstitions. Green magic. But neither of those things have the slightest effect without hope.

So she opens her apothecary chest and pulls out one of the yew shoots. Though inedible and toxic, legend says that the yew is the bridge tree between the living and the dead. A way to stay connected to a loved one even after they die. No one alive will ever know for sure if that's true, but she still puts a single shoot in one of her mason jars. There's no difference between a magic spell actually working and someone just thinking that it did.

"Tell your son the grief is . . . inevitable," she says. "But if he buries this with you, it will be the . . . link between you. Tell him when it's his turn to go, you'll be right there."

The man sighs peacefully, more like a baby who's just come into this world instead of father on his way out.

"I could brew up something for you," May adds. "A mild . . . painkiller, to make you more comfortable."

The man shakes his head and, with a trembling hand, puts twenty dollars on the table.

"My dear," he says, "I'm as comfortable as a man can be."

May walks him out, slipping the twenty dollars back into his jacket pocket as he steps out the door. He will die within weeks, and his son will never stop missing him. But maybe, in each of their last days, they'll have hope that they'll see each other again.

Heartache is unbeatable for business, if only May would take the cash. But when teenage girls arrive begging for love potions, she returns their baby-sitting money and leads them to the woods instead. People desperate for witchcraft have a litany of woes only trees and witchy women are willing to listen to. May learns about the boys who leave, the parents who don't understand, the bodies that will never be thin or beautiful enough. She's not sure the young women even realize that every breath they take in is cleaner than the one they let out, but they all run out of tears and words eventually. And look around them, at the still, silent trees, at how far they've come.

May stands at her back door, watching another girl walk away from the woods sore and tired, but with her head a little higher than it was before.

"You're a good woman, May," Edward says.

May turns to find him leaning against the kitchen counter. His eyes are bright, the way they are whenever he lands a job or throws out the whiskey. He's stopped telling her when good things happen, so he won't have to explain when things go bad.

Maybe this time he'll find a way to be happy. She steps inside and wraps her arms around his waist. He runs his lips across her collarbone, then down to the rise of her breast before scooping her up and carrying her to the bedroom.

Later, he pulls her close and falls asleep almost instantly. May lays her head on his chest, as comfortable and content as a woman can be.

Maybe this time.

✦

Francie buys a rugged, thick-wheeled stroller so she can walk with May and Paul through the woods. She complains that Paul is up at all hours of the night, but if that's the case, exhaustion suits her. She's dropped the baby weight and let her red hair grow in stunning spirals past her shoulders. Even Bill has been struck dumb a time or two when his knockout of a wife has walked into the room. He's now taking two afternoons off a week, and bringing Francie flowers every night.

"White daisies and orchids yesterday!" Francie tells May on a crisp October afternoon. "Three dozen!"

May smiles as they climb the narrow mountain trail. Francie is strong enough now to push Paul's stroller all the way to the grove, which is ablaze with golden needles. Next to the dusty green pines, May's sisters look like divas, but are actually sucking the color and nitrogen from their own needles to store it for winter. Beauty is a brief and frenzied thing.

Francie gasps in delight as they enter the grove, and May's skin warms. Her sisters have liked Francie from the start. Francie lifts Paul out of his stroller and sits on the ground with him on her lap. He's got a head of black hair, chubby legs, and likes nothing better than putting sticks and dirt in his mouth. May adores him.

"Did Edward interview for that sales job?" Francie asks.

May sits beside her, her back against one of her sister's trunks. A tree's rings mark not only how many years they've survived, but every stress, calamity and attack they've suffered. It's literally impossible for them to forget what's been done to them. The moment Francie mentions Edward's name, May's skin grows cold.

"He did," May says, but doesn't elaborate. Francie knows as well as she does that Edward is no salesman.

"Oh, May," Francie says. "I'm sorry. I can ask Bill if he knows of any openings."

Paul grasps a handful of larch needles and promptly stuffs them into his mouth. Francie screeches and uses her pinkie to scoop them out, even though May could have told her that they won't hurt him. In fact, larch needles are rich in vitamin C and taste like a mixture of lemon and wood. Paul only smiles, showing off his first tooth.

Once Francie assures herself that Paul's mouth is empty, she says, "I know it's a sore subject, but has Edward tried going to his father? Maybe if he just apologized . . ."

She trails off as May gets to her feet. Trees can never forget who the villain is, and neither can May. The fear and abuse Edward suffered from his father is unfathomable, unforgivable—a deep taproot that, even as grown man, won't let Edward go.

"Do you know what I am?" May asks suddenly.

Francie furrows her brow at the question, then laughs. "Don't be silly, May. Of course I do! You're the woman who saved my life once. A true healer. And Paul's godmother."

Tears sting May's eyes. She wants to talk about where she came from the same way that Francie speaks of childhood friends and elementary school teachers and growing up with parents who adored her. But May's story is fantasy, something none of them will ever believe in.

Then Francie is there, holding Paul in one arm and wrapping the other around May.

"If you mean that you're different," Francie says softly, "I've always known that. At first, I liked thinking you were some kind of exiled princess., but a fairy or a wood sprite would fit you better. A beautiful creature from another world."

She's kidding, of course, but the words are enough for May to catch her breath. To speak one truth.

"What about a woman who used to live in that tree over there? The one with the hole down its trunk."

Francie cocks her head at May's tree. "Oh, I see it! It does look like a woman's shape, doesn't it? I love it! How about I get to be the princess and you're the dryad?"

Francie's laugh echoes through the woods. A joke is enough. One true friend in this world is enough—the princess and the dryad.

Francie squeezes her waist, then suddenly pulls away.

"May!" she says. "You're pregnant!"

May has yet to tell Edward. She thought she was only waiting for the right moment, but now she realizes she's waiting for a number of things. For Edward to value what kind of man he is more than what job he has. For him to greet a single day with joy instead of dread. For a sign that he's ready to become a father. Turns out she's as helpless and human as a lovesick teenager, waiting and waiting for a man to change.

"It's a girl," she says. "I'm going to name her Faith."

Francie hugs May tightly as the larches drop golden needles at their feet.

"You just watch," Francie says. "Faith and Paul will fall in love and get married, and their children will be wood sprites of their own. You and I will spoil them rotten!"

Just one day, May thinks, that Edward greets with joy instead of dread. That's all she's asking.

"We'll live happily ever after," May says.

"Oh May, of course we will!"

The whiskey bottles return. Along with vodka and gin.

Edward once promised to never leave her, but the longer he stays, the less of him remains. His laugh is the first thing to go, followed by the touch of his hand. Telling the truth, it seems, was a burden he carried, so he learns to lie. The job applications he claims to have sent out sit in the garbage can. The coffee he drinks smells exactly like gin. What hurts May most is the physical distance he puts between them—walking inside when she steps into the garden and falling asleep in his chair in the living room rather than lying beside her at night. The curve in her belly is obvious now, but he never looks at her long enough to notice.

May gets a steady stream of clients. Day after day, she hands out salves and tinctures then puts the money in the tin box Edward gave her. He glances at the cash without speaking, and May stares at him until he acknowledges her. He knows she was born to outlast him.

One night, as Edward sits bleary-eyed at the kitchen table, she walks toward the sink. The television isn't on yet, so she hears the click of his fingers on the table, followed by his sudden gasp. She pours herself a glass of water and stares out the window he positioned perfectly to frame a view of the woods. It's so quiet, he could put his head on her belly and hear the beating of his child's heart.

"You're pregnant," he says at last, his voice raw with disuse.

May could have said, "Obviously," but she only watches a deer creep from the forest to nibble at her echinacea.

"You should have told me," he continues. "I had a right to know."

She nods, because he's right. She should have told him, but he also should have noticed. She should have asked how she could help him, but he should have talked to her more. Even worse than the things they should have done are all the things they shouldn't. He shouldn't drink. She shouldn't put up with it. She shouldn't have to act weak to make him feel stronger. He shouldn't stay.

She promised to love and support him. He vowed to be worthy of her every day. Making a promise when you know full well that everything will change is, she thinks, the most foolish and endearing part of being human.

"It's a girl," she says.

He stares at her as if he's never seen her before, then picks up his coffee mug, the one filled with gin, and flings it against the wall. The cup shatters, Edward's favorite drink sliding down his beautiful log siding. May tries not to react, but can't help placing a hand protectively over her belly.

For a split second, she sees the rage in his eyes and knows that if he stays, she will leave him. She won't sneak out the window the way she did at his father's house; this time, she'll walk right out the front door. She shakes her head at what he's brought upon himself, for what he's become, and it's the pity in her eyes that makes him cry out like a wounded animal.

"Please, May," he says. "Don't give up on me."

He begs for her understanding, for her love, for everything except to stay.

"This is just a season," she says. "Let it pass."

He packs nothing but his clothes and a picture from their wedding day. He tries to leave without looking at her, but she grabs his hand.

"'I'll have Faith," she says. "Come back whole."

Then he steps out into the night and is gone.

Fourteen

Bristlecone Pine
(Pinus longaeva)

The Great Basin Bristlecone Pine is 5,000 years old—the oldest living being in the world. It has survived to this ripe old age not because it's been pampered, but for exactly the opposite reason: It's had to survive in the harshest of conditions—dry soil and very cold temperatures along with high winds—which slow its growth rate and create extremely dense wood. Resistant to insects, fungi, rot, and erosion, even the needles of the bristlecone pine can live up to 40 years before being shed. When the tree does finally die, its carcass will endure, standing on its hardened roots for centuries.

✦

Edward does not come back.

Francie and Angel fuss over May but, strangely enough, she prefers the company of Bill. After assuring himself that there are no tears in her eyes, Francie's husband mutters, "Good riddance," then asks what he should do about his wilting begonias. Begonias crave slightly acidic, humusy soil, and excellent drainage is a must. May shows him how to repot the blooming plant in a mixture of leaf mold, peat moss and sand, then she positions them in an east-facing room, with bright but indirect sunlight. Root rot, at least, is an easy fix.

Harder to tackle is how to live alone in the house that Edward built. May sees him in every beam and notch; as her belly grows, the only shirts that fit her are the few Edward left behind. Sometimes, without thinking, she pulls his collar up to her nose and inhales his scent, but then a branch from the purple ash scratches the window. When she sits in Edward's chair, trying to figure out what he looked at for so many hours, her feet twitch, as if yanked by roots far beneath her. She stays inside for days, standing vigil with Edward's scents and handiwork and possessions, knowing that when she finally does walk out the door, he'll come with her. And he won't be allowed back in.

After a week without fresh air, May wakes to a heaviness in the middle of her chest. She struggles to sit up, the raspy cough coming on suddenly. If she stays inside one more minute, she's certain her lungs will collapse. She's not sick; she just has sisters—the domineering kind who can flood her with oxygen. At extreme levels, even the air people breathe can be toxic, causing their lungs to fill with fluid, damaging the liver, heart, and eyes. Still coughing, May puts on Edward's heavy jacket and throws open the front door.

The pressure on her chest lifts instantly.

"Okay, okay," she says. "I'm coming."

With her growing belly, she uses a fallen pine branch as a walking stick, carefully trudging through the first snowfall of the year. Her slow pace up the mountain makes Faith's flutters more noticeable—a gentle, rhythmic tapping, like a tiny fist knocking on wood. Up they go, May cracking through snow and ice, making a racket in the winter quiet. Most of the trees are dormant, their metabolism slowed to conserve energy, but her sisters have stayed awake. Waiting for her.

May steps into the grove, her hands on her belly. Without their dazzling autumn needles, the larches are a coven of forest witches—bony, barren, all-knowing. They were right about Edward.

May cocks her head, listening to the rustling of their branches. No one is more tree-like than a pregnant woman, when the changes on the outside are nothing compared to what's going on inside. She looks at the sister Edward's crew used for target practice, her trunk riddled by so many axe blows she's split down the center. Miraculously, her two halves still thrive. Superstition says that, if you're weary or broken, to pass through a living tree's cleft is to be healed. As long as the tree survives.

A gamble, for sure, but May knows about trees. How they battle for survival, how much they can endure.

Superstition. Magic. Hope.

May approaches the splintered tree, touching the golden healing sap on either half that smells like home. As she lifts her foot and steps through the gap she feels almost silly, but there's no one but her sisters to see. Nothing changes on the other side; she's as pregnant and alone as before. But as Faith taps her belly, May knocks on the wood of the tree. They're all in it together now.

On the way down the mountain, the wind blows, and May swears her body creaks like old wood.

For the next few weeks, May makes the long, hard walk to the grove every morning and tends to her clients each afternoon. Her bestsellers are, oddly, canker sore compresses and tinctures to soothe the nerves. By nightfall, her pregnant body is so tired it takes all she has to clean up the eggs that someone has taken to throwing against her house

At first, she assumes the vandals are bored teenagers or someone who wanted an instant result with one of her remedies, not the slow, subtle healing of plants. But then she gets a glimpse of unfamiliar men—some of them stumbling—outside her window. She hears their mutters of "Witch." After they leave, she finds broken beer bottles amongst the eggs. She learns quickly that it's best to remove the egg splatter before it hardens, so she spends hours outside in the dark, scrubbing the log siding and picking up shards of brown glass.

Vandalism is nothing special, so May doesn't speak of it. Some walk on four legs, some on two, but there are predators everywhere. She can't take on a pack, but one evening, when a teenage boy steps into her garden, May slides her knives into her pockets and steps outside.

Then she notices the teenager's unruly hair and the way he stares, transfixed, at her black henbane.

"Hello Gregory," she says.

He turns and smiles. He's grown another foot since she last saw him, or maybe he simply looks taller because he's stopped slouching. He hops over the garden fence to greet her.

"Wow," he says, looking aghast at her girth. "You're really pregnant."

May grins. Francie hated losing her figure to her pregnancy, but May once weighed 8000 pounds. She's been heavy and light, tall then short—the shape she takes is the least consistent thing about her.

"I am," she says.

Gregory takes a letter out of his jacket pocket and holds it up triumphantly. "I got into Harvard!" he says. "I'm going to study botany!"

He's as lit up as he was when he first saw her belladonna. May has no idea what Harvard is, but she's glad it makes Gregory so happy.

"That's wonderful," she says. "Congratulations!"

He practically dances as he slips the letter back into one pocket while taking something shiny out of the other.

"I wanted to give you something," he says. "It's nothing big. I know it's dumb."

The glass orb in his hand is not dumb at all. Inside of it is a perfectly preserved belladonna blossom. May takes the delicate orb from him, her eyes filling with tears.

"It's beautiful," she says, her voice catching.

"I just wanted to, you know, thank you. For trusting me with a little poison."

May beams at him and he gives her a quick, awkward hug.

"I'll write to you," he tells her. "Let you know what kinds of plants I'm studying."

He won't, but it hardly matters. She clutches the orb to her chest.

After Gregory leaves, May places the orb on the table where Edward's television used to rest. A week ago, May took that monstrosity out to Edward's work shed, where she found a mallet and promptly smashed it to bits.

During her third trimester, May scales back her walks to the grove to once a week. When her legs begin to swell, she stops visiting her sisters entirely. At least the weather cooperates, with February turning warm and dry so she can sit beneath the purple ash. What a pair they make—she with her swollen belly and ankles, the ash with greenish-purple buds ready to burst. But it's only February, and nature will not be rushed.

May is still sitting there, her back against the ash's prickly trunk, when the large white truck turns the corner. It's hard to get to her feet now; she's certainly not going to go to the trouble of standing for Cameron Cousins.

Edward's father still smokes his cigarette inside the cab and doesn't get out. May simply closes her eyes. What bothers her most is not that he keeps showing up, but that he's the most tree-like person she's ever met. Hard, still and silent. Time means nothing to him as he smokes cigarette after cigarette. Her legs grow numb and tingly before he finally drives away.

First thing in the morning, he's back again. This time with his window rolled down. May escapes to her greenhouse, but when the stench of cigarette smoke slithers in after her, she heads to the creek. Sitting amongst the river birches, she takes a deep breath and slips her hands into her pockets, where she still keeps her knives.

Cameron turns on the radio. Soft music can stimulate tree cells, but the racket he blasts will stress their cells, causing them to harden. Minute by minute, Edward's father increases the volume, until May grits her teeth and lumbers to her feet.

Cameron smiles as she approaches, his grin as wolflike and unsettling as before.

"How ya doin', pit bull? You're lookin' ready to pop."

He sucks on the last of his cigarette.

"Turn the music off," she says.

He shrugs and turns off the radio, grinding out his cigarette on the dashboard, then chucking the stub onto the floor.

"What do you want?" May asks.

"Who says I want anything? Can't a man come see his favorite daughter-in-law?"

May says nothing, but when he leans toward the window, she steps back.

"That fool boy left you," he says. "Can't even manage to take care of his own family."

May is never going to talk to Cameron Cousins about Edward. She'll keep her husband's silence, even if he never comes back.

"I didn't raise Edward to run away from his problems," he continues.

May glares at him. "You didn't raise him at all. You just beat him into . . . submission."

She turns to go, but Cameron reaches for her through the window. Her hand's already closed around the knife in her pocket by the time he pulls back.

"Wait," he says. "Please."

May shakes her head. One soft word doesn't excuse a lifetime of curses. Everything else about him is the same—the same cigarettes, same half-empty whiskey bottle on the passenger seat, same violent hand he clenches into a fist. But this time, he spots her watching him and unclenches it.

"Step back," he says as he reaches for another cigarette. "Smoke will hurt the baby."

May stares at him warily, but steps away when he lights the cigarette. Cameron inhales deeply, then blows the smoke away from her.

"I was hard on him," he says. "I didn't know how else to be."

May sighs, done with him. "Then do better," she says before walking toward her front door as quickly as her pregnant body will allow.

"Pit bull," Cameron calls out. "May."

May stops on the stoop but doesn't turn back.

"My wife left me once too," he says, "before Edward was born."

May looks over her shoulder. "Did you love her?"

He sucks on his cigarette. She can't even imagine how black his lungs must be.

"I did," he says as he exhales, "but not very well."

At least his words are honest, so she offers a truth of her own.

"Then you taught your son something after all," she says before disappearing inside the house.

✦

The night Faith is born, someone throws a rock through May's window. It wouldn't concern her except that a flaming rag accompanies it, which sets the lace curtains on fire. May battles a contraction while putting out the flames with her watering can. When there's nothing left but smoke and ash, she spots Pastor Maloney glaring at her through her kitchen window..

"Satan take you!" the minister screams before running off into the night.

May bends forward, trying to keep her breathing even and slow. She never did get her midwifery license, but she's helped three more women give birth beneath the purple ash. Vern must have had something to do with the fact that no sheriffs have ever returned to cart her away.

Her contractions started hours ago and are still five minutes apart—plenty of time for her to find a sheet of plywood and board up the window. But it takes close to an hour to locate the hammer and nails in the shed and a large enough sheet of plywood by the wood pile, and by then she's bent over in pain. A contraction hits just as she's hammering in the plywood, causing her to smash her finger instead. She cries out and brings her hand to her mouth, leaving the plywood hanging precariously.

May gathers her supplies as quickly as she can—warm water, towels, a pair of cord clamps, a pint of 180 proof alcohol, trash bags for the mess—then heads outside to the purple ash. It's three in the morning, the birthing hour. No one up to yell at her to be quiet and no one, thank goodness, who will faint at the gore.

But it's cold. The snow may be gone, but a cold March wind roars in its place. She should have brought blankets, but when she tries to go back for them, another contraction hits so hard, she has to cling to the ash to stay upright. She's stunned by how much things hurt—not only the pain in her stomach and hand, but her jaw as she keeps clenching it, all her fears about what's coming next. Faith will be the daughter of the town witch. She may never know her father, and May has no idea how to be a good mother. Who knew it would be so much harder to live here, with a million comforts, than it ever was in her woods.

She cries as she holds onto the tree a moment longer, knowing she has no choice but to go back inside. She'll freeze to death in these conditions, or something will go wrong and there will be no one to help her. Defeated, she turns to go, only to feel someone slipping a blanket around her shoulders. Vern shoves thick wool mittens onto her hands.

"What kind of idiot comes out here without mittens?" he asks.

When he sees the tears on her cheeks, he wipes them away and smiles. "You didn't think we were going to miss this, did you? Angela saw you out here. She's calling Francie right now. I imagine she'll be here in record time."

In addition to the blanket, Vern lays two pillows on the frozen earth and eases her down. The softness makes May cry again before another contraction comes on.

"Breathe," Vern says. "Easy now."

There's nothing remotely easy about it. The women who gave birth beneath this tree were warriors, and May isn't made of the same stuff. She knows nothing about enduring human pain. Her sisters can offer no solace as the contractions claw at her belly, building without pause until a tortured scream escapes her lips. Vern's constant admonition to breathe is useless. Whether she gasps or cries or holds her breath, there is only pain.

Then Angel is there. May has no idea when Francie's mother arrives. She's simply beside her.

"Easy-peasy, right?" Angel says with a wink.

May sags against her. She regrets that she couldn't have offered the women who gave birth what they must have needed far more than her herbal cures—someone who's been there.

"I can't do it," May whispers.

Angel hands her a towel to bite down on. "None of us can. But we do."

The next contraction starts slowly, then never stops. May screams into the towel in her mouth; at some point, she flings off the blanket. She doesn't realize Vern is talking until his story is halfway done.

" . . . on a daily basis," he says. "Crooks, thieves, arsonists, killers—you'd be amazed how normal they can seem. People are weird, difficult creatures."

"Vern," Angel says, "I don't think May needs to hear this just now."

But as another contraction comes right on top of the last, May gestures for him to go on. She bites down on the towel again and grabs Angel's hand, squeezing so tightly she fears she'll break the woman's tiny bones.

"My point is," Vern says, "no one's born a criminal. Even when they turn into one, most still cry when they're reunited with their dogs. Everyone comes into this world a little squishy and thankfully it takes quite a while for most to harden up. People are slower to change than trees."

Their eyes meet and Vern's eyes are twinkling. The man who faces harsh realities on a daily basis welcomes a fairytale or two. May can't imagine life here without him or Angel or the people barreling up the road in Bill's car.

Francie jumps out before Bill has even parked. "I'm here, May! I'm coming!"

Then Bill emerges, still in his silk pajamas and robe, carrying little Paul, who sleeps on peacefully in his fuzzy white blanket. Edward may not have stayed, but he made sure that that May was near others who would.

So she bears down while Angel dabs the sweat off her forehead and Francie tells her, over and over, that despite the pain, this will be the best night of May's life. And when the time comes at last, May yanks the towel from her mouth and lets loose a scream that flushes the nighthawks from the trees—and maybe even rides on the wind to her husband. To let him know that he gave her so many things, but the best of all of them was Faith.

Fifteen

Bay Laurel
(Laurus nobilis)

No other tree can compete with the Bay Laurel. Its Latin name, "Laurus nobilis," literally means praise and nobility. In Ancient Greece, a wreath made of bay laurel leaves was considered a symbol of victory and prosperity, and was given only as the highest honor. But like many creatures that strive for perfection, the bay laurel has a dark side. The Greek god Apollo insulted Eros, the God of love, causing Eros to fire two arrows—one to kindle love, and the other to dispel it. The first hit Apollo, who immediately fell in love with the naiad Daphne, and the latter hit Daphne, who just as quickly ran from him. When Apollo took Daphne against her will, her father, the river god Peneus, turned Daphne into a laurel tree to keep her safe from Apollo forever. Love and victory don't always go hand in hand..

✦

As a gift for Faith's birth, Vern replaces May's broken window with double-paned glass. Though not as beautiful as the original bubble glass, it's far harder to break. And now that Vern makes frequent patrols around May's house, he quickly arrests Pastor Maloney for setting a rattlesnake loose in May's greenhouse and painting pentacles on her front door.

Bill solemnly presents Faith with a $100 savings bond, while Francie and Angel buy the baby clothes in newborn sizes clear to 4T, enough to last nearly until kindergarten. A cardboard box also appears on May's front porch, without a return address or a note. May opens it tentatively, afraid of another snake, but instead of a viper inside, there's only an old photo album, its edges worn and frayed.

She takes the album to the kitchen, where Faith is sleeping peacefully in a hand-me-down bassinet given to them from Francie. May sits at the table and opens the album to a photo of a boy she would know anywhere—short brown hair, eyes the color of heartwood, freckles speckled across his nose and cheeks.

"Edward," she says out loud.

Her hand trembles as she turns the pages. Edward just after he was born—his face red and blotchy, then propped in a sudsy bath in the kitchen sink, a strong, callused hand holding him upright. He grows adorably chubby, his grin exposing his first two teeth, then slowly thins out as he takes his first step, swims, and poses proudly with his first big kid bike, holding up the training wheels he no longer needs.

Obviously, Edward's mother is the adoring photographer, because Cameron is the only other person in the album—first holding his infant son effortlessly in one arm, then hoisting Edward onto his shoulders at some distant beach, both of them smiling and covered in sand.

They were happy. A woman loved them, loved seeing them together and wanted to mark the moments—until she couldn't hold the camera any longer.

The last photograph is of Cameron and 10-year-old Edward standing side by side with their shirts off, flexing their muscles in the sun. The remaining thirty pages are blank. May wonders if Cameron threw away his wife's camera after she died, the same way Edward threw away his playing cards. Or perhaps there was simply nothing worth photographing after that.

May closes the book and stares at Faith, her tiny fist pressed to her mouth. The most surprising thing isn't that Cameron Cousins left pictures of Edward on her doorstep, but that he was willing to expose a part of himself—the best of himself—almost no one would believe once existed.

May sets the book aside and walks to her apothecary chest, taking out the dried marigold blossoms she usually uses as an anti-inflammatory tea. She heats a pot of water and drops the blossoms in to simmer. Two hours later, she has enough yellow dye to brush along the bottoms of Faith's hands and feet.

Faith sleeps soundly, even when May presses her tiny hands and feet to parchment. In the morning, May puts Faith into a sling and walks across town to Cameron Cousins's house. His truck is in the driveway, but she doesn't knock. She's quite certain that if they meet again, he'll still call her "pit bull." Now that she's no longer pregnant, he'll once again blow cigarette smoke in her eyes.

She slips the parchment under the mat and steps away, thinking of another man who fell in love and was happy, but couldn't rise above his demons for his wife and future daughter. May can't send Faith's footprints to Edward, so offering them to his father will have to do.

As she walks away, she hears a cough from inside the house, but Cameron doesn't open the door until she reaches the road. She feels his gaze on her back as she keeps walking. The last thing she'll ever hear from him is the rustling of parchment in his hands.

✦

A month later, the first envelope arrives in the mail. There is no return address, but May recognizes the writing instantly. It's possible this is the fastest her human heart has ever beat.

But when she tears open the envelope, there is only a fifty dollar bill inside. She appreciates that it might be all the money Edward has, but she would have traded every penny for a question about their daughter. A single word of affection or remorse.

The postmark is from Spokane, not even a hundred miles from her. She could easily walk the entire distance in a few days, if Faith wasn't screaming every step of the way.

Her daughter has developed a form of colic that May can't cure. She's tried linden, catnip, and a usually foolproof concoction of chamomile, lemon balm and dill, all to no avail. She knows that Gregory's belladonna, when given in carefully controlled dosages, reduces an infant's stomach cramping by relaxing the muscles of the gut, but for the first time in her life, she doesn't trust her own remedies. There's a fine line between medicine and poison, and until now she's confidently walked it. No one told her that having a child makes you afraid.

So she settles for putting a warm compress on Faith's belly, swaddling her in a blanket, then crossing the street to beg for help. No doe or sow has ever needed advice on how to care for their young, but Angel takes one look at May's tear-stained face and shoos Vern away.

"I'm surprised it took you this long to break," Angel says. "I called my mother to come save me exactly 16 hours after Francie was born."

They talk about colic, diaper rash, spit-up, and the benefits of formula—after May admits that Faith still resists breastfeeding and screams after every feeding.

"Francie was formula-fed from the start," Angel says. "There's no shame in that."

Angel settles May and Faith on the sofa, then rushes to the market, returning an hour later with baby bottles, three giant cans of formula, and a glossy magazine with an impressive herb garden on the cover.

"You need something to read, and I'm sorry to tell you that you won't have the time or energy to finish an entire book for the next 18 years."

After a few days of bottle-feeding, Faith sleeps six hours a night. The moment May feels strong enough, she carries her daughter to the grove and sets her inside her old bear wound to sleep. It's May's own high-pitched cries that her sisters try to absorb into their bark and branches.

Belladonna wasn't the herb May should have been worried about. The real poison, she thinks, is her.

Faith looks like her father. Same unruly brown hair, same heartwood eyes. She's quick and slippery, squirming away whenever May tries to change her diaper. She babbles at three months and says her first word at nine. There's nothing remotely tree-like about her.

May invests in a backpack, but whenever she totes Faith to the grove, her daughter spends the whole time fussing. She hates to be constrained, but she's not keen to explore the grove either. A floor of larch needles is prickly. When May lays her down to nap, Faith takes one look at the towering trees above her and screams.

Faith takes her first steps not in the grove, but on the concrete sidewalk outside their house. She likes inside things—grocery stores, carpeting, Angel's kitchen, the dusty space beneath the bed. When one of May's customers knocks on the door, Faith hides in her bedroom closet. The only one who can coax her out is Angel.

"La," Faith calls her. "LaLa."

May's child snuggles Angel for hours. She falls asleep with her face pressed to Angel's chest.

"It's a grandma thing," Angel says, but May isn't so sure.

For Faith's first birthday, May takes her to the grocery store to buy a cake and lets her daughter eat it inside her bedroom closet. After Faith falls asleep, May slips her into the backpack and walks in the dark to the grove. Oddly, now that Faith is sleeping through the night, May struggles to fall asleep at all. She wanders the house and garden, planting onion seeds at midnight and making stew at dawn. Sometimes, she wakes on the floor in the greenhouse with no memory of how she got there.

So it's easy to think she's dreaming when she stumbles into the moonlit grove to find her sisters stepping from their trees. Naked and beautiful, with hair that falls past their shoulders in shades of brown and gold, they marvel at their feminine transformations, bending and stretching their new, shapely limbs.

May would know them in any form. Thick and thin, smooth-skinned and pockmarked, they embrace her and kiss the dark hair on Faith's head. The oldest of them lifts the sleeping child out of May's backpack and holds her tenderly. Tears of gratitude slip from May's eyes as she crawls into her bear wound and sleeps and sleeps and sleeps.

She wakes hours later to Faith's screams.

The baby is clawing at May's legs, her eyes red and swollen from crying. May's sisters have retreated to their trees, if they ever even left them. May tries to reach out to comfort her daughter, but her arms resist, too heavy and wooden to move.

There's a whorl on the back of her hand that wasn't there before, and she fights her rising panic. A frantic mother can lift an automobile off her child; surely she can crawl a few inches. The tree's wound wood is tight around her hips, but May kicks once, twice, until something in the hollow shatters. Flinging herself out of the tree, she reaches for Faith.

But her daughter jerks away at the prickly feel of her.

"Faith," May says. "It's me. Mommy."

Faith sobs, her eyes searching the grove as if her real mother is hiding behind a tree somewhere. May breathes deeply, forcing herself not to scoop her daughter into her arms. She knows no lullabies to soothe her; the best she can do is be silent and still.

It's a while before Faith's cries start to ease, and still May waits. Then, suddenly, Faith throws herself into May's lap and clings to her.

"It's okay now," May says. "We're okay."

She won't bring Faith back to the grove for three years.

Because Faith loved her birthday cake so much, May asks Angel to help her make one from scratch. First, Angel explains the way the oven works, since May has yet to use the appliance Edward installed in their house. Then she shows May her cake recipe, which has a list of ingredients that May has never stored in her pantry.

"Why don't we go to my house?" Angel says. "We'll invite Francie and Bill and make it a party."

Vern plays with Faith in their living room while May learns to measure ingredients, sift flour, and beat eggs until they've tripled in volume. And that's just the cake. By the time she decorates her homemade vanilla buttercream frosting with confetti sprinkles, May's almost as big a fan of buying things at the grocery store as Faith.

Faith squeals with delight when May sets her in Paul's high chair and offers her a large slice of cake. May hears Francie's voice in the other room as Angel leans tiredly against the counter, her skin a little gray under the bright kitchen light.

"Angel," May says, touching the woman's arm, but just then Francie walks into the kitchen, holding Paul.

"Bill had to go meet a client. And I smell cake!"

Paul lunges for his grandmother, but when Angel scoops him up, the coughing fit starts. Francie takes Paul from her and gets her mother a glass of water while Vern comes into the room. There are worry lines on Vern's brow that weren't there before.

"Fresh air," May says, taking Angel by the hand. "And goldenrod syrup."

Angel is still coughing as the two of them head outside. May eases the woman down on the front porch swing, then hurries across the street for the cough medicine she makes with goldenrod flowers and honey. When she returns and holds up a teaspoon of the syrup, Angel opens her mouth obediently, like a little girl.

Indoors, May might be forgiven for overlooking the dark circles beneath Angel's eyes, but outside things are always clearer. Angel is swimming in clothes that used to fit her snugly, and her skin is not only gray, but flaking away. Trees and people die the same way they live—the former so slowly you might not even notice it's happening and the latter in a rush.

"I should have noticed sooner," May says.

Angel shakes her head. "You couldn't have done anything. No one can. It's cancer, May."

May sits on the swing beside her, holding Angel's clammy hand. There will be plenty of time to cry later. For now, for Angel, she won't show even a quivering lip.

"I'm so sorry," she says.

Angel leans against her. "I'm the one who's sorry, May. I don't want to leave any of you."

They sit in silence, without tears, strongest in their weakest moments, as most women are.

When Faith opens the door and cries, "LaLa," May barely feels the sting.

✦

May and Faith visit Angel every afternoon—first in her kitchen while she can still cook, then in the darkened living room and, finally, at her bedside, where she sleeps twenty hours a day.

Francie cries often, even after a cup of strong valerian tea, but whenever May arrives, Vern disappears. May hears him pounding things in the garage, and spots him digging up perfectly healthy hydrangeas from the garden. Angel tells May that he's still struggling to come to terms with her diagnosis, but they both know this is a lie. On the rare occasion when May catches his eye, it's obvious that the only thing Vern's struggling with is fury. There's one person, in his mind, to blame.

On a cool, spring evening, he shows up on May's doorstep.

"Just answer me one thing," he says without preamble. "Did you tell her you could cure her? Because she admitted she's had that lump for ages, long before I finally dragged her to the doctor."

May had been expecting this, but his words are still a blow. She'd rather he called her a witch than believe she would hurt them.

"I did not," she says.

"Did you offer her some crazy tincture or poisonous plant you promised would burn away her tumors?"

He towers over her, the way he must stand over suspects at the police station, trying to get them to confess.

"No," she says.

He stares at her a moment longer, then turns and leaves without a word. The next time May makes Angel tea, he demands an ingredient list and samples it first. He hauls Angel back to a second doctor, then a third, hoping for a more positive diagnosis, but they all say the same thing: The time for treatment has long passed. The important thing now is to make Angel's final days as comfortable as possible.

On the way home from the final doctor visit, Vern stops at the police station and hands in his badge. He stops answering the door when May knocks.

Faith cries for "LaLa" every day. Whenever May opens the door, Faith bolts for Angel's house and May has to carry her home, screaming. May tries to find her own solace in the purple ash and river birches, but the trees, along with her sisters, are markedly silent. When no one opens the blinds across the street for three days, May goes quiet too.

One morning before dawn, someone pounds on May's front door. Pulling on her flannel robe, she glances out the window to the house across the street, where the blinds are now wide open, every light ablaze.

She hurries to the door, expecting Francie or Vern, but it's Bill standing on her front porch, looking grim.

"Angela's asking for you," he says. "Francie needs you, too."

May lifts Faith out of her bassinet and follows Bill across the street. Vern sits in a chair in the corner of the living room, his head in his hands. He doesn't look up until May nudges him and places her sleeping daughter in his arms. She's ready for a fight, but there's only agony in his eyes. He looks down at Faith, a tear sliding down his cheek as he tucks the child gently against his chest.

Bill checks on Paul sleeping in his playpen while May walks down the hall. Angel's door is ajar, but all May can see is Francie's curled back and uncombed hair. When May steps into the room, her friend looks up from her perch at Angel's bedside, her eyes red and swollen from crying. For once, she says nothing at all.

Angel barely takes up any space in the bed. Every part of her has shrunk or sunken; her once smooth, pink skin has become mottled and blue. Even if death will be a welcome relief from her suffering, she still has to get through the dying—a process that may be longer and messier than she'd like. Hands swell, bladder control vanishes, and a musty, metallic odor—almost like acetone—takes over. Every inhalation is wet and gurgling, more like drowning than the breath of life.

Francie makes room for May to sit beside her on the armchair, and May reaches for Angel's skeletal hand.

Angel opens her eyes. They're a little cloudy, but she smiles. May makes the tiniest drowning sound, too.

"Don't . . . get mushy . . . on me now," Angel says.

May's mouth twitches and she lets out her breath. The room is suffocating. Hot and stuffy, the delectable aromas of Angel's cooking replaced by wilting flower bouquets and decay.

May stands and pulls back the blanket. Angel is wearing a thin pink nightgown that doesn't cover up the fact that most of her is already gone. May slips her hands beneath the woman's bony hips and back and barely feels the weight of her. It's no burden to lift an angel.

"May," Francie says, "I don't think you should—"

May is already out the bedroom door. Angel is too weak to lift her arms around May's neck, but she can whisper.

"Thank . . . you."

It doesn't matter when Angel starts coughing and can't stop. Or when Vern looks up from his chair in alarm. May points to the blanket he should bring and doesn't even pause before carrying Angel outside. Today, there's no need to get across the street to the purple ash. This is no birthing;

for death and dying, there's only the yew. The tree often planted in graveyards to protect the dead.

The old, particularly gnarled one growing in the corner of Vern and Angel's yard beckons them. May carries Angel across the lawn and sets her down gently beside the rippled trunk. Angel smiles, but looks positively ghoulish—skeleton head, black, sunken eyes, a drop of blood on her chin.

Vern rushes out after them, carrying both Faith and a blanket. Faith is awake and calling for LaLa, but Vern holds her squirming body tight.

"Let's get you back inside," he says to his wife. "This is no time for May's foolery. Let me—"

"Hush, Vern," Angel says. "Please."

She gestures toward Faith. Vern glares at May before, reluctantly, easing Faith onto Angel's lap.

"LaLa!" Faith cries, throwing her arms around Angel's neck and clinging to her. Angel releases a long, contented sigh. Vern tucks the blanket around the two of them. The larks are just beginning to sing.

"We should really—" Vern begins, but Angel merely shakes her head. She closes her eyes and leans her head back against the yew's trunk as Faith burrows deeper into the crook of her arm.

"LaLaLaLaLa."

Vern looks at May as if she ought to do something, but of course there's nothing left to do but wait.

"She can't . . ." Vern whispers, then hangs his head and says nothing more.

"Cold," Angel says. "More . . . blankets?"

Vern looks from his wife to May, then heads back to the house. Angel winks at May.

"Is he gone?"

May nods. She has yet to speak. The last words you say to someone, she thinks, must come out like shards of glass.

"Tell me," Angel says, "who . . . you are. Quick, before he . . .comes back."

Or maybe the last words are like water. One drop and then everything you've ever held back slips out.

"I came from a grove in the mountains," May says, looking at her daughter instead of into Angel's eyes. "I was . . . different. A tree. I changed for Edward."

She braces herself for scorn and disbelief, but when she looks at Angel, the woman is merely smiling at the twisted boughs of the yew.

"What kind of tree?" Angel asks.

What kind? The tears fall before May can stop them. Happiness is sharpest, even cruel, right before it ends.

"Larch," May says, swiping at her tears.

"Oh!" Angel replies, closing her eyes. "Good. That's a beautiful tree."

A stack of blankets in his arms, Vern hurries back with Francie right behind him. Bill, holding Paul, brings up the rear. Vern gently tucks three more blankets around Faith and his wife. Surprisingly, he drapes the last one on May's shoulders.

The larks sing for a while, then go silent as Angel dozes. The dark, needle-like leaves of the yew tree rustle consolingly in the light breeze. When Faith falls back asleep, May takes her from Angel's arms and turns to go, knowing it won't be long.

"Stay," Vern says suddenly. "She'd want you to."

Vern is the strongest man she knows, but she's uncertain how he'll go on alone. She nods, but stands in the background while Francie kneels beside her mother.

"I love you, Mom," Francie whispers, her voice so broken May isn't sure it can ever return to normal. "I know you're tired. It's all right to go."

It's hardly even noticeable when it happens. Just a raggedy breath, a long relieved sigh, then nothing at all. Vern presses his ear to Angel's chest; Francie cries softly, leaning into Bill and Paul.

The luckiest tree in the forest is the one they cut first.

Sixteen

Hazel

(Corylus avellana)

Nine magical Hazel trees are said to line the border between the human realm and the home of the gods. When these trees drop their nuts into streams, the salmon who eat them gain glistening spots blessed with all the knowledge of the world. Humans who then eat these salmon gain prophetic abilities and lifelong wisdom. On the other hand, the Hazel tree doesn't grow right. It can live up to 80 years, but without human coppicing—chopping the tree down to its stump to make it regrow—it's not particularly impressive. You'd think that, with all that wisdom, the hazel wouldn't put all its nuts in one basket—growing primarily in Turkey, where it's particularly vulnerable to climate change.

✦

Month after month, the cash-filled envelopes arrive. There is never a note inside. With Edward's money and what she earns from her herbal remedies, May is able to buy the food she can't grow and get Faith a red wagon for her second birthday. May pulls her up and down the block, Faith singing the same nonsense song.

"Lola, lulu, lalala."

She no longer realizes she is saying Angel's name. They pass the house across the street without Faith throwing herself to the ground and wailing, as she did for months after Angel's death. Whenever Faith gets a cut or scrape, it's May she turns to for comfort, an act that warms May's heart but also saddens her. People are far better at forgetting than trees.

As she grows, Faith also adapts to the steady stream of customers who arrive at their door. She still whimpers at the ones covered in boils, but she no longer hides in the closet. The only thing that doesn't change is her hatred of May's garden.

"Bad," Faith says when May hands her a homegrown carrot. "You grow bad things."

May purses her lips and wonders if her two-year-old daughter is stealing away in the night to listen to Pastor Maloney's sermons.

"It's a carrot, Faith," May says, but Faith wrinkles her nose and won't take it. She'll only eat the flavorless ones May buys from the store.

The long days pulling Faith in her wagon and checking on Vern pass in a blur. After Angel's death, the man doesn't return to work. The laundry and dust pile up in his house, as do the pictures of Angel. Every time Vern catches himself feeling anything other than grief, he takes out another photograph of his late wife and stares at it until he's heartbroken all over again.

"I can't go on," he says to May whenever she carefully places the photographs back in their albums.

"What hurts the most," she replies, "is that you can."

When Faith turns three, she begs for dance lessons. At four, Francie buys her a pink tutu, which she wears day and night for months. Faith dances through the yard, past the creek, and eventually, with a little coaxing, all the way up the mountain. After three long years, Faith and May finally return to the grove.

May steps warily into the ring of larches. The whorl on her hand has faded. She's come back to claim her history, and nothing more.

But Faith has no memory of their last visit and runs from trunk to trunk.

"Mama, look at them!" she squeals. "Their needles are made of gold!"

Two sisters have lost their crowns to lightning, while a dozen golden saplings tickle Faith's legs. When Faith reaches May's tree, she doesn't hesitate before peeking inside the bear wound.

"Is this where the fairies live, Mama?"

"Hmmm," May replies. "What do you think?"

Faith grins. "I think they're here. Be quiet so we don't scare them."

They sit in the center of the grove, Faith's eyes wide at the rustling of golden needles, as if it's really the fluttering of fairy wings. May's sisters are busy breaking down the chlorophyll in their needles to store for winter, but to May it feels like a cool, calming hand on her forehead. She's still not sure what happened the last time they were here—if what occurred in her bear wound was real or some frightening dream born of exhaustion—but she knows she's safe now. Faith is safe.

May weaves her daughter a crown of fallen larch boughs and places it on her head.

"Queen of the larch fairies," she says.

Faith touches the crown, careful not to dislodge a single golden needle. She wears it home and puts it on every morning for two weeks, even as the needles start to brown. One afternoon, when May is laying straw in the garden for winter, Faith runs to her in tears. The last needle has fallen from the crown and she throws the bare twigs at May's feet.

"You lied! Fairies aren't real at all!"

Well, now, May thinks. That all depends on who you talk to. Still, she was hoping this conversation would come a little later, when there would be less chance of breaking her daughter's heart.

"They are if you believe in them," she says.

Four-year-old Faith rolls her eyes and scoffs like a teenager. "That's what all parents say. And I don't believe you."

Already, Faith can out-talk her. Her daughter, in her tattered tutu, will win every debate they have, so May simply takes her hand.

"Come," she says, leading her inside to the kitchen.

May has replenished her apothecary chest multiple times over the years. Filled to the brim with seeds, cuttings and, at this point, quite a bit of dirt, the bottom drawers are reserved for her most precious possessions—the seeds from the trees that Edward cut. She takes out one of winged larch seeds and puts it in the palm of Faith's hand.

"A gift," she says, "from your father."

Faith rarely asks about Edward. Perhaps it was better that he left before she was born because there is no particular man for her to yearn for. No richer, better life she's missed. She's seen Bill with Paul, but the man also buys her dolls and ballerina slippers. Vern couldn't love her any more if she were his own.

"He's gone," Faith says, flicking away the seed. "I don't care about him."

May watches the winged seed flutter to the floor, then stoops to pick it back up. They're not going to have an easy time of it, her and Faith. Not in the witch's house. Faith once threw out all of the poppy seeds May was cold stratifying in the refrigerator because they were in the way of the cookies. On the kitchen shelf is the canister of potting soil that May enhances with coffee grounds, no matter how many times Faith tells her that no one else's mother keeps dirt in the house on purpose.

Now, May grabs that can of soil, as well as one of the terracotta planting pots she keeps next to her mugs, and fills the pot with dirt. One day, she will tell her daughter that magic is everywhere—in healing plants and true love and tree roots that whisper of drought, disease and need, but for now she just holds out the seed.

"Look at it," she says.

Faith rolls her eyes again, but finally glances at the seed. It takes her a moment, but at last she gasps.

"It has wings!"

May nods and sets the delicate seed in the palm of her daughter's hand.

"We need to be gentle," she says. "We don't want to hurt her."

Faith gives May a half-hearted scoff, but can't stop staring at the winged seed. May can almost see the battle between scorn and yearning going on inside her. It's a full minute before wishfulness wins and she carefully buries the seed in the pot.

"Is it really a fairy, Mama?" she asks in a tiny voice.

May thinks that's a very good question. Faith's idea of fairies might be fanciful, but so are groves of sisters and wishing on stars. Who's to say that people—even the ones who believe in nothing—aren't simply fairies without wings.

"Hmmm," May says, picking up the pot.

She leads Faith out to the greenhouse, where she places the pot on the sunniest shelf. She hands Faith her watering can and her daughter carefully waters the seed.

They stand in silence for a long time, much longer than Faith usually does. May wonders if her daughter feels the same thing she does, a tingle of gratitude that rises from the soles of her feet to her head. The sisterhood of the larches.

"Why did he leave us?" Faith asks at last.

The tingle fades suddenly, leaving May and her daughter alone in the greenhouse.

May looks through the kaleidoscope of windows Edward painstakingly installed. There are the things you know, and the ones you tell your daughter—the former sure to break her heart, the latter to mend it. So now, as always, she tells the truth, but not all of it, and one day when Faith has daughters of her own, she'll understand and do the same.

"So he could come back," she says.

By the time Faith starts kindergarten, every window in their house has been smashed. May replaces the last of Edward's beautiful bubble glass with modern double panes and sleeps with a baseball bat under her bed. Although, to be fair, the rock-throwing culprits run away faster when she comes after them with a broom.

The vandalism is irksome, but also surprisingly good for business. Any house worthy of a brick through the window must contain a powerful witch. Word of her prowess with plants spreads from Laramie to neighboring towns, and May has to triple the size of her garden. Even Pastor Maloney's wife stops by one night to buy the strongest sleep tonic May makes. Her husband has been arrested three times now for trespassing and still preaches against May's unholy medicine, but Eva Maloney just wants something to help her sleep through her husband's snoring.

"You try sharing a bed with that blowhard," she says.

In addition to the broken windows, the rocks people throw shatter Faith's nerves. For a while, she crawls into May's bed to sleep, but the night after her three best friends decide to sit at a different table at lunch, Faith hides in her bedroom closet once again and refuses to come out.

"Everyone hates me because of you!" she cries from behind the door.

For the last five years, May has devoted herself to learning the words that will comfort her daughter, yet there is nothing she can say to refute the truth. The only thing Faith wants is a mother nobody notices—not the one who stands apart in mud-coated boots.

May stares down at the dirt she can never scrub clean from beneath her fingernails, then walks to the kitchen. By now, she's gotten quite good at using the phone; she even knows Francie's number by heart.

Francie answers on the first ring. May always pictures her sitting beside the phone, willing it to ring—particularly if it's someone who's got gossip.

"Would you be willing to take Faith for the night?" May asks. "There's something I need to do."

After Francie agrees to come pick up Faith, May searches the phonebook for a number she never thought she'd call. Thankfully, it's the person she wants to talk to—Eva Maloney—and not her husband who answers.

"I just wanted to tell you that I mean you no harm," May says. "But something has to be done."

Eva is quiet for a long time before she chuckles. "Do your worst," she says.

That evening, while Faith sleeps peacefully in Francie and Bill's guest bedroom, May gathers cattails and twigs from a thicket of mountain ash and fashions them into a broom. She waits until well after midnight to dress all in black, then carries her creation, along with a matchbook and a large bag of salt, across town to Pastor Maloney's house. In the middle of his lawn, she draws a large heart in salt, then stabs the ash-handled broom into the center of it. She raps on their bedroom window., and by the time Pastor Maloney and his wife stumble out of bed, May has already lit the match.

The couple peers out their bedroom window as the broom catches fire. The salt will scorch the grass and keep anything from growing there for years, but the real spell is making Pastor Maloney wonder if he's made a mistake, antagonizing a witch. He shouts something she can't hear, but he doesn't come outside to put out the flames. May's fine with him hating her, as long as he fears her more.

As she turns to go, she swears that Eva winks. The woman might have even realized that a proper sorceress wouldn't make a broom handle out of mountain ash—the very wood that, for centuries, has been used for the protection of women and to ward off evil witches.

May walks home slowly, watching the sky lighten like a healing bruise. This is the first time she's walked alone in five years and, when the curve of the sun rises above the horizon, she stops to take it in.

A tingle runs down her spine, not at the blood-red dawn, but because there's a footstep behind her.

Without turning around, she slips her hands into her pockets, closing them around her knives. Her sisters send their warning signals down the mountain, but minutes pass and no one attacks. A familiar scent of wool and sawdust flits past her and May whirls around.

Maybe she sees a man's tousled brown hair and wool coat disappearing around the corner, and maybe she doesn't. The only thing she knows for sure is that his name sounds foreign on her tongue.

"Edward."

✦

Pastor Maloney stops throwing rocks, but isn't against a little hate mail. Half a dozen letters arrive in May's mailbox each week, though she wouldn't object to more. Where else is she going to learn so many swear words? She burns the letters after reading them and adds the ashes to her compost. Her belladonna grows like mad.

Faith is no longer afraid of the garden; she's declared war on it. Every chance she gets, she stomps through Poison Alley, crushing every plant in her wake. When May scolds her, Faith kicks the garden fence for good measure and runs to her room. She refuses to walk to the grove and, once her friends return to her lunch table, begs to ride the bus to school with them—even though Francie's son, Paul, rides the same bus, and Faith doesn't like him one bit.

"He's weird," Faith tells her. "Always off by himself, climbing trees. And he smells like mud."

May's mouth twitches. "That's a good smell."

At five years old, Faith has already mastered a withering stare. "You only think that because you're weird, too."

Francie tries everything she can think of to help Paul make friends—throwing him elaborate birthday parties, enrolling him in soccer camp, insisting on play dates with boys he hardly knows—but her son still climbs trees by himself at recess. She sits on May's front porch most afternoons, sucking down May's calming teas, occasionally spiked with a dash of bourbon.

"I know I shouldn't," she says, tucking away the whiskey bottle beneath her chair. "But whoever said motherhood is bliss must have had a drink in her hand all day long."

Across the street, Vern putters in his yard. He wanders from garden bed to bush, but never seems to prune or plant anything. His once meticulous lawn is now six inches tall and overrun with dandelions, a fact which delights May and horrifies the neighbors.

"All I do is worry," Francie continues. "I just want Paul to fit in, you know, but I tell you that child glories in being an odd duck, the one no one understands. And Bill's no help. All he says is that Paul will be fine."

May pats her friend's hand consolingly, even though she agrees with Bill. Paul will be fine; Paul *is* fine. When did it become a crime to like trees better than people?

"And then there's him," Francie says, gesturing across the street toward her father. "The station has asked him again and again to come back to work, but he's not interested. He barely eats. He just wanders around the garden and stares at her pictures. It's like he's willing himself to die so he can be with her. It's been four years, May. Four *years*."

It's been well over five years since Edward left, and lately May swears she sees him everywhere. In the woods, bending low over her garden, turning a corner just as she calls his name.

"Sometimes time just makes things worse," she says.

Francie stares at her, then hands her the cup of spiked tea. "To worry and sorrow," she says.

May takes a sip, the tea burning as it goes down. She struggles to keep from coughing as Francie laughs and takes back the cup.

"It's an acquired taste," she says.

May never gets used to the taste of whiskey, but she grows quite fond of their ritual of afternoon tea on the porch. An hour before the school bus brings home their children—in separate seats, of course—Francie arrives to tell her the latest town gossip. May brews everything from dandelion to white willow tea, and more often than not Francie spikes it. They laugh about the elderberry wine May leaves on Pastor Maloney's doorstep after every hateful letter, and commiserate over everything from wayward children to insomnia and garden pests.

"You should see the aphids on my roses," Francie says on a warm spring afternoon. "Bill won't lift a finger to help me in the garden. His hands are softer than mine."

May glances at her, and they both laugh. They're still chuckling when the school bus turns the corner and Francie pushes the whiskey bottle farther under the seat. Paul usually sits in the back row and is the last to get off, but today they spot him near the front, sitting beside a smiling, brown-haired girl who won't stop talking. It takes May a moment to realize that the happy girl is Faith. The two of them get off together, Faith still talking and Paul giving her a small, shy smile.

May feels Francie go still beside her, but when the children reach them, all her friend says is, "Good day at school?"

Paul shrugs as he glances at the purple ash he normally climbs. Today, instead, he follows Faith inside the house. Perhaps he showered this morning, or Faith has taken a liking to a boy who smells of the earth. Either way, Francie leans into her.

"I told you they'd fall in love."

May laughs again as Francie takes the bottle of whiskey out from under the chair and screws the cap back on.

"I'm going to save the rest," she says. "I have a feeling we're going to need it."

Seventeen

Otholanga
(Cerebra odollam)

Otholanga, also known as the Suicide Tree, belongs to the oleander family, and is excessively toxic. During the 19th century, thousands of people in Madagascar were forced to ingest the tree's fruit to determine if they were guilty of witchcraft—a hugely successful trial by poison, as the vast majority of defendants died quickly and painfully of heart failure. The Suicide Tree's fruit contains cerberin, a digoxin-type toxin that disrupts the heartbeat, usually fatally. More people—the vast majority of them women—have taken their own life by Otholanga than by any other plant in the world.

✦

When Vern stops coming outside, even just to putter in his yard, May shows up at his door. He's not looking well, but May simply tells him she's forgotten the rules to gin rummy. Pushing past him, she sits down at his kitchen table and refuses to leave until he plays.

The next day, she asks for another refresher, and by the end of the week, they have a standing date to play cards every morning after Faith leaves for school. The two of them pass hours laying down sets and straights and never speaking of Vern's swollen hands and ankles. May assumes it's kidney failure. He's been starving himself; there's not a single can of food in the pantry. Sometimes, in the middle of a game, he'll fall asleep.

You can't will your kidneys to fail, but there are steps a desperate man can take to make sure they do. Starvation, dehydration, alcohol poisoning. Francie has threatened hospitalization and feeding tubes if Vern doesn't start eating and taking better care of himself, but May knows there's only one way Vern is leaving this room.

"Would it make a difference if I told you I need you?" May asks him one morning.

Vern stares at his cards. Every day he takes a little longer to decide which one to discard. Sometimes he even discards two of them, and May never says a word. He finally chooses one to put on the discard pile, then looks May in the eye. He talks the way May used to, with more gestures and pauses than words. The language of the young and the dying.

"You don't . . . anymore."

She sighs as she draws a new card from the deck. He's right. She can fix her own windows and scare off those who would break them. She is May; she's always been able to get what she needs It's getting what she wants that's the tricky part.

She stares at the card she drew. A Joker, which she quickly sets on the table with two Aces. At first, she rarely won a hand, but now she beats Vern easily. She discards her last card and wins the game by over a hundred points, though, as always, she declares Vern the winner.

She reaches for his bony hand. "Thank you," she says, "for everything."

✦

The following week, it's Vern who forgets the rules. He furrows his brow as he stares at his cards, eventually playing the queen of hearts, even though it doesn't match any other card on the table. May takes her turn, while Vern searches through the deck, taking out various cards and laying them in front of him. Once he hands her all the cards he doesn't want, she calls him the winner. Vern smiles, but there are tears in his eyes.

When they're not playing no-rules gin rummy, Vern dozes on the couch while May sits on the chair beside him, staring out the window at the yew tree in the yard. She comes each morning right after Faith gets on the school bus, while Francie takes the afternoon shift. Francie restocks the pantry, but Vern presses his lips together whenever May offers him food. There's no point in forcing him; what's done is done. Trees and people can only take so much damage before they fall.

One morning, Vern is sleeping when May arrives, but an hour later he awakes with a gasp. He looks around in terror, as if he has no idea where he is. May kneels beside him and takes his hands in hers.

"Everything's okay," she tells him. "You're almost home."

He clings to her, opening and closing his mouth a few times before he's able to say, "Takes . . . long."

She nods. "Bodies are as stubborn as old men. They don't give up easy."

May savors the long silence that follows because she dreads the words that she knows will come next. She's expected them for days. Vern squeezes her hands with the last of his strength.

"You . . . help?" he asks.

She wonders why she doesn't cry. For him, for Angel. For the things that love and mercy compel her to do.

"S'okay," Vern says, struggling for every word. "You . . . don't . . ."

"I don't have to," she whispers for him.

But she does. His pain will increase and he'll have trouble breathing. His last days will be a horror show of pain, delirium, and fear. She's taken no oath; she has only her plants and conscience to guide her. Nature can ease pain or end it—if you know where to look, and you're strong enough to do it.

She takes a deep breath and lifts a hand to Vern's cheek. He's crying, yet his eyes are clearer than they've been in a long while.

"Do you think you'll see her?" May asks.

A huge grin breaks through his tears and she has her answer. Heaven, for him, isn't a place, but an Angel.

May stays with him until he sleeps again, then slips out quietly. She planted the tree she'll need over five years ago in a rocky canyon that no one in their right mind would care to reach. More than a mile from the nearest trail and surrounded by sage brush, May has managed to keep the tropical plant alive and thriving through a mixture of straw mulch, blankets, and the warmth of the canyon's red rocks.

Ironically, it was Angel who provided the seed. Years ago, when the woman gave May her apothecary chest, she included a seed meant to grow in lush rain forests and coastal swamps. A seed Angel thought looked pretty, but knew nothing about. Otholanga, the suicide tree.

May reaches the canyon an hour later. The tree is still small, but intensely fragrant inside its circle of protective sage. This spring, it erupted in gorgeous white and yellow blossoms, but it's the green, mango-like fruit that she needs. Inside each fruit are highly toxic kernels that will cause death within three to six hours. Even one kernel can be fatal, especially to a man whose kidneys are already failing.

May harvests five.

Back home, she puts the kernels on a tall shelf Faith can't reach and waits for her daughter at the bus stop. Paul must have gotten off earlier because Faith isn't smiling and shrugs off May's hug. May tries to win her over by telling her she can choose what they'll have for dinner.

"Anything?" Faith asks.

May glances across the street at the dark windows, then nods. "Anything."

Faith asks for ice cream and pickles and, without a word, May starts walking toward the grocery store. Faith catches up to her.

"You're really going to get that?" she asks, her eyes doubtful even as she starts to grin.

"Chocolate syrup, too," May says.

That evening they sit at the kitchen table eating dill pickles and vanilla ice cream with chocolate syrup. Faith can't stop smiling and talks more than she has in ages, about her friends and school and how Paul sent her a Valentine—the same one that he sent to everyone in his class, but still. She even agrees to a game of gin rummy before letting May tuck her into bed.

Once Faith falls asleep, May stares out the window at the house across the street. Francie came and went this afternoon and there's been no sign of lights or movement since. May bows her head, offering up a wretched prayer that fate has already taken this burden off her shoulders.

But when she looks up again, a light burns in Vern's living room window.

May retrieves the kernels from the upper shelf and pulverizes them with a mortar and pestle. It's ludicrous to worry about their bitter taste, but she still mixes them with melted vanilla ice cream and chocolate syrup, then pours everything into her nicest glass.

Her hands don't shake as she carries the deadly shake across the street. Pastor Maloney might be right about her: She's as capable of harming someone as she is of healing them. Vern took her in and treated her like his own daughter, yet what he needs now is not a daughter, but a witch.

She finds Vern on the living room couch, smiling like it's Christmas morning. He sighs contentedly when she sets the milkshake on the table beside him.

"You need to drink it all at once," she says. "Otherwise things could get messy."

She hardly recognizes her own voice, the icy calmness. She wonders if she'll ever speak lightly again. She walks to the window and stares once more at the dark needles of the yew. If Edward hadn't entered her grove, she would have remained a dispassionate, silent witness to the creatures who died at her feet. She never would have killed or comforted anyone. The price of love, it seems, is guilt and pain.

When the glass shatters, she whirls around, but Vern hasn't changed his mind. There are glass shards and the final drops of the shake on the floor. Vern drank the rest; a rim of chocolate coats his upper lip.

"Oops," he says without any difficulty at all. "There goes the evidence."

When he smiles mischievously, it all rushes in. Grief, anger, horror and, even in this terrible moment, gratitude for this good man she has to lose. She was once made of wood; she can stay strong for him a little longer.

"I'll stay until it's done," she says.

He nods and pulls a blanket over his legs, like a little boy settling in after a long day's play.

"Thank you, my May," he says.

She doesn't cry until he stops breathing. It's hours before she stops.

The warning from her sisters comes suddenly, a month after Vern's funeral. May has just crossed the creek behind her house and is heading up Battlecreek Peak when a sharp pain shoots up her legs. She senses no threat to the grove—no infestation, disease or drought. Her sisters simply don't want her to come.

May squints up the mountain. Faith is at a sleepover at her friend Carrie's house, and rather than sit home alone, May had wanted to spend the evening in the grove. But when she takes another step, the pain rockets to the small of her back. There is danger that way, they tell her. Not for them, but for her.

The pain doesn't bother her as much as knowing they've set her apart. She tries to keep going, shaking off the throbbing in her legs and even a sock to her stomach, but when her chest tightens alarmingly, as if someone—or something—is squeezing it, May wonders just how far her sisters will go to keep her away. The pressure builds until it's nearly impossible to breathe, let alone walk.

"Okay," she says, gasping as she turns back. "Okay."

It isn't until she enters her house and sags against the door that her sisters relent. The pain fades quickly, but she aches all over.

They don't want her.

For the next few weeks, whenever May forages in the woods for fir tips and nettles, the stabbing pains return. She gathers her supplies quickly and glares up the mountain before hurrying home to soak in a warm bath. One excursion leads to a horrible rash on her arms and neck, even though she's certain she didn't brush against poison ivy. She applies a jewelweed mash to her skin and spends a sleepless night trying not to scratch herself. In the morning, when even a casual glance out her window causes a jolt of pain down her legs, she grits her teeth.

Enough.

Throwing open her closet door, May dresses in her heaviest boots, wool pants, and one of Edward's thick coats to protect her from the forest's barbs and poisons. Then she stomps to the kitchen and tells her daughter they're hiking to the grove.

Faith looks up sleepily from her bowl of cereal. For her sixth birthday, she asked to paint her bedroom hot pink, the same color her friend Carrie chose for her own room. May's eyes hurt for days after painting. It's no wonder her daughter doesn't sleep well in there.

"Why don't we have a car?" Faith asks.

She asks May the same question every day. Why don't they have a car? Why do they walk miles when normal people drive? Why do they always have to be so *odd*?

"I like walking," May replies.

"Carrie's parents have two cars! They don't walk anywhere."

May takes a deep breath. Yesterday, Faith informed her that Carrie's mom never wears men's clothes and won't allow a speck of dirt in the house, let alone a bag of potting soil.

"Walking is good for us," May says. "We can spend the day together."

Faith wrinkles her nose. "Can't I just go to Carrie's? The grove is boring. It's just a bunch of dumb trees."

That's what she calls them now. Dumb trees. The stupid forest and boring grove. May has every intention of telling her daughter where she came from, but not yet. Not when she's six years old.

So she only nods and says, "If that's what you want."

Sleepiness and cereal forgotten, Faith leaps out of her chair to give May a brief hug. It's so fleeting, May doesn't even get her arms around her before Faith breaks free and scurries off to get dressed.

May feels fine as she walks Faith across town to Carrie's house, but the moment she reaches the unpaved back road, her head aches. Everything's going to hurt today, so it's no surprise when her first step onto gravel feels like walking barefoot over broken glass. She grits her teeth and sprints, aiming for the gully that will give her a steep but quick route to the grove.

Agony rips through her legs and torso, but she veers off the road and begins climbing, determined to reach the summit before her sisters squeeze all the air from her lungs. The higher she goes, though, the more intense and chaotic their signals—stabbing sensations that jump from hip to shoulder, a throbbing in her jaw, the feeling of something clawing at her feet. One minute her legs go numb and she stumbles, and the next she can hardly breathe. May reaches a knoll twenty feet below the grove before the pain in her head becomes excruciating. She slumps to the ground and lets loose a scream that flushes even the fearless ravens from the trees.

She holds her head and can't stop the tears. Her sisters want her gone or they want to break her. Either way, when she looks toward the grove, all she sees is a wall of thorns.

It's a moment before she realizes that it's not an illusion. The wild grasses and yarrow that once grew around the grove have been replaced by a six-feet tall thicket of spiny devil's club. The plant is an effective treatment for diabetes, but most healers won't go near it due to its 12-inch wide leaves, each one sporting brittle yellow spines that embed themselves in the flesh of anyone who passes.

May drops her hands and narrows her eyes at the plant. Normally, it grows in moist, dense woods, not on the arid side of a mountain, and never in such an orderly arc. The hedge encircles the grove perfectly, sealing off her sisters before stopping at a cliff not even mountain goats could navigate.

This is no wild thing. Someone planted it.

The moment May feels a flutter in her chest, an answering shock of pain surrounds it. There's a wall around the grove now, and she's no longer on the right side of it. Nevertheless, she gets to her feet—small and human though they are.

"You can't stop me," she says and, despite her aching head, steps toward the grove. Even the most majestic trees are helpless to stop what's coming at them.

The pain her sisters send her now is almost a side note as May climbs, the last, pitiful thing they can do. She reaches the hedge and notes the placement of each root ball—close enough to form an impassable wall. Where did the devil's club come from? Why is it here now? Why plant a thicket no creature can pass through without being torn apart?

Her sisters are hiding something.

The afternoon shadows lengthen as May follows the green barrier around the grove. The hedge is already too tall for her to peer over—certainly planted from mature root stalk, not seed. She bloodies her hands parting the barbed leaves, in search of an opening, the slightest gap where she can squeeze through, but there's not so much as a peephole to the grove beyond. The armed wall is not only tall, but at least three feet deep. Impenetrable.

They've sealed her out.

The moment she accepts the truth, the pain fades away. May's sisters would have emerged from their trees as long, lithe gardeners, planting the barricade that will keep out not only May, but loggers and bears and the rest of the world. On the outside, unable to even look in, May sits alone by their creation, unsure how she's going to find the energy to hike down the mountain, especially when there will be no point in ever coming back.

The sky darkens like a bruise, from red to purple. It's nearly bedtime for the robins, not yet breakfast for the great horned owls. Quiet enough to hear the rushing of the distant river, along with the faintest footstep on the other side of the devil's club.

The hairs on the back of May's neck instantly stand on end. She leans toward the thicket, straining to hear another step, but there's nothing but the sound of the river and her own beating heart. She could have imagined it, except that when looks down, she spots what she missed before—not a gap in the devil's club at all, but a hollow in the earth beneath it, deep enough for a person to slide through.

She doesn't need her sisters' warnings to know that she ought to head home. She was lovestruck when she left the grove, so there's no telling what she'll become if she returns to it. Yet her heart pounds against her chest, her impatient body is already moving.

The only way through the hollow is flat on her stomach. May wriggles beneath the spears of devil's club, hardly feeling it when the spiked leaves rip clumps of hair from her head. There's light ahead, a glimpse of the trunks of towering larches. She shimmies toward them, finally emerging in the grove wearing a crown of thorns.

Getting to her feet, the first thing she notices is the hush. Her sisters stand silently as always, watching. And leaning against her old tree, Edward stands and watches, too.

✦

May doesn't move an inch. Edward's hair is shorter, his heartwood-colored eyes brighter. He steps toward her cautiously; he could have been waiting in the grove for a day or for years. Perhaps he was here every time she visited.

He stops a foot away—fully a man now, clean-shaven, well dressed, remade. She can almost hear her sisters grumbling. He removes a canvas bag from his shoulder and offers it to her. She narrows her eyes, but he merely waits, silently, for her to take it.

She snatches the bag, if only to throw it back at him. But there's just enough light left to spy the letters inside—hundreds of them—all written in his hand, in tiny, pained script. She pulls one out, scanning the long ago date and the first few lines, and looks up at him. Every word he never said. Every letter he should have enclosed with the money he sent, but chose not to. It's all there—his struggles, love and despair laid bare, apology after apology while he fought for work and pride and sobriety. May picks out another, and another. Five years of precious love lost.

"It's been years," she says at last, her voice like a thunderclap in the woods.

He bows his head and says nothing.

"A lifetime," she continues. "Faith doesn't even know you."

She sees the tears on his cheeks and is glad.

"People throw rocks at our windows," she goes on, grateful for every harsh word she's mastered. "Angel died. I put poison in Vern's drink so he could die, too. All while you were busy writing letters you were too cowardly to send."

She doesn't know what she wants from him. What could possibly be enough? He looks at her, his face tortured; she has no idea why he's even here.

"I'm so sorry, May," he says at last.

The statement is so inadequate, May laughs. She used to appreciate his brevity, but now she doubts that he's ever had the words to make things right.

Surrounded by the wall of devil's club, darkness comes quickly to the grove. Just before it engulfs them completely, May notices the hedge's pruned branches, the telltale signs of a human hand. It wasn't her sisters who planted it, but she stares at the person who did.

"So you've been here? Doing this?" She waves her hand at the imposing barricade, imagining the effort it must have taken to haul dozens, if not hundreds, of spiny plants up here, how his callused hands must have been torn to shreds. He found solace in the earth while she and their daughter were just down the mountain, boarding up broken windows without him.

"Just this last year," he says. "I wanted . . . It's an offering, to protect this place. I know it's not enough to make up for what I've done."

Of course it's not enough. He missed Faith's birth, her first steps, every night when he should have tucked his daughter into bed and made her feel safe and protected. Just because they could survive without him doesn't mean he should have let them. And now what? His ring of devil's club might hinder a lone woodcutter, but it won't stop a bulldozer. She's surprised Edward doesn't sense her sisters' animosity. Their rings mark every storm, drought and scar that they've suffered. They're literally standing on the hurt and damage done to them.

May turns back to Edward. "Regret helps nothing," she says. "If you're only here to say you're sorry, I don't care."

He stands as tall and strong as she remembers, but his eyes are pained. It's obvious that the last years have created a bear wound of his own.

"I'm sorrier than you'll ever know," he says quietly, "but that's not why I'm here. It took me a while to set things right. The letters will tell you . . . I wish I could have been quicker. I wish I'd never been who I was."

She shakes her head at his useless words. This very moment, her sisters are marking their rings with another calamity—the return of a villain. Despite Edward's good intentions, they would have felt every thump of his shovel as he planted the devil's club. There's no telling how many of their lateral roots he cut.

"I've found a job here," he continues. "A steady one, surveying land for a local builder. I haven't had a drink in three years. And neither of those things mean you ever have to forgive me, but I want you to know I'm building a cabin down Elk Creek. Within walking distance of our—of your house, if you or Faith ever need me. I won't impose. I don't expect anything. But nothing's going to make me leave you again. Not even you."

It's not his speech or the tears in his eyes that cause her to lean toward him, almost against her will. She's simply drawn to him—she's always been drawn to him—the way a plant turns toward the sun. She understands that he's a danger to her sisters, but she's no longer one of them. Nor is she the lovestruck girl Edward first met here, or the wife who let him go. She's a woman who needs only food, light, and water to survive, but who has also come to want more. She is May.

Edward lifts a hand, then drops it. A man who leaves for five years knows exactly how little he's needed.

So May is the one to take his hand, not out of need, but because she'd like to meet the man he's become, see if he suits the woman she's turned into. She feels his shudder of relief, the calluses on his fingers. She can't say where they'll go from here, but she knows it will be forward.

"The moon's is up," she says. "Let's take a walk."

Eighteen

Pear
(Pyrus)

The pear tree is intolerable. Feeding humanity since 2000 B.C., over three thousand varieties of pears are grown worldwide—each one more fair and beautiful than the last. If the apple is the forbidden fruit on the tree of knowledge, the pear is her voluptuous but wholesome cousin, the one who beguiles you but never steers you wrong. The shape of the fruit is suggestive of the female form; humans paint her as a symbol of fertility and bounty. In most cultures, the pear is referenced as a symbol of divine sustenance, abundance, even immortality. No other fruit can compete.

✦

So they walk.

To frigid alpine lakes and the meadows where the one-eared bear still forages. To a pretty bend in Elk Creek, where Edward shows her the simple cabin he's already begun framing, to the grove to check on his thriving hedge of devil's club, despite May's sisters' unrelenting silence. May's pain is gone entirely; she hasn't felt so much as a twinge since she and Edward left the grove.

One time only, they walk to the elementary school, where May insists Edward stand in the shadows. During recess, Faith sits at the base of the monkey bars while her classmates climb past her to swing from the topmost rings. Even her best friend, Carrie, can't coax her upward.

"She's a little fearful," May says quietly, but Edward merely smiles.

"Smart girl. She'll never fall."

Of course he wants to meet his daughter, but May insists that they wait. First they need to figure out what they're going to be to each other, this time around. Then there's Faith's timidity to consider, not to mention her upcoming dance recital, the cold she battles for a week.

"People are going to figure out that I'm back," Edward tells May as they hike up the north side of Simpson Peak. "I'm afraid if you don't tell her about me, someone else will."

May stoops to collect the fiddleheads that are unmatched for managing heavy menstrual flows. "I just want it to go well," she says, not looking at him. "I'm not punishing you."

He says nothing, but she can feel him watching her. They both know she's learned how to lie.

Unsurprisingly, one of the first people to learn that Edward is back is Francie. She shows up breathless on

May's porch one day to announce that Edward is building a cabin on Elk Creek.

"Hank Wilson told me Edward hired his electrical crew. And he's got a job in town, May! Some kind of land assessment thing."

Francie waits for her reaction, but all May says is, "I heard."

May has not only learned how to lie, she can also bottle up the truth. She didn't tell Francie about her walks with Edward because she knows her friend won't approve. Nor will she ever share what happened in Vern's last hours. Their friendship might survive it, but May's not convinced that Francie would.

Francie takes May's hand. "You haven't talked to him, have you? How can he just waltz on back here? If Bill disappeared for five years, I'd never give him another chance. What are you going to do?"

May sighs. She's not looking for approval, but that isn't going to stop Francie or anyone else from offering their opinions and advice.

"I'm not going to do anything," she says. "We'll just see where we end up."

Francie squeezes her hand before letting go. "Well, you know best," she says, even though her pursed lips say otherwise. "I just worry about Faith."

May worries about Faith, too. Losing sleep over her daughter is as unhelpful as unsolicited advice, yet there seems to be no cure for it. If her daughter is afraid of strangers, imagine how terrified she'll be to meet the father she's never known.

So May dozes fitfully at night and walks with Edward every morning before he heads to work. Francie would be happy to know that Edward has not so much as kissed her. He's careful to keep a respectable distance between them and always says goodbye formally, with a tip of his hat. It's driving her mad.

This morning, they sit on a sunny hillside, picking fireweed and eating the stalks raw. Edward has spent so many years working outside his skin is already turning leathery, while May's gardener's back has developed quite a stoop. They're a pair, the two of them—the cowboy and the crone.

She laughs out loud and though Edward smiles at her, he doesn't come any closer. Men, honestly! She almost tells him to go plant more devil's club until he's ready to woo her, but instead she leans forward and kisses him, hard.

His arms, at least, know what to do, winding around her waist instantly. Then he takes control of himself and draws away.

"I don't want to rush you," he says. "I can wait if . . ."

He's charming, but ridiculous. She simply pulls her shirt up over her head and pushes him to the ground.

"May," he says, and then thankfully runs out of words.

He kisses her neck, then the hollow between her breasts, and though she loves how he lingers over every inch of her, she murmurs, "If you go this slowly, you'll be late for work."

It isn't until he chuckles and yanks off his own shirt that she admits to herself she's in love again. She's always been in love with him. She's stronger alone, but what kind of life is that?

"May," he says again, kissing her shoulder, the crook of her arm, every part of her. There are tears on both their cheeks as they lay amidst the fireweed

Let the world judge them. Love, however brief or flawed, is rare.

Every morning, May waits for Faith to get on the school bus before meeting Edward in the woods.

It's bliss to feel the cool earth below her and Edward's heat above. Whenever he whispers that he loves her, she squeezes him tight and says, "I love you too, I love you too, I love you too."

When he talks about Faith, she kisses him. She's not exactly sure who she's protecting—Faith, Edward, or even herself. She fears that Faith will hate him, but where will May stand if she doesn't?

One Sunday afternoon, while May plants a row of milkweed in the backyard, Faith squeals from the front. May is on her feet in an instant, but Faith is already running toward her, uninjured and beaming. She clutches a glittering tiara to her chest.

"I love it, Mama!" she says. "It's just like Carrie's!"

May glances quickly toward the woods. She didn't buy that tiara, but she thinks she knows who did. She should have wondered why, in the last few days, Edward has stopped asking when he can meet Faith. Why wait for permission when you can simply go get what you want?

"Faith," she says, but her daughter is already running inside to call Carrie.

May squints toward the trees, but sees no flash of heartwood eyes. She's certain she hears a man whistling, though, as he takes the forest path toward home.

The next morning before school, Faith finds a ruby-colored necklace on the sidewalk in front of their house.

"Ooh!" she cries, snatching it up and examining the glitter and faux gemstones. "Carrie doesn't have one like this. Thank you, Mama."

May shakes her head. "The gifts aren't from me. You must have a secret admirer."

Faith's face lights up. "Really? Do you think it's Paul?"

Faith still has a crush on Francie's son, even though Paul has finally found a couple of outdoorsy boys to hang out with, and rarely sits beside her on the bus. May helps Faith put on the necklace.

"Could be anyone," she says. "You have a lot of admirers."

May doesn't meet Edward in the woods that day, or any day that week. Still, every morning another trinket appears in their yard—rings set atop the dandelions, hair clips in the lawn and, today, a rhinestone belt hanging from a branch of the purple ash. After May loops the belts around her daughter's waist and walks her to the school bus, she stands in her garden, hands on her hips.

"Come out, you coward," she says.

Edward slips from the trees, his hat in his hands, but a smile on his lips.

"You can't bribe her into accepting you," May says.

Edward's grin doesn't fade. "I'm not trying to. I'm just one of her many admirers."

May shakes her head. "This isn't a game. You're not allowed to hurt her, and I can't stop her from breaking your heart."

Edward nods. "I'd say I owe her a broken heart or two."

The jewelry keeps coming, each gift located farther away than the one before. Pearl clip-on earrings on the mailbox, beads strung up in the corner elm, a golden crown ringing the fire hydrant on the next block—each present a sparkly breadcrumb that, May knows, will lead right to Edward's front door.

"Paul said they're not from him," Faith tells May. "I don't know who else it could be."

May should tell her, warn her, but Faith is so delighted with the treasure hunt, she hardly notices she's being brave. She practically skips down streets she's never seen before, wades right into Elk Creek to retrieve a sequined choker, and walks straight up to a man sitting on his front porch, a gold locket on his knee.

Faith stops in her tracks.

"It's your father, Faith," May says quietly, though she's quite sure the whole forest can hear.

Edward smiles as he gets to his feet, but Faith has already turned back toward May, eyes blazing. May should have realized that if Faith was going to hate anyone, it would be her. Before May can say another word, Faith turns and runs for home.

✦

May finds Faith in the garden, beheading the motherwort.

"I should have told you," May says.

Faith doesn't look up from her hatchet job. It's a shame that she went straight for the motherwort, since it's the only herbal medicine she'll take. The plant is a gentle tonic for heart disease, menstrual cramps, and the anxious tears of a six-year-old when she can't fall asleep at night.

"You know I'll just plant more, right?" May says.

Faith glares at her and throws the remains of the plant at her feet.

"Carrie said my father was dead."

May's inborn stillness first gave way to walking, then to rocking her daughter to sleep, and now to flinching at the things Faith says.

"He's not dead," May says.

"I wish he was."

May shakes her head. "Well, then, thank goodness not all wishes come true."

Over the next few days, Faith kicks over May's garden sign, tramples the jimsonweed and upends every pot in the greenhouse. Just when May thinks she's gotten it out of her system, her daughter sneaks out before dawn with May's apothecary chest and dumps every precious seed in the stream. Later that morning, May finds the chest overturned in the dirt, half of the tiny drawers missing and probably washed away. Faith is sitting at the kitchen table, dressed for school, when May returns and sets what's left of the chest on the counter. The defiance on Faith's face fades into wariness when May stares at her, but says nothing, a bit of stillness left inside her after all.

Faith swallows. "The bus is coming."

May nods and picks up her daughter's backpack. They walk outside in silence, Faith stealing glances at her. As the bus rumbles toward them, Faith scans the windows for Paul, while May tosses her daughter's backpack right in front of the bus's tire.

The crunch of Faith's books, lunch and the pretty gold mirror she takes everywhere snags not only Faith's attention, but also the bus driver's. The man hits his brakes and opens the door.

"Are you crazy, lady?" he shouts.

She might be, because she grabs the backpack out from under the bus and stomps on it herself.

"Mom, what are you doing?" Faith cries.

The children on the bus strain to get a good look ats May gives the bag one last stomp of her heel before holding up the skidmarked remains.

"Mom!" Faith says, her cheeks flaming as she scans the windows to see if Paul is watching.

May smiles wickedly at her daughter; she'd even cackle if she thought it would do any good. A mother plays a hundred roles, and one requires a witch's hat.

"You can hate me all you want," May says, "but we're not going to hurt each other like this anymore."

She hands Faith her dirty backpack and walks back inside the house.

For the next few days, neither one of them speaks. May buys Faith a new backpack, and her daughter stays out of the yard. In fact, Faith barely comes out of her room at all. The only time May sees her is at dinner and breakfast, when they sit at the kitchen table and listen to each other chewing. Faith is as good at this game as May is. It's almost like being back in the woods.

Then one night, when the wind is howling, May wakes as Faith crawls into her bed. Years ago, May kept the window open all night, serenaded by the sound of rain and thunder, but as soon as Faith was tall enough to reach it, she closed the sash. May puts an arm around her daughter's trembling body and pulls her close.

"It can't hurt you. It's just the wind."

Faith burrows into May's side anyway. May can't remember the last time she was this close to her daughter and buries her nose in her hair. She rocks her gently until Faith's trembling subsides.

They're both nearing sleep when Faith whispers, "This is the witch's house. He doesn't belong here."

For a fleeting moment, May senses her sisters' interest, but the feeling is gone as quickly as it came. She pulls her daughter closer.

"Agreed."

✦

After three months peace in the witch's house, Faith agrees to meet her father again.

She and May walk in silence to the cabin Edward has completed on Elk Creek. The man is standing stiffly on his front porch, no sparkly bribes in sight.

"Faith," is all he says.

Faith squeezes May's hand tightly and narrows her eyes at her father. It's something to see a six year old make a full grown man flush with shame.

"You left," Faith says at last.

Edward gets down on one knee. "I wasn't the person you needed, but I hope to be that now."

Faith stares at him dubiously. "I don't need you," she says. "I'm six, you know. And she's a witch. We can take care of ourselves."

May sees the pain in Edward's eyes as Faith presses herself against her, but what did he expect? Children can only lean on the one who's there.

"That's true," May says. "We can do anything, including giving your father a chance. But not until you're ready."

May gives Edward an encouraging smile as they turn to go, but Faith never looks back.

Edward stops leaving trinkets around their house, though every once in a while Faith scans the bushes, as if she expected her father to put up more of a fight. It would be nice if Edward actually *did* leave something new because Faith has broken everything else he gave her. The garbage can is littered with sequins and fake gemstones, every last hair clip snapped in two. Faith has given up on the silent treatment and now peppers May with questions.

Where has he even *been*? Why couldn't he come back before? What does he want with them now? May gives Faith an abbreviated history of her relationship with Edward—minus the grove and the worst of Edward's behavior. One thing at a time.

"We both felt," May says, "that the best decision for our family was for him to leave for a while."

"But why?" Faith asks.

May pulls her daughter into her arms. "Because we're human, Faith," she says. "We make mistakes, some of them terrible. Everyone does. We need to give each other a little grace."

Seeing Faith so confused and upset, Edward and May stop meeting in the woods.

"It's just a season," May reminds him as she kisses him one last time on his front porch. She skirts the forest walking home, but senses nothing from her sisters except a distant satisfaction that she and Edward have vacated the woods.

One evening, a few weeks after their visit to Edward's house, May finds her daughter examining herself in the bathroom mirror.

"His eyes are the same color as mine," Faith says.

May nods. "That's true. The color of heartwood."

Faith meets her gaze in the mirror. "Carrie says they're mousy brown."

May tucks a lock of Faith's hair behind her ear. "Your poor friend needs glasses. I know heartwood when I see it."

"I didn't notice his hair color," Faith says. "Is it the same, too?"

"Hmmm," May replies. "I'm not sure. You'd have to stand side by side."

A few days later, Faith asks if they can return to Edward's. "Just to see."

May's mouth twitches as they sit on Edward's front porch, waiting for him to return from work. He loves his new job, and has proudly shown May his maps and elevations as if the mountains aren't real without them.

Half an hour later, Edward pulls up in the driveway and practically leaps out of his truck, his gaze going straight to his daughter. They do have the same tawny-colored hair, as well as matching frown lines and a certain love-hate relationship with the outdoors. Once they forge a relationship, May knows she'll be the odd one out.

It's not for the faint of heart, being odd.

When neither of them speak, May tells them, "Talk to each other or don't. I'm taking a walk."

When Faith reaches for her, May forces herself to keep moving. In a few quick steps, she reaches the creek and jumps across. It's easy enough to disappear into the woods, but harder to block out Edward's tender, but trembling voice. She keeps going until she reaches a ridge where the only sounds are the wind through the trees and her own shallow breathing.

The luckiest trees may be the ones cut first, but the luckiest people are the ones with the most to lose. Look how much she's lost already! Her sisters, Vern and Angel, Edward, for a while. Even if he and Faith don't reconcile,

Faith will grow up and not need her. A full life is riddled with holes.

She returns down the mountain in time to see her daughter and Edward building cairns along Elk Creek. Edward looks up with such a light in his eyes, May catches her breath. At last, he's one of the lucky ones, too.

✦

"People talk, you know," Francie says.

She and May are sitting in Francie's newly remodeled dining room—Bill wanted a more modern feel, opting for cold metal chairs and a glass table that Francie struggles to keep free of fingerprints. Outside, Edward and Bill barbecue chicken wings while Paul convinces Faith—who just turned seven—to climb to the lowest branch of the towering red maple. Paul still spends most of his time with his friends, but this hasn't dampened Faith's feelings for him one bit. A month ago, she told May in no uncertain terms that she and Paul were going to get married.

"When I say so," Faith declared, "because boys can be dumb."

Now, May turns back to Francie. "People have always talked about me," she says. "I'm popular."

Francie elbows her and laughs. "At least you don't have Cameron to worry about anymore."

May nods. When Edward returned to Laramie, he never contacted his father, and Cameron never welcomed him home. Edward's father died alone in his house a few months ago, probably of a heart attack, though no one knows for sure. It was days before one of his workers checked on him and found the body.

"I'm serious about people talking," Francie continues. "It's been almost a year since you and Edward got back together. You're married, so why not live together? Word is he's going to skip out on you again."

May stares out the window at her husband. Since his return, he's grown a beard, put on ten pounds, and somehow made her heart race even faster. She laughs when he flips the chicken wings only to have Bill tell him he's doing it wrong.

"I don't want him to move in," May says. "It's the witch's house. Faith and I want it this way."

"Really?" Francie asks.

May squeezes her friend's hand. "Is there only one way to love someone? Edward and I have our own story. It doesn't have to be like everyone else's."

"Of course not. But Faith—"

"Faith is fine," May cuts in. "She's still getting to know her father. And Edward and I like running around like a pair of lovers. What's wrong with that?"

May can see that Francie thinks there's plenty wrong with it, but thankfully her friend merely purses her lips and says nothing. Outside, Paul keeps trying to lure Faith up to the higher branches, which eventually makes her dissolve into tears.

When Bill puts a second batch of chicken wings on the grill, May realizes that Faith isn't the only one crying.

"Francie, what's wrong?"

Francie shakes her head. "Are you happy with him?" she asks. "With Edward?"

May no longer thinks Francie cries too much. If anything, she worries about her smiles. The forced laughter when it's obvious she's in pain.

"I am," May replies. "Not every minute or every day, but if someone offered me a lifetime of bliss with someone else, I wouldn't take it."

Francie swipes at her hears as the men's voices drift through the window. Bill is still lecturing Edward on the proper way to flip wings.

"I'm happy for you," she says quietly. "I don't know if I'd say the same."

Twenty minutes later, with salad and perfectly seared chicken wings on the table, they sit down to eat. Both Francie and Faith have stopped crying, but only Faith is back to smiling, chattering happily with Paul. Francie pokes at her chicken and, for once, barely says a word.

After dinner, Edward walks May and Faith home. He may not live with them, but they see him every evening—when he brings truckloads of mulch for May's garden and reads a story to Faith before tucking her into bed. Sometimes, when May knows he'll be surveying land on Battlecreek Peak, she walks until she finds him, luring him from his work by pulling him down on a bed of pine needles. An hour, sometimes two, later, he'll kiss the sweat between her breasts and say, "You're always getting me into trouble."

May laughs loud enough for the whole forest, including her sisters, to hear.

"If you're not getting into trouble," she says, "you're doing something wrong."

Over the years, Faith takes a liking to science.

"People who mess with plants," she says while May's hands are six inches deep in the garden bed, "should know what they're doing."

May grins wickedly, yanking up a clump of stinging nettle, a plant which can cause a terrifically painful rash but also restores important nutrients after childbirth.

Faith rolls her eyes. She's 12 going on 30, her greatest ambition to be the opposite of May in every way. She scorches her naturally curly hair into pin-straight lines every morning and comes home from sleepovers with her eyelids painted blue. She still loves indoor things, but also rock music, horror movies, and magazines of shirtless, long-haired boys. Though she plans a medicinal herb demonstration for the science fair, she tells May in no uncertain times that she doesn't need her help.

"This is *science*," she says. "How plants grow and actually help people, not some snake oil you sell on your front porch."

May barely flinches now, but she does rub at the pain in her head that accompanies each jab. No amount of willow tonic can dent it. It doesn't surprise her when Edward shows up that night with peat pots, poster board, and a variety of common herbs—chamomile, calendula, lemon balm and lavender. Over the years, he's made it his business to know the words to Faith's favorite songs and which teen heartthrob is worthy of a poster on her wall. He and May attend every piano recital together, but it's Edward who Faith searches for in the crowd. The one who wins her affection by simply showing up.

Edward denies Faith nothing.

"Haven't I given her enough unhappiness already?" he says to May after buying their daughter an entire new wardrobe and letting her bring half a dozen friends to his house, where they stay up all night painting each other's toenails and eating ice cream.

When Faith sleeps at her father's house, May walks into the woods. Not to the grove, but to a ridge that was so scorched by wildfire, not even fireweed can take root. Oddly, it's in a place where nothing grows that she feels most at peace. Nothing to fix or nurture or offer a sip of water. Just black earth, dead trees, and a rip-roaring wind in her ears.

Until her sisters come knocking, breaking their long silence with a rush of adrenaline through her veins. May leaps to her feet, her heart hammering against her chest.

She wants to slide down the cliff and run, but she has no idea where to go.

Her sisters are taunting her. They have a secret, and she's the last creature on the planet they'll tell.

✦

May isn't surprised when Faith's crush on Paul stalls. At 18, Francie's son graduates high school and immediately buys a beat-up van to live in while he bops around the country. A year behind him, Faith is the top student in her class and has her pick of colleges. The few times Paul comes home for a visit, Faith is too busy to see him.

What does shock May is the day Paul abruptly comes home for good. Thirty states and six months of open roads and freedom are enough for him, apparently, because suddenly he's going to follow in his father's footsteps and become an attorney. While Bill and Francie throw a party to celebrate their son's bright future, May corners Paul by the buffet to ask him if he's out of his mind.

"Since when did you have any interest in the law?"

The young man shrugs and runs his fingers through his newly shorn dark hair. She preferred it long and scraggly, preferable sporting a pine needle or two.

"Turns out you can't live on fresh air alone," he replies.

May wrinkles her nose at his spicy aftershave. It's pleasant, but she preferred the smell of mud.

"You used to climb trees," she says.

"That was a long time ago, May." He grabs one of the crab cakes and pops it into his mouth. "People grow up."

May narrows her eyes. She doesn't care for his fancy, new suit either, or his shiny shoes.

"You can never outgrow who you are," she replies.

But perhaps she's wrong. For the next four years, Paul studies hard and graduates summa cum laude with a degree in business, then applies to the University of Idaho College of Law. His transformation from nature child to future esquire captures Faith's fancy all over again, and a year after Paul enters law school, May's daughter and Francie's son go on their first date. Six months later, they announce their engagement.

Their wedding takes place on a crystal clear autumn day. Edward walks Faith down the aisle, holding back tears until she turns to hug him. When he finally takes his seat beside May, she squeezes his hand, her own eyes bone dry.

She's wouldn't be anywhere but right here, watching her daughter marry Paul, yet when Edward whispers in her ear, "I'm so happy," she can't say the same. She won't tell him that her bones ache; they've ached for years. She still walks miles, but every step is a struggle, as if the ground beneath her has turned to mush. Once, when she was deep in the woods, it even rumbled and knocked her from her feet. No tree limbs or needles fell with her. The tremor was just for her.

It's been easy to hold it all in, to keep what's happening to her locked away behind a silent, crusty exterior. She was born for this, after all. Edward's surveys have been transformed into plat maps for forest subdivisions, and May's equilibrium is off. She needs a walking stick to keep her balance—two, if Edward's with her. The warnings are incessant.

Get away. You're not safe with him anymore.

After the ceremony, May slips out of the church. Autumn belongs to the larches, who gild the mountainsides with swaths of gold. Edward comes up behind her and wraps his arms around her waist. "It's a perfect wedding day," he says. "Faith is so happy."

May nods. She's becoming more tree-like by the minute. Losing her words again. All her secrets tucked inside.

"It's almost time for the father-daughter dance," he continues. "Faith and I have been practicing."

He turns her around in his arms, his face shining with such joy that of course she doesn't tell him.

Trees do not forget.

Nineteen

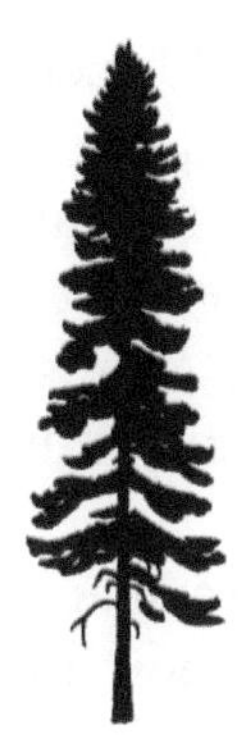

Sitka Spruce
(Picea sitchensis)

More than a century of logging has decimated the spruce forest, but the trees that remain are a sight to behold. The Sitka Spruce is the third largest conifer in the world and can live more than 700 years. Native Americans utilized the spruce's pitch for canoe caulk, glue, and varnish, but more importantly, they believed the boughs held mystical powers. Studies of Sitka spruce trees in Scotland suggest they have traces of supernovae in their trunks.

✦

The winter after Faith and Paul's wedding, northern Idaho receives a record snowpack. The summit above May's house accumulates over 120 inches, three times the usual amount, keeping Edward in the office instead of out in the field. After work, he comes to May's house to split and stack firewood—still from downed trees he finds in the woods—and often stays the night. May snuggles into his warmth, watching the snow fall outside her window, wishing that winter would never end.

But March brings warmer temperatures and daily rainstorms that turn the snow to slush. When the clouds finally clear, people emerge from their homes, smiling and blinking at the sunlight. May, on the other hand, feels only dread. Her garden beds dry out, but she doesn't plant her pea seeds. She moves slowly, stiffly—if she moves at all. Her legs creak with every step, her tongue feels wooden. Once again, she can go days without speaking a single word.

It's only when she and Edward are making love that her skin warms, and she remembers that she's made of blood and bone. With him, slowness is her saving grace, a chance to imprint the feel and taste of him on her brain. She keeps the light on, running her fingers and lips over every inch of him. He laughs and tells her she's incorrigible.

"Can't get enough of me, huh?" he asks.

"Not even close," she replies. "Maybe it's time you move in here."

"And tame the witch?" he asks, smiling. "I don't think so."

She gives him a house key, but he never uses it. The nights he sleeps alone at his cabin, he knocks on her door first thing in the morning—an overeager suitor coming to call. While the forest roads remain washed out and impassable, he lingers in her bed. Then one morning, they hear the rumble of motor graders clearing the roads.

"Time to go back to work, I guess," Edward says, even as he kisses the sweat on her neck. "I'm going to be putting in crazy hours until I catch up."

He starts to rise, but May pulls him back. It's not hard to convince him to stay. She's thankful he hasn't shaved, so she can savor the feel of his whiskers on her lips. It's not pleasure she feels when he slips inside her once more—that's for people with time—but focus. She's in a race to memorize it all—the downy hairs on the back of his neck, the feel of his hips rocking against hers, the whisper of his breath in her ear.

He comes slowly, in the way of a man who believes he has all the time in the world, and she clings to him. Edward holds her tightly as her tears slip onto his shoulder.

"Was I that terrible?" he asks.

Even now, he can make her laugh. Every day, he grows more boyish, as if he's going back in time, making up for all of it.

"Edward," she says, "don't go up the mountain."

He pulls back to look at her, but his smile doesn't falter. "I'd love to stay with you, but I really do have to get up there. I promise I'll come straight back to you after work."

She knows how crazy her next words will sound, but she says them anyway.

"Something's going to happen. In the woods. I don't know what, but I think you need to stay here. Please stay."

He takes her face between his hands, smiling tenderly. "You don't have to worry about me. I know the woods almost as well as you do."

"Edward, you have to listen to me."

But he doesn't have to do anything. He's the man she's always wanted him to be—confident, unafraid, sure.

"I told you no one will ever make me leave you again," he says.

No *one*.

He kisses her lightly, breezily, then gets up to dress. Jeans, jacket, his work boots laced tight. May's throat closes; even if she had more words, she doubts she has enough breath left to say them. And the truth is that she could be wrong. Even if her body feels wooden and slow, she's no longer privy to all of the forest's secrets.

So she lumbers to her feet and puts on her clothes. Edward presses one more quick kiss to her forehead before stepping away from the bed.

"Should I bring something home for dinner?"

She forces a smile and says, "No, I'll make your favorite. We'll celebrate you getting back on the job."

He winks at her and is out the door without another word.

She watches from the window as he drives away, then closes every blind in the house. She spends the day doing chores in slow motion—dusting the mantel for 15 minutes, taking hours to clean the toilet and sink. When the wind picks up, she turns on the television. She sits on the couch, eyes closed, trying to find comfort in the sound of human voices.

A client comes to the back door for a bottle of goldenrod cough syrup, but otherwise May doesn't open the door. She feels a dull ache all over, but nothing like the stabbing pains she gets when she walks through the woods. It's hard to accept that, after all these years, she's safer inside.

Hours pass and thankfully even dread grows a little tiresome. After imagining a dozen worst case scenarios, May's stomach rumbles for a bowl of pea soup. After lunch, she changes the bedsheets and picks up her apothecary chest—which Edward repaired for her with a new set of drawers. Afternoon sunlight peeks around the blinds as she sorts this year's seeds and tells herself that, when Edward comes home, she will decide what she will plant tomorrow. She starts preparing his favorite meal—spaghetti and meatballs, with her homemade sauce rather than the one he used to pour from the jar.

The people on the television launch into an elaborately choreographed dance, so it's a moment before she realizes the jingling sound is coming not from the music, but from the phone on the wall.

She sets down the bag of pasta. It could be Faith or Francie or a salesman peddling a shiny new vacuum. She doesn't even have to answer it; she can watch another dance number and go on pretending that fate can't slip through the door.

Except that she feels like she's falling. The floorboards are solid beneath her feet, but she sways. She takes a deep breath and snatches the phone. It's Edward's coworker on the line, a 250 pound man with a booming voice that has shrunk to a whisper. May slumps against the wall.

"May . . . it's about Edward," the man says. "I was headed to my truck. I thought he was right behind me. I . . . I don't know why he stopped. Wh-when I looked back, he was just standing there, looking out over the view. It's a beautiful view. And then . . . the whole slope gave way —trees, rocks, Edward, all of it. It must have been all the snow we had this year, then the rain on top of that. He had no time to run . . . It was a massive avalanche. It's going to take time to even find his . . . May? I'm so sorry. He's gone."

May has no memory of ending the conversation. She might have hung up on the man; she doesn't much care. She makes a sound—more like a bleating than a cry. At some point, she finds herself on the floor, curled up tight.

Her sisters return without satisfaction or glee. No signals or warnings—just the presence of other living things. Edward took what they loved; they took who May loved. The forest is cruel, but it's balanced. They won't leave her again.

She will have to call Faith, but not yet. First, she will sit in silence with the family she came from. Wait until she can summon the strength to be a mother again.

It's dark before she uncoils her body. The television has turned to news that doesn't matter at all. She stares at the coffee table in the living room—the one Edward bought even though she told him it was made of black walnut, a tree that forms a death zone around itself so nothing else can grow. May wonders now what she was thinking, allowing it into her house. Or why she never told him plainly that trees, like calm water, might look gentle, but they can kill you just the same.

Faith and Paul rent a modern condo across town that May is fairly certain Paul hates. Dark and sleek, with concrete floors and a dizzying mirrored backsplash, it's no place to tell a daughter that her father has died. And even if it was, Faith is rarely there. With Paul still in law school, May's daughter is the main breadwinner, working long hours at some environmental regulatory compliance agency, where she finally gets to tell people, and nature, what to do.

So May picks up the phone.

"Paul," she says, when her son-in-law answers, "can you bring Faith here when she gets home from work? Edward's dead."

She could try to soften her words, but Paul is a hard man to shake. After the smallest gasp, he says only, "I'm so sorry, May." He's never been one to ask questions or fuss. Even as a baby, his tears stopped the moment you took him outside.

He'd have made a splendid tree. A ponderosa, perhaps. Silent, thick and sturdy. But she's doubtful that he'll make a very good lawyer.

"Please let me be the one to tell Faith," May continues.

"Of course," Paul replies. "I'll bring her over as soon as she gets home."

After she hangs up, May looks around her living room, hating everything in it. The toxic coffee table, the pile of magazines Edward likes—liked—to read, the grandfather clock he fixed, his half-finished cup of coffee still sitting on the counter. May stomps across the room to turn off the television and, in a burst of fury, swipes the magazines onto the floor. She lets loose a scream she hopes the whole mountain can hear.

Everything has changed, including her sisters. Instead of the silence she's after, they chatter and gab nonstop. May knows the temperature in the grove and which of them are currently being defoliated by sawflies. Her oldest sister is hogging all the rainwater; the plastic water bottles a hiker discarded leach chemicals that keep the earthworms away. May's husband dies, and they send each other signals about root rot. Sociopaths, the lot of them, but a cold comfort nonetheless.

May grabs the edge of the coffee table and drags it across the floor. She means to be rough, thumping the monstrosity out the back door and down the steps to the patio. With a shriek that echoes up the mountain, she heaves the table onto her compost pile.

Then she gathers kindling—wood chips, needles, the newspaper she uses to keep the weeds down—and stuffs it between the compost and table. She finds the matches by the barbecue. She'll never again be squeamish about watching wood burn.

The walnut is dense and resistant to fire, but the kindling and compost beneath it erupt. May adds more newspaper until the table begins to smolder. Black walnut produces juglone, a chemical that's toxic to some plants and animals, but May still takes a good long breath. How much more can she possibly hurt? She drops a rotting fence post on top of the table, then one of her wooden Adirondack chairs for good measure. The bonfire is ten feet tall and raging by the time Faith walks into the yard.

"Mom?"

May glances past her to the road, where Paul sits in their car, waiting to pick up whatever pieces of his wife he'll be left with. May's tears sizzle like sap when they fall into the flames. Years ago, Faith wanted to know if fairies and magic are real. There's no better time to find out than when the world has gone dark.

"Mom, what's going on? Is that your furniture?"

Faith complains about being the witch's daughter, but May thinks what she really hates is having no magic of her own. The witch's *daughter*. The one who wore a crown of larches when her mother was the larch herself. But daughters are the ones who carry on the story. Or, if they're like Faith, they write something entirely new.

"Your father found me up there," May says, gesturing toward the mountain. "For months, he tried to tell himself I was just foreign or suffering from some farfetched amnesia, but he knew. You know, Faith."

"Know what, Mom?" Faith replies. "It's late and I'm tired."

Some people wail when they grieve, some rage, but May will grow stronger again without Edward, and also more brittle. A number of her sisters are diseased and decaying from the inside out, yet they'll live for years with holes in their heartwood. You don't have to be whole to survive.

May's legs creak again as she heads to Edward's work bench. He'd been working on shutters for her windows, carving a larch tree into each one. He'd hiked to the grove himself to find one of her fallen sisters for the panels. When storms came, he told her, he wanted her to be protected by the ones she loved.

But she's always been protected. She has the strength of the forest behind her, while Faith has only her.

So May picks up the shutter Edward had been carving just yesterday, the larch missing half its crown, and throws it on top of the flames. Faith cries out and, without thinking, reaches for the shutter. May snatches her daughter's hand from the fire the way she did when Faith was a child.

"Don't be silly," May says. "It's already gone."

Faith looks from her to the fire. Science has gotten her this far, but it'll take a leap of faith for her to admit that her mother's hand now feels rough as wood. It's intuition, not science, that allows her to look at a burning shutter and know that her father is gone.

"No," Faith says. "Mom, no!"

Children don't grow up, not really. Oh, they do adult things—get married, find jobs, raise their own babies—but when you take away the parent they loved best, they still cry out as if they're all alone in the world. May gathers Faith into her arms, holding her tightly while she explains what happened. The avalanche, the last view he had. The beautiful view. Faith shakes her head and sobs.

"No," she keeps saying. "It's not true."

But she knows it is. Edward left her again, left her with the witch, the one who she knows, deep down, is something different, the parent she loves least. Even with the vast vocabulary that May has amassed, there are no words that will bring any comfort. So she merely waits until her daughter's sobs subside into quiet, heartrending whimpers. Then she speaks of the trees.

"The forest is a living thing," May says, "but the thing most people don't realize is that the core of every tree is dead."

Faith pulls away and shakes her head. "Mom, please. Not now."

May smiles at her. When has she ever listened to anybody?

"They call the core heartwood," May continues. "It had its day in the sun, but as it ages it grows inward and is no longer a part of the tree's daily functions. Yet it's the very thing that holds that tree up in a storm."

As the fire pops, the charred skeletons of the shutter, chair, and walnut table glow red with embers. Faith's shoulders tremble, but she doesn't make a sound.

"Human or tree, the longer you live, the more weight you bear," May says.

May returns to Edward's bench for another shutter. She is about to throw it onto the fire when Faith grabs her arm.

"I'll never be as strong as you," her daughter says. "He hasn't been dead a day and you're already burning his things."

May wishes Faith was right—that she'll never need to carry her family's burdens and sorrows, but that's not the way of things. Trees, as they say, hold up the sky.

"You'll do fine," May says and holds out the shutter. "You really think you need this to remember him?"

Faith hesitates, then takes the shutter as May steps back into the shadows—where trees and mothers live. With a cry of rage and despair, Faith launches Edward's beautiful creation into the fire and stands tall as she watches it burn.

Twenty

Western Hemlock
(Tsuga heterophylla)

Western Hemlocks don't realize how beautiful they are. Long and lean as ballerinas, they never take center stage. The gawky teenagers of the tree world, they slouch and lurk in the shadows, hoping you'll pass them right by. Their root systems are shallow and, at the first sign of trouble or wind, they'll often give up and simply fall over. Which is a shame because hemlock bark is useful for tanning hides, and the wood has an even grain that resists scraping, making it easy to turn into doors and staircases. Tsuga is from the Japanese Tsu-ga, which means tree mother.

✦

May's core turned to heartwood the day Edward died. Francie fusses over her, pitying her loveless, lonely existence, but there's a benefit to going a little dead inside—the rod of steely wood at the heart of her holds the rest of her sorry self up.

She burns everything. After the walnut table, she torches her wooden bowls and all her clothes—every last piece she owns. She prefers to wear Edward's wardrobe anyway. His clothes don't bind her and they smell of him. His leather boots, wool coat, boxy cargo pants. Now that she's no longer the object of anyone's desire, she burns her hairbrush and breaks all the mirrors. She lets her hair grow long and wild and stops cleaning the dirt from beneath her fingernails. The grooves on her fingertips grow steadily deeper; her elbows sprout rough, brown gnarls. She throws away her gardening gloves and harvests stinging nettle without pain.

Angel, Vern, Edward. Yes, she's one of the lucky ones, with people still left to lose, but she's had quite enough of human sorrow, thank you very much. One afternoon, she walks to the stream, where the black hawthorns grow rampantly, and snaps off a dozen of their one-inch maroon spikes. It's a bloody business, crisscrossing the thorns into a star shape and tying them together with red string, and she's glad. A mother's blood is said to add to the protection spell. After dark, May walks across town to slip the amulet under Faith and Paul's doormat. Her daughter will likely find it and throw it out, but May will just make more. The hawthorn has long been linked to the fairies, its thorns a barrier to sorrow and loss.

The only thing that scares her now is living without Faith. She's no longer fazed by earthquakes, or even the burly neighbor who chains half a dozen dogs in his yard.

May simply stomps onto his property with a bolt cutter and sets them all free.

She has a bonfire every month. When she runs out of furniture to burn, she dismantles Edward's workbench and shed for firewood. Faith calls her a ghoul and secrets away all the pictures of her father.

"I can see him better with my eyes closed anyway," May tells her. "Trees never forget a thing, you know."

Faith rolls her eyes. "You're not turning to wood, Mom."

But even she must notice the wrinkly rings that have formed around May's neck.

Of course May is changing. Before the avalanche, she belonged to Edward. Now she belongs to no one—not to Francie or Faith or even to her sisters, who fill her mind with visions of starlight and nourishing rains. She won't go back to the grove to face her sisters and Edward's thorny wall until her daughter comes with her.

Faith, however, isn't interested.

She's busy, still working long hours despite the fact that Paul has passed the bar and landed a job as an associate attorney at a mid-sized firm. She's safe, the amulet still under her doormat, but Faith remains as unimpressed as ever by the secret and sometimes sensational lives of trees.

So May shows up on her doorstep every Saturday morning, Edward's hiking boots on her feet.

"How about a walk to the grove today?" she asks.

"I told you, Mom, I use the treadmill at the gym."

May merely shrugs, and returns the next day. For two months, they play this dull game, until one morning Faith is waiting by her door, dressed in her gym clothes.

"You're not going to stop, are you?" Faith asks.

May grins. "Never."

Faith still hates walking, but her pace to the grove is quick. "Let's get this nonsense done," she says.

May's heart skips a beat when she sees the hedge of devil's club, now over nine feet tall. The tunnel Edward carved beneath it has been filled with debris, but May merely pulls a hand shovel and pruning shears out of her pockets.

"Are you kidding?" Faith says. "This will take hours."

Only two hours, in fact, before May clears a new path beneath the spiky leaves. After they crawl through and emerge in the grove, May looks first at the tree she came from, the old bear wound starting to rot. When she finally turns to her sisters, she waits for a fury that never comes. Human hatred is as exhausting as sorrow, or perhaps her heart has simply turned to wood, too. Either way, she's no different than them—a little rotted in places, but still standing.

Faith rustles around behind her. "Can we get on with this?"

May takes a deep breath and turns to her daughter. "Your father planted all this devil's club," she says.

Faith looks at the hedge and reaches for one of the large leaves, only to come away with yellow spikes in her flesh.

"Why on earth would he do that?" she asks, wincing.

"For me," May replies, then gestures at her sisters. "For them."

She could tell her daughter that the root systems of trees look eerily similar to the bronchi of human lungs, but Faith already knows this. She'd call it science, not evidence of some fantastical connection between people and trees.

So May speaks, instead, of a fact that can't be refuted.

"You're pregnant."

Faith hangs her head. She wants children, but didn't plan on one coming so soon. She and Paul just made an offer on a house on Sheep Creek and, as May predicted, Paul isn't happy with his job. She doesn't know what the man expected, but apparently drafting briefs isn't it, and he and Faith fight about it. Their plans were to save their money, buy a new car, take some time to solidify their relationship before devoting themselves to someone else.

"A baby is a blessing that ruins all your plans," May says. "This one's a girl. There's some sass in there, that's all I know."

Faith walks along the circle of devil's club, reaching for it the way she once reached for her father's hand, then drawing back.

"We were waiting until after the first trimester to tell everyone," she says. "I've already seen Dr. Seymour. We're doing this the normal way. I doubt he'll let me take any of your remedies."

May doesn't mention that Dr. Seymour himself has shown up on her doorstep a time or two for something to give him a little more oomph in the bedroom.

"You can do this any way you please," May says. "It's your baby."

Faith puts a hand on her hip. "If you knew I was pregnant, you shouldn't have made me walk all the way up here."

These days, when May sighs, it sounds like the rustling of needles, but Faith hasn't paid attention to her for ages.

"Walking is good for you. I used to hike here all the time when I was pregnant with you."

Faith snickers. "Yes, but you grew up in a tree, right? So maybe you had a bit of an advantage."

"Ah," May says, "you figured it out."

Faith throws up her hands. "I didn't figure out anything except that you lie. You're not going to tell my child this ridiculous fairy tale. The crazy stops with me."

Words, May hopes, will soon mean nothing to her. They'll filter through layers of bark and wood until they're nothing but a sound wave, bouncing off her and echoing somewhere else.

Faith keeps one hand on her stomach and the other clenched in a fist. She'll have her own battles, no doubt, with the daughter she'll bear. It's possible she'll even raise a believer.

"Let's head back," May says. "I'm sorry I put you out."

Faith unclenches her fist. For a moment, it looks as if she might say something, but then she bites her lip and silently follows May out of the grove.

✦

Seven months later, May sits in the hospital waiting room with Francie and Bill. She offered to help Faith with her delivery, but her daughter prefers Dr. Seymour's arsenal of forceps, anesthesia, and heavy pain medications.

Francie frantically knits two pairs of socks, one pink and one blue, despite May's adamancy that the baby is a girl. Her friend wears her red hair in a bun now that she's working at Bill's firm, managing the front office. Sometimes she puts in more hours than Bill does. The secretaries all call her Mrs. Greene and do everything she asks.

Bill, on the other hand, plans to take a whole month off to help with the new baby. The man who never changed his son's diaper is suddenly asking May's opinion on onesies versus footsie pajamas.

"I was so busy working when Paul was little," he tells May. "I didn't do right by him. I know I didn't. I'm hoping Paul gives me a chance to do better."

Francie sets down her socks and glances toward the labor and delivery wing.

"You don't think Faith's having a problem, do you?" she asks. "It's been hours."

"It's always hours," May says. "I'm sure everything is fine."

But the clicking of Francie's knitting needles gets on her nerves. In truth, she has no idea what's happening in the delivery room. In the last month, Faith stopped returning May's phone calls and refused the red raspberry tonic that would have toned her uterus and perhaps even shortened her labor. Paul explained that late pregnancy had worn Faith down and made her brusque with everyone, but that was a lie. Faith stopped talking to May during the baby shower, when May showed up wearing Edward's jacket and clunky boots.

"Thanks for dressing up for me, Mom," Faith had said when May stepped onto the porch.

May looked down at her outfit. Clothes had been the last thing on her mind when she'd been buying toys and blankets and tiny shoes for her future granddaughter. But when she offered the gifts to Faith, her daughter merely shook her head.

"I'll open them later, okay? I think you should go home or on one of those walks in the woods that you love so much. I'm worried about you, you know. You've really let yourself go."

May stood on the porch with her shower gifts as her daughter went back inside. She could have argued, but Faith was partially right. May hadn't let herself go; she'd let go. Of her sisters and Edward and ever becoming the kind of mother Faith wants. All that's left now is meeting the little person who might be the last love of her life.

The baby comes in the middle of the night. It's a girl, of course, and they name her Brianna. Francie is allowed in first, then Bill. May stares out the window at the parking lot, so no one will see the face of the woman who might not be allowed to hold her own granddaughter. Finally, Bill and Francie reemerge, grinning from ear to ear.

"Go on in now, May," Bill says. "They want you."

Air rushes back into her lungs as Francie hugs her. Bill kisses the top of her head.

"How lucky are we?" he says.

Faith is in bed, holding the baby. Paul stands beside her, beaming. Brianna looks like every other newborn—battered and bruised, with a cone-shaped head. May already adores her, but she keeps her hands in her pockets and doesn't ask for a single thing.

Then Faith holds the baby out to her and starts sobbing.

"If she ever treats me how I've treated you, it will break my heart," she wails. "I'm so sorry, Mom."

✦

Brianna is colicky, willful, and impossible to soothe. She startles easily, hates her crib, and never sleeps longer than two hours at a time. Faith and Paul try white noise, pacifiers, and a variety of swaddling techniques and formulas, but they still stumble around the house like zombies, serenaded by Brianna's screams.

May arrives one afternoon to find Faith slumped on her porch stoop with Brianna in her arms, both of them sobbing.

"Oh, for Pete's sake," May says. "Let me take her home with me for the night. I promise she'll be alive in the morning."

Faith must be desperate, because she instantly hands over Brianna and races for the diaper bag. May wrangles Brianna into her stroller, where she screams as if she's been set on a bed of nails.

Kissing Faith goodbye, May heads toward the hills. They'll go the long way, out past the cottonwoods, where no one will complain about the racket. Brianna's got pipes, that's for sure, screaming for 90 minutes straight before sinking into a deep, bone-weary sleep. She was born with a head of black hair that fell out quickly and is now coming in blonde. When she's not pinching up her face to scream, she has dimples and shockingly blue eyes. Obviously, she's going to be trouble. May can't wait to see what unfolds.

When they finally reach home, May maneuvers the stroller into the kitchen so Brianna can slumber on. Perfect moments pass the quickest, so May savors this one, sitting quietly in her warm kitchen while her granddaughter sleeps. She doesn't stir until Brianna does, then makes a tea of fennel, chamomile and ginger, along with one drop of the belladonna tincture she was too afraid to give to Faith. There's no fear now; she knows what she's doing. Witches only grow more powerful with age.

The moment Brianna cries, May adds a spoonful of the tea to her formula and carries the baby to the front porch. Brianna suckles greedily before letting out an enormous burp. She's quiet and alert for all of five minutes before her shrieking begins anew. Faith wasn't lying; Brianna's go-to mood is abject misery. She screams before she even opens her eyes, her face already red and furious. May brings her into bed with her, gently patting her back and offering another spoonful of tea with every feeding. May has a sleepless night, but when Brianna wakes at dawn, she takes one more bottle and doesn't cry for a full hour.

Faith arrives at nine to find Brianna on her back on the rug, laughing as she plays with her feet. Faith's shoulders slump as she turns to May.

"Give me the tea," she says.

Turns out Brianna isn't the last person May gets to love. Faith gives birth to a second daughter, Polly, three years after Brianna is born. Polly is everything Brianna is not—dark-haired, quiet, easy to soothe. Brianna takes no interest in her chubby little sister, but Polly lights up whenever Brianna walks into the room.

Bill's plan to help out for a month after Brianna was born turned into two months, then six, then indefinitely after he quit the firm. The man who starched his shirts and wore polished wingtips to the grocery store now dons sweatpants and a hoodie that reads "World's Best

Grandpa." He babysits every day, making homemade play dough and changing a dirty diaper in thirty seconds flat.

May meets him by the river most days, collecting herbs while Bill pushes the double stroller. May shows her young granddaughters every root and flower, but whenever Polly asks for the petals, Brianna swipes them out of her hands.

"Brianna!" Bill says for the umpteenth time, giving Brianna a stern glare—which their oldest granddaughter patently ignores.

"She's as prickly as I am," Bill says to May, though they both know that's no longer true. Brianna wear the bristly crown now; Bill is too busy making hand puppets and huckleberry animal pancakes to even compete.

The World's Best Grandpa soothes Polly with one of the ever-present lollipops in his pocket.

"Me too, Papa," Brianna says.

Bill sighs, but hands her a sucker. "I go home everyday and fall asleep instantly," he says. "I never thought that would be a good thing, but it is. Francie thinks I'm crazy."

Francie has been promoted twice and is now an executive secretary to one of the founding partners at Bill's old law firm. It's surreal to see her in a suit every day while Bill sings along with Snow White.

He and Paul watch the game together every Sunday. Paul must not have told his father that he's unhappy with his job because every time Bill talks about Paul's law career, he beams. The man practically oozes contentment, which is all you can ask for if you're going to die suddenly in your sleep. The coroner rules the cause of death a heart attack; May likes to think that it happened in the middle of some tender, grandfatherly dream.

Francie throws an elaborate funeral, complete with gold leaf programs and a men's choir, followed by a catered dinner at her house. She chooses the same tablescape she had at their wedding—blue floral china and silver goblets—and doesn't shed a single tear the whole day, not even when

Paul delivers the eulogy while holding Polly in his arms. But when May stays late to help her clean up, Francie goes into the bathroom and beats her fists against the wall.

May keeps vigil doing the dishes and gathering the photos of Bill they set out, most of them taken recently, when he would actually smile for the camera. The banging in the bathroom eventually trails off, but Francie doesn't emerge.

May steps up to the door. She can hear Francie sniffling, but when she asks her friend if she's okay, there's no reply.

"Francie?"

Francie throws open the door, her fists as swollen and red as her eyes. "There were some days when I didn't even like him."

May's mouth twitches. "Only some days?"

Francie elbows her, chuckling, then her face falls.

"That's love," May says, pulling her friend into her arms. "You love Bill."

Sobbing, Francie replies, "I r-really do."

Loving someone who is no longer with you is like trying to remember your favorite book by heart. You'll never forget the ending, but over time you'll get parts of the story wrong. In the year after Bill's death, Francie talks about him as if he always had lollipops in his pockets and never once drove her mad. It's a happy, carefree tale that tidies up the first chapter of her life so that she can move on to the next one. In California.

His name is Manuel, and though Francie wasn't looking to fall in love again, she says she couldn't help it because he's divine. Dark-haired, a few years younger than her, with a dancer's physique and a luscious Portuguese accent. They met backstage after one of his ballets and have been dating long distance, but now Manuel wants her to move in with him in Los Angeles. Francie cries when it's time to leave her granddaughters, but a few weeks later, she sends a postcard.

'*We eloped!*' she writes. '*Hopefully Paul will approve.*'

Paul thinks they're acting like hasty, lovesick teenagers, but he's glad his mother is happy. Nevertheless, Francie's absence lets the air out of the room. Not only did she fill the silences, she gossiped and gushed and laughed more than the rest of them combined. No secret was safe when she was around, but now they're riddled with them.

Paul has stopped complaining about his job. In fact, he doesn't talk about the law firm at all. Faith drops the girls off at preschool every morning—even though Brianna hates it—then works a full day before picking them up again and making dinner. She's far too tired to worry about the things her husband won't say.

Of course, no one finds May's long silences odd. Nor do they wonder at her absences. There's no one left to notice that she rarely sleeps at home anymore. The summer nights are warm, and the grove more welcoming than her empty bedroom. Tonight, as always, she sleeps on a bed of needles and wakes to a tug on her hair. She's partial to the crooked sister whose branch shyly snags her, since the larch tree shouldn't even be alive. A large patch of brown rot is feasting on her trunk, turning her wood to brittle cubes that break away at the slightest touch. At this point, the hollow in her sister's core is nearly large enough for a bashful girl to hide inside.

May enjoys the morning with her, then heads home as slowly as she can. The longer she stays in the forest, the more words she forgets. First to go are the fluffy adjectives, followed by the fancy names of plants better identified by their stems and leaves. She hums a tune she once knew the words to, her mind blissfully blank, until she crosses the stream to find Faith standing by her back door, a howling child in each arm.

"I need you," May's daughter says.

As May's granddaughters rush toward her, Faith explains that the preschool won't accept Polly anymore. While Brianna is nearing kindergarten and likes to show off by reciting the alphabet backwards, two-year-old Polly speaks only one word: Baba. Everything is Baba, from her blanket to the sky to May herself.

"I couldn't believe it," Faith says, brushing back tears. "They're not equipped to handle her, apparently, like she has some kind of disease."

May kisses Brianna's forehead, then turns to her youngest granddaughter and taps her own chest. Polly's eyes light up.

"Baba!" the girl says with delight.

May doesn't understand the problem. The child is two; words will come. Maybe not at the speed the preschool or Faith would like, but at some point Polly will scream obscenities and complain about her parents like everybody else. But Faith is beside herself.

"I've already found a speech therapist," she says, "and I'll get her ears checked again. But if you can, I really need you to watch the girls during the day until Brianna goes to kindergarten and I can find another preschool."

It might be bliss to be alone in the woods, but it's better to be needed. So May—now Baba—stays away from the grove in favor of mornings at the playground with her granddaughters. After lunch, they wade into the creek behind May's house. The girls sit in the cool, shallow water, searching for water skippers and shiny stones. Brianna declares herself the diamond queen and tells Polly that, if she follows orders, she can be her ruby princess.

"Baba," Polly says.

One hot afternoon, Baba takes off her heavy boots and dips her swollen feet into the water. They burn all the time and are an odd shade of purple. She takes a daily tincture of rosemary, ginkgo and butcher's broom to help improve circulation, but so far it's not doing much.

She's tired. She loves her granddaughters, but they wear her out. Some nights, she's asleep by seven, and she dreams of quiet things—caves and burrows and long, dark winters when nothing stirs.

Today, the diamond queen marches confidently across the river while her ruby princess traces the whorl-like veins on the back of Baba's hand. Polly's hair is a rich, earthy brown, while her own has turned as stiff and gray as last season's needles.

The girl finally toddles off after her sister. Baba reads them fairytales every afternoon, but stays quiet about her own story. Not only because she promised Faith, but because she's old news. She's far more interested in what's going to happen next.

That night, after Paul picks up the girls, Baba stands in her backyard, staring at the woods. She sees things now—a pair of dark eyes in the dry rot of that larch tree, and Edward standing a few feet from her, leaning against the trunk of a river birch. She even smells his scent of sawdust and wool before the vision fades.

A week later, while Faith and Brianna are off registering for kindergarten, Polly looks up from stacking rocks in the stream and says, "There. Him." As if she's been speaking with ghosts all along.

Baba sees nothing but shadows. Edward is dead; he's not building a wall of devil's club or coming back to her ever again. Yet her heart races. *Him.* The scent of wool and sawdust builds as Polly smiles up at her.

"Yes," Baba tells her, even though she sees nothing. "That's your grandpa."

Over time, Edward grows bolder, slipping into Baba's dreams and staying a bit even after she wakes. Early one morning, when the bed sinks as if someone is settling in beside her, she dares to reach out. Edward's pillow remains empty, the air there ice cold.

"Him," she says, rolling closer. For just a moment, she sees a pair of heartwood-colored eyes.

Twenty One

Amur Maple
(Acer ginnala)

The Amur maple is the most prolific of the maples, content to lie low, shrub-like, while quietly producing over 5000 seeds a season—many of which travel long distances by wind to spring up in woodlands, bogs, and otherwise meticulously landscaped backyards. Unlike the sugar maple, which is magnificent but sensitive to compaction, heat, drought, and road salt, the Amur maple will take over your yard even in the poorest of conditions. With strong root systems, the trees are difficult to pull out; even when chopped down, the Amur maple will likely resprout.

✦

Certainly, Baba is the star of her own story, but her final chapter is hijacked by Brianna—or, rather, Bree, now that Faith's eldest daughter insists her given name is lame. At 14, Bree is a girl who eats pizza, laughs at knock knock jokes, and plans to go to college. By 15, she's a skeletal, stoned mess.

She met a boy. Baba doesn't care to remember his name. He's not important. What matters is how much Bree has been willing to give up for him: Family, friends, ambition, honesty, thirty pounds she can't afford to lose. There are drugs involved. Faith and Paul constantly debate which kind and the crimes that Bree might be committing to acquire them. Their only other topic of conversation is why, in the midst of all this, Paul abruptly quit his job.

They never argue in front of the girls, but sometimes Baba is so quiet, they forget that she's still in the room when they lay into each other.

"As if worrying about Bree every minute isn't enough!" Faith rails at her husband as Baba stands still as a tree by the door. "Now I also have to clean up the mess from my husband's midlife crisis."

"It's not a crisis, Faith," Paul says quietly. "That career was killing me. You know that. I'd have been no good to any of you if I stayed at the firm."

"You're no good to us now!" Faith cries. "Do you know the kind of looks I get when I tell people my husband wants to be a wood carver? That's a hobby, Paul, not a profession. What are you trying to prove? That you're not your father? Say what you will about Bill, but even on his worst day, the man took care of his wife and child!"

Paul stiffens. "I've talked to shops and buyers. I know I can make money at this. I wouldn't have quit if I didn't think I could provide for you and the girls."

"Well, that's great, Paul, but meanwhile I'm out there working my tail off and making excuses for you."

"I never asked you to do that," Paul snaps. "Why does it even matter to you what other people think?"

Baba has been asking Faith this question for years, but when her daughter starts crying, she knows Paul won't get a clear answer either. She slips out of the house, unnoticed, fairly certain that there's not a thing Paul can say to comfort his wife.

Her feet are killing her. The swelling that started years ago has worsened, spreading clear to her knees. She means to head straight home and take a warm bath, but instead she stops abruptly by Paul's workbench.

"Oh," she says, her heart racing as she reaches for the young female form that's taking shape in a trunk of larch wood. Paul has roughed in the girl's body and face peering out of a hollow. Baba glances back at the house, where Paul and Faith's argument is ramping up again. What has Faith told him? How much is he willing to believe? It could just be a bit of whimsy, but Paul is not a whimsical man.

She wonders if Faith understands that it won't be only Paul's heart that breaks when she leaves him.

In the weeks that follow, the arguments continue and Baba stops coming over to witness them. But one afternoon, Polly bursts through Baba's front door.

"They're separating!" she cries, throwing herself into her grandmother's arms. "My dad's moving out!"

Baba holds her granddaughter tightly. Polly no longer has trouble with words, which is a shame because all of the ones spoken lately are awful. Nothing's forever. Love fades and people leave. Baba waits for Polly's wails to subside before leading her silently down to the creek, where Edward is waiting.

Baba is the one who sees him now. Years ago, Polly's ability to glimpse ghosts changed into something far lovelier: A talent for discerning the colorful auras that emanate from every living thing. She loves to shout out what she sees—green for the trees, yellow and pink for the grass and flowers, a once vibrant ruby red for Bree that grows darker every day.

But she's silent today. Edward leans against a tree, colorless and still. Baba doesn't have time for him as she cups Polly's chin in her hand.

"It's when people leave that you discover how strong you really are."

"I don't want to be strong," Polly replies tearfully. "I want my dad."

Baba nods. "I know. Your mother wanted her father, too, but parents can be slippery things. Might be wise to figure out who you are besides a daughter."

Paul doesn't invite her, but a week later, Baba wraps her swollen ankles in gauze and walks four miles along a little used mountain road to find the house he's renting—a small log cabin that reminds her of the hunter's hut where she and Edward once lived. When Paul leads her into a cozy room of gleaming logs and rough-hewn fir floors, it's like stepping inside a tree.

"You and Faith better move here after you work things out," Baba says as she takes a seat on his sofa.

Paul sinks into the couch beside her. The sweet boy she remembers is now a monster of a man—tall, broad-shouldered, and growing out a beard.

"What's going to happen with me and Faith?" he asks.

"What always happens," Baba replies. "You're going to say a bunch of things you don't mean, then see if you can forgive each other."

"She hates who I am now," he tells her.

Baba snorts. "Welcome to the club."

"I shouldn't have quit without telling her. I just . . . I couldn't take it one more minute. Maybe I can beg my boss for my job back. It's not worth it to be out here on my own without my daughters."

Baba stares at him. He's never strung this many words together before, so it's a shame they're all lies.

"Don't be ridiculous," she says. "You acted on instinct, and that's never wrong. Give Faith a chance to come to terms with things."

"You think she'll come around?"

Baba has no idea what her daughter will do, but she smiles reassuringly.

"Faith has never loved anyone but you."

Paul may have moved to the woods, but he spends his nights in town, tracking down Bree. The girl's been grounded for a month, but she still manages to sneak out to cocaine dens, keg parties and, once, a crowd of drunken skinny dippers at Quinn's pond. Last Baba heard, Faith had installed a padlock on the outside of Bree's door.

Nevertheless, one morning before dawn, Paul's truck barrels up Baba's driveway. She would leap to her feet, but her ankles are so swollen now she has trouble getting out of bed. She manages to pull on a robe and open her bedroom door only to have Bree charge through it.

The girl is dressed all in black and doesn't even look at her. She stomps across the room and throws herself face-first on the bed.

"Rough night?" Baba asks, receiving nothing but a grunt in reply. Leaving Bree to her misery, Baba walks down the hall to find Paul slumped against her kitchen counter.

"I'm sorry to dump this on you," he says. "I didn't know where else to turn. Bree escaped out her second story window last night. No rope or bedsheets tied together. She just jumped."

Baba raises her eyebrows. The girl could have died, but you have to admire her pluck.

Paul paces across her kitchen floor. "I don't know what to do anymore. We yell. We sympathize. We ground her. We even force-fed her one night. Have you seen how thin she's gotten? Our daughter is literally starving herself to death right before our eyes."

Baba doesn't reach out to comfort him. Paul's a man who quit a lucrative job to carve wood. He knows who he is, so he ought to be strong enough to face who his daughter is, too.

"See now," she tells him, "that girl hates you. But she hates herself more."

The horror on Paul's face doesn't stop her. Things are what they are; softening a few words isn't going to change anything.

"You should be glad she's fighting you," Baba continues. "Better that than giving up and going quiet."

Paul's hands are in fists. "What do you suggest I do?"

Despite her swollen ankles and the pain deep in her bones, Baba smiles. She's been waking up to flecks of blood on her pillow. Every morning, she drinks a different tonic, but she knows that none of them are going to help. The cancer has been growing inside her ever since she stepped from her tree. She's an abnormality, after all, as much of a mutation as cancer itself. Every night, her bedroom walls fade and Edward's silhouette grows more solid and three-dimensional. Sometimes she hears him tapping his foot, impatiently waiting for her, but it actually takes quite a bit of time to die. In the meantime, a drugged up, anorexic teenager doesn't scare her one bit.

"Buckle up," she tells Paul. "And leave Brianna to me."

After Paul drives off, Baba barricades the front door with two heavy chairs, then drags a blanket and pillow to the door by the kitchen. It takes some work to lower her aching body to the floor, which gives her plenty of time to guess which objects are being shattered in her bedroom. The bedside lamps for sure, and perhaps the photos of Bree and

Polly in happier times. Baba chuckles as Bree hurls something massive—most likely the oak nightstand Edward hand built—at the wall. She should have thrown that piece on the bonfire months ago. Oak is dense enough to burn for hours.

When Bree finally runs out of steam and clicks open the bedroom door, Baba closes her eyes. Her granddaughter tiptoes to the front door first, then, with a curse, heads toward the back. She pauses beside Baba, probably trying to determine just how deeply she's sleeping, then tries to slip past her to make a run for it.

"Oh no you don't!" Baba says, easily grabbing her granddaughter by her skinny ankle.

Bree kicks, but it's pointless. She ought to have eaten enough to at least overpower a dying grandmother.

"Get out of my way, you old hag!"

Baba only smiles and sits up against the door. Bree glares at her murderously. The girl wears so much makeup it's hard to tell if the darkness beneath her eyes is intentional or the result of no sleep. Baba lets go of her twig-like ankle and gets slowly to her feet.

"I've got plans for us," she says. "I suggest you bring a snack."

Bree purses her lips, as if even the mention of food adds calories. Baba grabs Edward's jacket and puts it on over her robe and pajamas. As she slips on her boots, Bree eyes the door.

"If you run," Baba tells her, "I'll just hex you."

Bree scoffs, but there's a flash of uncertainty in her eyes that keeps her rooted.

"Let's go then," Baba says, opening the door and heading out into the crisp autumn dawn.

Once she shakes off her bed rot each morning, she can still walk for miles—albeit less gracefully and at a far slower pace than she set before. Not bothering to check if Bree is behind her, Baba picks up her walking stick and crosses the yard. She steps right into the shallow stream to reach the forest path beyond.

Bree finally trudges down to the creek, but refuses to cross it.

"I'm not going for a *hike*," she says.

When Bree was little, Baba took her into the woods, but even then the diamond queen refused to go very far, certainly not all the way to the grove. She complained about mosquitoes and renamed Battlecreek Peak "Death's Mountain." Once she hit her teens, Bree labelled anyone who walked for pleasure a maniac.

Baba merely shrugs. "Suit yourself. I can show your sister my secret later."

She sets off without another word. The sparrows and bluebirds are so boisterous, their chirping nearly drowns out the sound of Bree grumbling as she splashes across the stream.

"I'm not going all the way up there!"

Baba chuckles, even as Bree insists on resting every hundred feet. Let her granddaughter think she's gained the upper hand; with Baba's ankles swelling to twice their normal size, she welcomes every opportunity to sit and rest her feet. Bonus points, every time she gets up again, she's dizzy enough to see stars—her favorite cancer symptom by far.

Bree walks behind her, huffing and puffing and, on the steep climbs, shouting, "You're a monster!"

Baba is breathless, too. She's gone from sleeping in the grove to visiting her sisters weekly to rarely making it up the mountain at all. Tears sting her eyes when they finally reach the devil's club. The tunnel beneath the hedge is passable—just barely. It'll be a painful, thorny crawl.

"This way," she says.

She eases herself down beneath the barbed leaves and shimmies forward. With all of her aches and pains, she hardly even notices the thorns in her back. But when Bree reluctantly crawls in after her, the girl shrieks as if she's under attack.

"Where the hell are you taking me? You're out of your goddamned mind!"

Baba exits the tunnel slowly, struggling to her feet, while Bree rockets into the grove, red-faced and furious, her hair and coat studded with yellow spines.

"What the fuck, Baba?"

Baba ignores her. Dressed in the last thing he had on—work boots, jeans, and a flannel jacket—Edward leans against the crooked larch, whose patch of brown rot is spreading steadily up her trunk. Edward smiles at the sight of his eldest granddaughter. When Bree grabs hold of Baba's arm, even the larch's golden needles quiver.

"This is my mom's idea, isn't it?" Bree asks. "Dump me in the woods somewhere so I can eat beetles and figure out my life?"

For a skeleton, the girl has a pretty firm grip.

"Actually," Baba says, "that idea is mine."

A flash of shock, and perhaps a little fear, cause Bree to let go of her. The girl scans the grove, wrinkling her nose at the woody scent of the trees. She overlooks the most beautiful things, from the late-blooming goldenrod to Edward's shadowy ghost and the slender larch beside him, extending a wispy branch toward Bree's hair.

"I hate the woods," Bree says.

Baba nods. Some people do. There are kooks in every family.

"The woods don't care how you feel about them," she says. "They'll hide you just the same."

The crooked larch is as much of a troublemaker as Bree, landing a few needles in the girl's hair. Bree swats them away as she slowly turns toward Baba. With all the makeup she wears, it's easy to forget how beautiful she once was underneath it.

"Are you actually telling me to run away?"

Baba shrugs. "Did I say that? I'm just showing you a place where the hares are plentiful and the bearberries last all year. Down that slope is a river, not to mention a miner's cabin, if you know where to look. All you need to survive are shelter, water, and food, Brianna. The rest is just fluff."

Bree gawks at her. She doesn't even correct her for using the wrong name.

"You really are crazy," she says, the slightest bit of awe in her voice.

Baba and Edward chuckle. One of the crooked larch's tiny roots, the barest of things, wriggles out of the soil near Bree's foot.

"I do try," Baba replies.

The night Bree runs away, she makes a brief stop outside Baba's bedroom window. Baba is sitting up in bed, reading, when her granddaughter's pale face—for once scrubbed clean of makeup—peers in. The girl looks like the child she is, scared but determined, and Baba nods, even though doubt creeps in. The hares are plentiful in the grove, but Bree has no idea how to hunt them, nor did she ever listen when Baba pointed out the difference between edible and poisonous berries. The girl is hardly a survivalist, but then again, she can't survive here either.

A second later, Bree vanishes into the night.

Baba closes her book and stares at her gnarled hands. Her skin is turning bark-like and brittle, but she wishes the rest of her would harden, too. What a relief it would be to become indifferent, once again, to everything except fire, infestation, and disease. If something happens to Bree, she will never forgive herself. Faith will never forgive her for letting Bree go.

Edward slips into bed to comfort her. He's never far away. Lately, her body has taken to shivering for no reason, so when she curls up against his shadowy shoulder, she actually feels a little heat. Everyone who's been loved knows magic, but what if you believed you weren't worth that love in the first place? What kind of magic does a girl like Bree have?

The police are called. Paul spends his days driving through town, fruitlessly searching, then sleeps fitfully on Faith's living room sofa. A rumor begins that Bree was pregnant when she left. In the days that follow, Baba starts out for the grove a dozen times, but always turns back, breathless and cold. She could make it up the mountain if she really pushed herself, but what's the point in trying to save someone who's not yet ready to live?

The walk to Faith's is nearly as daunting. Baba finds her daughter slumped on the sofa, her head in her hands. They're all breathing tears instead of air.

"Honey," she manages to say, but nothing more. She's the reason they're all drowning.

So she stands sentinel by the door, once more a silent witness to sorrow. Love brought her to life, but it burns her. She was safer in the woods; Bree is safer.

Faith looks up through her tears and says, "Mom?'

That word burns most of all. Bark resists fire, but skin, it seems, is meant to be branded—by love and fear and loss combined. Baba crosses the room to hold her daughter.

"Where is she?" Faith asks.

Baba struggles for breath and says, "The grove."

Faith pulls away instantly, swiping at her tears.

"Don't be ridiculous. This is Bree we're talking about. Not you or Polly. That's the last place she'd go."

Baba strokes Faith's cheek and says, "Are you sure?"

That night, when Edward sits on the side of the bed, she snaps at him to go away.

"I'm not done yet. Not until Bree comes home. Can't you see that?"

He reaches for her hand, and tears come to her eyes when she feels the weight of his fingers.

"Please," she says. "Wait."

The problem is that Baba herself may have waited too long. More often than not, her longest walk is from her back door to the garden. Cancer pain is far worse than anything her sisters threw at her; deep and visceral, like she's being squeezed to death. But when Polly shows up at her house, desperate for news of her sister, Baba takes a deep breath and puts on her boots.

The first thing to do is grab the steel cutters. She leads Polly across the street, where her neighbor has chained another dog to the tree. The poor creature's barks have turned to pitiful cries.

"Your mother would want me to tell you that this is illegal," she says.

It takes only seconds to cut the dog free. A mangy, purebred husky, he immediately shakes his neck in relief and rolls over onto his back.

"No need for that," Baba says, but she rubs his belly. "Best to run for the trees this time, Bronco. Head for the deep woods. That's what I'd do."

The dog lingers for a few pets, then finally heads, rather reluctantly, toward the hills. Baba turns to Polly.

"Now I assume you're here for Bree. Let's see if we can find her."

Baba can't move at more than a snail's pace, so it takes all afternoon to reach the wall of devil's club. The next time she comes—the last time she'll come—it will take most of the day. Then, though, she will finally rest, lying down to die amongst her sisters, the way trees do. Not only will her nutrients return to the soil, she will leave no mess for Faith and her granddaughters to clean up.

With a wink at Polly, Baba slips beneath the devil's club and leads her granddaughter into the grove. When they step amongst the larches, the sun is setting and her sisters glow like spun gold. Polly looks around, awestruck.

"What is this place?" she asks. "Is Bree here?"

"I showed Bree this grove once," Baba replies. "A long time ago. At least it feels that way."

While Polly searches the grove for Bree, Baba's sisters do what they can to lessen her pain. There's no need for blasts of nitrogen and phosphorous. They simply give her what they give everyone—a constant, unnoticeable flow of oxygen. No one is ever really alone. Not even at the end.

Polly's shoulders slump with disappointment at finding no trace of her sister. Baba steps over a mound of fallen, cubed wood to tap the trunk of the rotting larch.

"You know why people say 'Knock on wood,' don't you?" she asks. "It's not superstition. It calls the spirit of the tree for help and guidance. Knock lightly and you won't be alone."

Unless, of course, you tap a tree whose spirit has gone elsewhere—perhaps to a teenage girl's hiding place in the woods. The brown rot has hollowed out a slim, female form in the larch's trunk, and the wood that surrounds the opening is cool to the touch. Still alive, but empty.

"Bree's alone," Polly says. "We should go."

Darkness is settling in as they head back toward the devil's club, shrouding everything but the larches' golden needles. Good thing they glow a bit; otherwise, Baba and Polly might have stumbled right into the smoldering ring of stones. A lock of charred blond hair still sizzles on a bed of coals.

Polly looks up at her, and Baba's heart races. *Brianna,* she thinks. *My sweet girl.*

It's all she can do to hide her smile.

"Hmmm," is all she says.

She lets Edward come.

He lies beside her in bed, holding her gently while she struggles to find a comfortable position. He rubs her swollen ankles, his hands as cool and calming as ice. Either he's solid now or she's fading; it doesn't matter which. He never speaks, which is just as well because she's done talking. What more is there to say? During the day, they sit together on her porch, sometimes listening to snippets of conversations as people pass by, sometimes dozing. She's saving what's left of her strength for her final walk to the grove.

Until the day her sisters tell her, one last time, not to come.

Men and machines have returned to the mountain, this time with site plans and city permits a lone woman can't hope to fight. Even without her sisters' warnings, Baba feels the earth shaking as hundreds of ancient trees fall. Roads have gone in where only pine trees stood before. Trees don't panic, but they do wilt under stress. Her sisters will die before her.

Don't come.

Perhaps Baba was never meant to return to her sisters. This is, after all, the house that Edward built for her. This is the life she'd cling to, if she could.

She's as light as air as Edward carries her to the purple ash in the yard. The two of them sit against the sturdy trunk, waiting. It shouldn't be more than a few days. Baba sleeps through the night and much of the next day, even when a light snow falls. She stops eating and can't rouse herself until Polly appears in the yard.

If Polly notices Edward helping her to her feet, she gives no sign.

"Taking a break from gardening," Baba forces herself to say. No sense in breaking the girl's heart until the very end.

Polly bounces on the balls of her feet. "I've been leaving food and clothes for Bree in the grove. Everything's always gone when I come back. It's Bree. I know it is."

Baba nods, even though she thinks the culprit might very well be her own sister, the one who stepped from a rotted larch tree to follow a tortured girl. Either way, she's no longer worried. Her vain granddaughter was willing to burn her own hair—one of her prettiest features—to save herself. Bree is going to be fine.

"But the grove, Baba!" Polly continues. "The bulldozers are so close to it. We have to stop them! It's the only place where Bree will be safe."

Baba holds Polly as tightly as her withered arms will allow. Now is not the time to tell her granddaughter that everything must die. Polly is young and strong and called to battle. Baba has no doubt that she can face whatever comes. Without her.

She pulls back to stare at the girl who is nobody's princess, no matter what Brianna might say. There are only two words worth saying anyway.

Baba takes Polly's chin in her hand and tells her, "Have faith."

✦

The last day begins differently. For one thing, Baba feels no pain. She and Edward haven't left the purple ash in three days, and there's a layer of newly fallen snow over both of them. The purple ash stands leafless and sleepy, its trunk cold to the touch. She presses her cheek to the frozen bark, then dozes again, Edward's arms tight around her.

She wakes to the rumble of trucks on the mountain, then the echoes of buzzing saws. She feels it in the earth, in her bones, when her sisters fall. Polly appears in the yard, her face stained with tears. She's been in the grove, or what's left of it, Baba knows. The girl races toward her, the despair on her face turning to horror when Baba tries to get to her feet, but collapses instead. She's no more substantial than a tangle of rickety sticks at this point.

"Baba!" Polly cries.

Baba can no longer raise her arms to hold her granddaughter, but it's enough to see the girl's beautiful face. Edward sits with his back against the ash, his edges blurred with white light. She wonders if Polly can see it.

"Tell me what to do," Polly says. "Even with the snow, I can find any plant you need."

And she can, too. She's a wonder! But there's nothing else to be done. Nothing to worry about any longer. How marvelous is that?

Finally, a few words come. "I . . . loved to walk."

Polly's eyes widen, but she shakes her head. "No! Bree . . . we both need you. Please don't go!"

She sobs so hard, Baba wishes she had the strength to take her in her arms, or at least enough breath left to explain that she's wrong. They don't need her at all. Friends will walk beside them, Faith and Paul will offer love and guidance. A grandmother, well, she's a little useless. Just a mirror that shows nothing but your best self.

She manages to place a light kiss on Polly's cheek and whisper the few words she has left.

"It's been a joy."

She hears Polly crying, but all she sees are colors. White at first, then orange, lavender, yellow, and green. Such a beautiful world. What a gift to be able to walk around in it for a bit.

Epilogue

Magnolia
(Magnolia soulangeana)

Magnolia trees are the prom queens who give up their crowns to wallflowers. Popular, beautiful and surprisingly good-natured. Sporting massive white, pink, and magenta flowers before the emergence of waxy green leaves, the more the magnolia is cut, the more she thrives. Appearing on the planet before bees evolved, magnolias were first pollinated by the lowly beetle. In Chinese culture, the magnolia symbolizes purity and nobility. Used in a wedding bouquet, the blooms are said to bring everlasting love.

It sounds like machine gun fire as every tree in the grove snaps, one after the other.

The former larch hides behind the trampled devil's club, watching her sisters fall. The rotted tree she came from tumbles with barely a nudge, while her oldest sisters resist the longest, until cheering men in bulldozers ram them down.

The men pack up, satisfied that they've felled every tree in the grove, but somewhere down the mountain, one more sister says goodbye. She sends no distress signal as she dies, but simply a vision: Orange, lavender, yellow, green.

The men have to walk right past the former larch to reach their trucks, but they're too busy laughing and congratulating each other to notice that not everything in the grove is dead. She glances at the girl she follows, who's hiding farther away, in the snowy brush. The girl glares murderously at the men who drive away with their radios blaring. Apparently, butchering an entire family is all in a day's work.

A young girl and her friends have been coming to the grove for weeks now, calling out, "Bree," and leaving food and clothes behind. The girl called Bree snatched up everything they brought at first, but lately she's started leaving some of their gifts behind.

"I know you're out there somewhere," Bree says suddenly, her voice as smooth as sap. "If you can crawl over all that carnage, you can have the vegetables Polly left. They suck."

The former larch never lets herself be seen. She has already taught herself to walk and eat and dress in the clothes Bree leaves for her. A couple weeks ago, when Bree struck match after match but couldn't get the cold, damp wood to ignite, the girl who was once a tree yanked out her new, golden hair and set it ablaze on the last ember. When Bree returned to the firelit grove, she squinted at the flames, then turned to the larch whose brown rot had spread into the shape of a young woman.

"Hmmm," was all she said.

Now, Bree turns her back on the decimated grove and trudges back to the dingy miner's cabin she calls home. The bulge in her belly slows her pace, allowing the former larch to snag the bag of vegetables before following. She sticks to the shadows, wearing the castoff sweater and jeans Bree left for her that do nothing to block the cold. She's also ravenous, surviving mainly on the green beans Bree hates and bliss. Bree smells of vinegar and dank, closed spaces, like nothing else in the forest. Just the sight of the curve of her hip makes the one-time tree's newly formed toes curl in pleasure. Her sisters didn't send a single warning signal when she stepped from her tree, unwilling to lose another war against love.

But this time is different. The former larch is nothing like the one who waited more than 40 seasons to step out of her tree to be with the man she loved. That woman came from a bear wound, while she's been living in rot. The moment Bree stepped into the grove, a breath of desire blew away the larch's crumbling wood, making room for something far softer, and warm to the touch. She spent that night in blissful agony, tearing bark from cambium, willing sap and heartwood into blood and bone. She had one foot out of her tree by morning.

The night of the massacre, a bearded man toils alone in the grove, clearing fallen limbs and hacking through the frozen soil to dig a grave. The next day, he carries the body of the old woman who was once a larch home. A woman and the young girl who leaves food and clothes in the grove throw cold earth over the old woman's body. Bree watches them intently, even when the young girl's friends arrive with larch seedlings, planting one for every sister who fell. It's not until everyone leaves that Bree cries.

The snow starts in earnest that day and never stops. The former larch lives in a mostly dry hollow beneath a fir tree, covering herself at night with its warm, bristly boughs. One evening, Bree steps out her front door and flings a wool blanket onto the stoop.

"I'm the one trying to survive, you know!" the girl shouts, then slams the door.

The former larch's lips curl upward and her first chuckle tickles the back of her throat.

They survive. No one will ever understand how. In early spring, Bree waddles out of the cabin, her shirt and jacket barely fitting over her enormous belly. The former larch remains hidden in the trees, but Bree looks right at her.

"I'm going home now," she says. "You coming?"

The words may be meaningless, but the erstwhile tree's new heart races as Bree smiles for the first time. Bree holds out her hand and the larch who is now a young woman steps forward to take it.

Here or there, they've both been home for a while.

Dear Readers,

Thank you for joining me on a little walk through the woods. For those of you who discovered Baba in a book called *Girlwood*, thank you for coming back for a little more magic. I wrote *Girlwood* to bring a little wonder to my daughter and young girls everywhere. This novel is for the capable, strong women those girls have grown into, for maidens and mothers and grandmothers and crones, and of course for the men who adore them. There is magic and life in us yet.

Best wishes,

Claire Dean

www.ingramcontent.com/pod-product-compliance
Lightning Source LLC
Chambersburg PA
CBHW020323030826
48979CB00022B/847
9780998602554